Chasing Victoria

Chasing Victoria

E. Denise Billups

Learn from yesterday, Live for today, Hope for tomorrow
The important thing is not to stop questioning.
Albert Einstein

Acknowledgments

WITH MANY THANKS to the constants in my life, Ouida Billups, and James Billups, and to Marsha Bullock early readers for her feedback and to special friends who have shown me what friendship is truly about Mirna Hamilton, Julie Chan, Colette Bryce-Miller, and Par Balkaran—my Bella Sorelle.

Books by E. Denise Billups

Novels
  By Chance
  Chasing Victoria
  Kalorama Road
Short Stories
  Ravine Lereux
  The Playground
  Rebound

Prologue

The phone rings on the nightstand awakening my senses to a warm breeze fanning my hair, and a snug weight anchoring my legs and waist. Then I remember everything from the passionate beginning in my foyer to this entangled moment. The instant I turn my head to his breath's rhythmic rise and fall, the phone disturbs the silence and the sleeping man beside me again.

"The phone...babe, you awake?"

"Mmm-hmm," I grumble, annoyed someone's calling so late. Removing his arm from my waist, I grab the mobile and squint at the caller I. D., displaying anonymous caller. I accept the call and answer, "Hello."

Rapid breathing, footsteps, and city noise overshadow the caller's voice. "Hello."

A woman's voice sounds muted through the phone.

I can't hear you. Can you speak louder." I jump when his lips graze my neck, then tense and arch my back to silence an excited breath.

"Vicky, it's me, Kayla."

"Kayla? What time is it?" I ask, and squint at the time on the mobile. "It's one in the morning. Where are you calling from?"

"I'm sorry for calling so late, and I don't have time to explain."

A door creaks open and shut. Muted restaurant clatter replace city din.

"Kayla, where are you? And why are you whispering? I can barely hear you."

"I can't talk any louder. Vic, I need to see you. Can you meet me at the park in the morning?"

The distress in Kayla's voice stiffens me further. Concerned, I ignore his lips igniting my spine. "Are you okay?"

"Excuse me," a man interjects in the background.

"Sorry," Kayla mumbles. A door creaks and muted voices and clinking utensils grow louder then fade to silence as Kayla moves to another space.

"Kayla, what's going on?"

"I can't explain on the phone. Did you find the disc in your bag?"

"Disc?"

"Vic, I have to go, but please, wait for me at Engineers Gate at five o'clock, I'll explain everything."

"Okay. Kayla?" I stare at the silent phone a second then return it to the nightstand. "That's odd," I mumble. Before I can voice concern, his lips find mine and thoughts of Kayla suspend for the moment.

* * *

Four hours later, I throw on my running clothes and tiptoe toward the bedroom door. I turn and stare at his sleeping, sheet-shrouded figure and deliberate jumping back in bed. But I can't, not after that troubling phone call. "Damn it, Kayla," I grouse and close the door. When I step from the apartment, I realize this is the first time I've allowed a man to remain in my condo. I'm surprised how soon I've abandoned control in this incipient affair.

November's fog blankets the city a buoyant, ghostly white. Only a block from my condo and beads of mist already coat my vision. I shiver, not so much from the crisp autumn air, but Kayla's fearful voice. Was she trying to elude someone? And why couldn't she talk on the phone, why the park?

What's going on Kayla?

I pull my jacket sleeve over my fingers and rub my arms to generate heat. With a brisk walk, I begin a jog toward Central Park's Engineers Gate. My sports watch confirms it's five o'clock sharp, but there's no sign of Kayla. She's always punctual. Something's wrong, I've sensed it for days. Uneasily, I stroll inside the park toward the water fountain, disturbing a homeless man asleep on a bench. On the northern end of the gate, a biker zooms into the park. A woman appears through the fog, and I believe it's Kayla. I sigh and walk toward her. "Kayla, I was… oh, sorry, I thought you were someone else."

The woman smiles and starts a jog toward the reservoir.

Growing anxious, I release my mobile from the armband. Kayla's phone rings several times before going to voicemail. "Kayla, I'm at the park. Where are you? I'm worried about you. Well, it's five o'clock. I'll wait a few more minutes. If I miss you, I'm on the roads running."

After ten minutes, impatient and itching to run, I comb the entrance one last time before taking off on Central Park's running loop. Worry seizes my mind. Kayla would never get up this time of morning unless it's serious.

Kayla, what have you done?

Instead of crossing the 102nd street traverse to the western side of the park, I continue toward steep, rolling hills on the wooded northern end. Dense fog blurs slick leaf-covered roads, so I slow my stride, wary of slipping on dangerous footing. Eerily, taillights emerge through swirling mist. Alarmed, I slow to a stroll, scrutinizing Connecticut license plates and Greenwich Little League Baseball sticker surfacing on a black Lincoln Town car parked near the wooded ravine. The interior light illuminates a man behind the steering wheel. I stop, wary of the wide-open back door, and search for the ever-present police cruiser always present this time of the morning, but it's nowhere in sight.

Paralyzing fear grips my body when muffled voices, crunching leaves, and scuffling arise in the wooded ravine. Through sparse tree limbs, a murky trenched-coated man pushes a blurry figure to the ground. My instincts warn, flee! But I'm transfixed by the chilling scene.

The man threatens, "We warned you bitch to stop snooping."

"No, please..." the woman pleas and struggles from a fatal position. The man pushes her forward on her hands and knees. "Please don't do this. I won't say anything," she squeals with audible tears.

"We know you took the file. Where did you hide it?"

"Please, I told you, I don't know what you're talking about."

"We saw you take it. Now, one last time, where is it?"

"I don't know..."

Before it registers in my mind, the gun pops and her body falls into the ravine. *It's Kayla!* I jump, suppressing a scream. *No, it can't be Kayla. No—no—no, not Kayla!*

The man behind the wheel, steps from the car. I turn and speed uphill in terror, hoping he hadn't seen me. The steep, leaf-covered incline thwarts momentum, sending my feet slipping, sliding, and tumbling. I catch my fall in a downward dog, glance under my arm, and notice him looking in my direction.

"Hey, you!" He yells.

I scramble off the ground, speeding uphill with the force of adrenaline, driving me faster than I've ever run. I glance back and notice the man gaining speed. My heart thuds faster when I see the gun in his hand.

This can't be happening!

An instant sting brushes my leg.

He's shooting at me!

I pick up speed and run onto a dirt path. Weaving between trees, I stop and hide behind a wide tupelo tree. Peeking sideways, I find the gunman doubled over and heaving for air. Straightening his stance, he places the gun in his jacket and retreats in the opposite direction.

Uncontrollable shivers claim my body as I watch him disappear down the hill. I drop to my knees, examine blood-ripped running tights, and graze from the bullet on my calf. Waves seize my chest, escaping in choppy sobs. The image of Kayla falling into the ravine finally registers.

She's dead!

I grasp the tree and breathe deeply. When my mobile vibrates in the armband, I glance over catching Kayla's face on the screen. Terror snatches my breath again. Apprehensively, I press accept, knowing it's not Kayla on the other end. The callous voice from the ravine menaces.

"Ms. Powell, I know who you are and where you live."

He knows my name!

In my periphery, the blue and white police cruiser winds the curve. With flailing arms, I race in its direction, pointing toward the ravine. Words escape in jagged breaths. "Kayla ... My friend..." And the words to follow, unreal as they are, sound like someone else's words. "They killed her!"

* * *

At the ravine, the trench-coated man scours the area around Kayla's body, taking precautions to erase evidence of his presence. Kayla's reddish tresses, immersed in the shallow ravine, ripples with the stream. A beep buzzes from her pocket. With his foot, he turns her body sideways like discarded garbage, retrieving the beeping cell phone. A picture of a smiling woman with a voluminous mane of brownish curls and full heart-shaped lips displays with the name Victoria A. Powell. He presses play, and her voice echoes through the ravine. "Kayla, I'm at the park. Where are you? I'm worried about you. Well, it's five o'clock. I'll wait a few more minutes. If I miss you, I'm on the roads running."

He taps the photo and a number and address displays. "Well, well, well, Victoria Powell ... Wrong place, wrong time," he says with a chortle. He gazes at Kayla's body, shakes his head, and whispers under his breath, "What a waste." Placing the cell phone in his coat pocket, he struggles up the muddy ravine, just as the other man makes his way back to the car.

"She got away, Sir."

"Don't worry. She couldn't have seen our faces with this fog." He removes the cell phone from his pocket and waves it like a prize. "I retrieved this from Kayla's jacket. I believe I know our intruder."

As the car starts its descent, the man dials Victoria's number. The phone rings twice then dead silence greets him. She's listening, waiting for a voice, perhaps Kayla's. A grin skews his face, picturing her holding the phone to her ear like a cornered mouse. "Ms. Powell, I know who you are and where you live." Holding the phone to his ear, he listens to her quiet fear as the car creeps down the hill, out of the park, and onto Manhattan's dawn-lit streets.

PART ONE

Chapter 1

A Month Earlier

No one can predict where life will carry them. The most well-thought-out plan can go awry. I ponder persistent solemnness, daily rituals, and countless tasks, which take me nowhere but circles, never-ending, mind-numbing circles. When did it all become so mundane? I want to shake things up, create disorder in my well-constructed life. Do away with rituals and transform into something different. But fear of losing control, fear of the unknown, holds me in that mundane place bleeding for change.

Often, I've wondered if mom, Judith Powell, named me Victoria to signal a triumphant birth. At the age of forty, and after several attempts, she finally succeeded victoriously. Mainly, I believe she gave me this name to triumph the ordinary and live as remarkably as she had. Victoria is an impossible name to emulate, especially when you fail right out of the gate. But, as I see it, there will always be challenges to conquer. So, I decided to run. To train my body, prepare for life's challenges, and be physically and mentally ready when the time comes.

Although I'm just like Judith, I try not to be. Judith Powell a celebrated opera singer, achieved great success, great victories in a life that resembled a stage. My childhood was magical with singers, actors, and dancers, who entertained me at home and onstage. For hours, I'd watched Judith's rehearsals and memorize scenes and music pieces. From Judith's living room to the theater was a continuous act—entertainment on demand by her thespian friends. Sometimes I wondered if there was a division between reality and her stage life. If so, I couldn't tell. Onstage, she played the heroine well, but did she offstage? Would she have survived the real world, a job where vocal and acting abilities aren't measures of success? I assumed not.

Judith's second stage, her home in Martha's Vineyard, is filled with magical artifacts. She decorated my room like a castle with drawings of a forest, moon, and magical creatures guarding me as I slept. That seemed so long ago. A child no more, I've chosen a traditional life offstage, a life different from Judith's, my father's path, a career in finance. My father, Aiden Powell, loved Judith more than life. He showered her with love and a life of luxury. But dad always says, "*Judith was a free spirit.*" He understood and accepted her ways, but at what cost. His pain, I can't imagine.

In my mind, I hear Judith say, "*You should have had a career on stage, your first defeat.*" Maybe she was right. If I had a magic ball, would my life be different? Truthfully, I lost focus, my direction twisted, or am I rebelling against a life planned by Judith. Determined to lead a life different than mom's, I chose a career shocking to both my parents. Eager to conquer Wall Street, I donned the typical attire of the financial world, filled my closet with power suits, black leather pumps, and accessories alluding to wealth. I subscribed to the tools of the trade, Wall Street Journal, BusinessWeek, and Forbes, and became another Wall Street drone clad in designer clothing.

The rituals of hard work consumed me and even felt worthwhile. But Wall Street success comes quickly for those with good connections, family status, and sometimes sleazy improprieties my ethics can't stomach. However, I've determined with diligence and hard work I'd be victorious. Or would I? Soon, making it through mind-numbing days of numbers, market trends, and research left me questioning my purpose. At twenty-five, I assume I'm way too young to experience an existential crisis. *Or am I?*

Eventually, getting out of bed and going to a soul-draining job felt challenging. So, I decided to run. Running became compulsory, an endorphin-laced addiction, bolstering and melting mundaneness, and it would save my life.

* * *

It's morning again, and the alarm jolts me from the bed. I perform ritual one, two, and three, fumbling in the dark. Slightly awake, I dress for my morning run and exit the condo, ready to witness another sunrise. It's one of those foggy New York City mornings caused by early autumn's fluctuating temperatures. Five o'clock hum of early risers serenades me across the avenues. On the narrow streets between Lexington and Park Avenues, newspaper boys hurriedly toss papers inside building lobbies. At the corner, a taxi stops eager for a fare. I smirk at his disregard for my running outfit and shake my head. On Madison, I say a polite, "Good morning," to a sluggish dog walker.

"Good morning," he mumbles and yawns as the dog yanks him forward.

In front of the Episcopal Church of Heavenly Rest, a homeless man packs up his makeshift bed. Ahead, teenagers exit the park trailed by marijuana fumes. I feign disinterest, clutching steel keys in my hand. As I grow closer, the group part politely, allowing me to pass. With languid strides and glassy eyes, a tall, thin boy dressed in sagging jeans, takes a long drag on the waning joint, exhaling fumes through his thin nostrils. Narrowing his eyes, he intones in a strained voice, "Holy shit, you're out early."

"Not as early as you," I say.

His eyes follow, and his head bobs up and down with an approving smile. "Shit, she's got some balls. I like that. Can I join you," he asks, rubbing his hands in his masculine parts.

I keep walking, dismayed by his ignorance. *An opera of comedies*, I think as I turn my head, noticing the group disperse to different addresses along the street. The lingering, pungent scent grazes my nose, and I juxtapose a grassy high and endorphin-induced runner's high. Addictions, mine's not so different.

Skies turn indigo blue as I make my way inside the park's entrance on Fifth Avenue. I begin my run around Central Park's running loop and finish with an orange-magenta sunrise coloring the horizon. I head toward a bench to stretch at the entrance when footsteps approach from behind. Quickly, I turn my head toward a striking man nearing the bench. He stops and stretches beside me.

"How was your run," he asks, catching his breath.

His athletic built and sculpted calf muscles tell me he's a seasoned runner. A drop of sweat, commingle with morning mist, rolls from my chin, and I reply, "Wet," embarrassed by my profuse sweating.

"I watched you from a distance. You're a good runner, good pace. I had a hard time catching up with you. Do you get out every morning?"

His voice is so unguarded as if he's been speaking to me forever, not the typical wavering of strangers. However, I'm a little perturbed he'd been trailing and watching me from behind. Cautiously, I reply, "Sometimes."

Lifting his leg on the bench, he stretches more limber than any man I've met. Silence pursues as we each continue a ritual I perform alone after each morning run. It's unusual stretching in silence with a stranger. I catch the smooth, dark hairs and muscles etching his calf. An earthy musk grips my nostrils, and it's pleasing. He catches my eye. Embarrassed; I stretch deeper.

"My name is Chase," he says, standing straight with an outstretched palm.

I straighten and shake his hand, noticing his angled jaw, full lips, and intense, brown eyes staring at mine. It's odd, but shaking this stranger's hand is calming. I release my grip from his smooth hand's firm grip. He smiles, and I grin awkwardly. "Chase, that's a good name for a runner. My name is Vicky."

"Is that short for Victoria?"

"Yes, but I've always preferred Vicky, less formal. Victoria is so regal. That I'm not," I say, shaking my head.

"You should let someone else decide that. You're impressive when you're running. You have the form of a dancer and the spirit of a gazelle."

Laughter bursts from my mouth. "A gazelle. Hmm, I've never pictured myself running like a gazelle, but they are fast."

"I like your pace. You would be great to run with."

Wiping the sweat from my brow; I stand akimbo, uncertain how to reply.

"Will you be in the park tomorrow," he asks.

He seems harmless, but so did Jeffrey Dahmer. I start to worry and stumble, forcing a lie, which sounds obvious. "I'm not sure. I never know whether I'll make it to the park, depends on my morning." Of course, I'll be in the park as I am every day. It's the only way I survive a long workday.

"Well, it was a pleasure running behind you. Maybe one morning we can run together."

I flinch at his words, which seem intimate—together—I've always run alone. I can't imagine running and talking with a stranger. Occasionally, I'll run with friends, but find myself pulling ahead, leaving them struggling behind. My run is meditative, a time when the world outside the park doesn't exist. Nothing matters except my air-filled lungs, pounding heart, and sensation of flight as the wind rushes past. "Well, I run alone, but if you can keep up, perhaps one day," I reply with an emphasis on one, hoping he understands I prefer running solo.

"Well, Victoria, I hope I'll see you soon."

"Likewise," I say with a smile. He turns to leave, and my eyes follow his long, muscular legs toward the exit until he disappears around the corner.

Finishing my stretch, I head back across the avenues, recalling Chase's earthy scent arousing dormant desires. Quickly, I dismiss thoughts of a stranger I'll probably never see again and assume a jog home.

Chapter 2

The GE building's Byzantine lobby transports me to another era. Rippled-pink-marble walls, vaulted-golden ceilings, and hidden wall sconce's diffused sunburst remind me of a perfect sunrise. On the thirty-eighth floor, pristine, marbled halls and a crystal chandelier lead me toward Wheaton Asset Management's imposing bronze double doors. I pause in front of the gilded entry and press my thumb on the security console. The door unlocked prompting a deep inhale and exhale before I enter.

As always, I'm struck by the window view up Park Avenue to the George Washington Bridge, adjoining New York to New Jersey's jagged cliffs like an artistic mural. Morning silences the opulent reception area, décor styled for Wheaton's wealthy clientele. The room feels empty without Amber the receptionist who I've grown fond of the last three years, a female presence I appreciate among Wheaton's Ivy League men.

Past the reception area, I'm surprised to see the owner of the firm, Bruce Wheaton, seated with a guest in the conference room. He's rarely in the New York office, except for special meetings, and rarely sees clients before the market opens. His guest, seated across from him at the conference table, hasn't removed his trench coat, and I assume the meeting will be short. With his back turned toward the door, only his profile is visible, but the distinct slant of his eye reveals his Asian heritage.

The Asian man pounds his fist on a thick manila folder and slides it across the table. Bruce opens his mouth with angry words silenced by glass walls. His eyes catch mine as I hasten down the hall toward male voices emanating from the trading room. I attempt to pass unnoticed, but Bob O'Connor turns his head before I cross the door.

"Hey, morning Vicky..."

I pause, leaning on the door frame. "Morning, guys."

Two lethargic responses trickle through the door.

"Morning..."

"Morning, Vic."

Wheaton's three traders sit back-to-back, monitoring trades in the medium-sized room overrun with computer consoles. Bob O'Connor, seasoned head trader, has been with the company since its inception. Born from one of the wealthiest families in Greenwich, Connecticut, his persona speaks of old money. His dusty-gray hair has lost its youthful, golden color, but a hint of attractiveness remains. When will he decide he's had enough of this life of thirty years? Loving Wall Street's hectic pace, he'll probably work past retirement, although, he could have retired years ago.

"How was your run this morning?" Bob asks.

Bob's engaging personality and genuine concern for colleagues always engenders admiration. A family man with three grown children and a pampered wife, I suspect he uses his career to escape marriage's confines.

"Endorphins still pumping, you should try it one morning."

"I'll pass, but my wife would like nothing better than to see me in running shoes," he says, jiggling his belly with his hands.

I picture his ticker and organs smothered by fat but forgo my opinion; certain he's heard it before from others. "How is Linda?"

"Linda is Linda, always got her hands in some new endeavor. Last week it was the New Age Health Spa in the Catskills, and now she's on some cleansing diet."

I remember Amber mentioning Bob's wife started a holistic diet of juicing, and the green drink on his desk is probably her concoction.

"More of Linda's juice?" I ask, tilting my head in the drink's direction.

"Yep, and it's God-awful," he says with a cringe. "I don't know what's in this stuff, but it's like drinking swamp water and smells worse."

I chuckle, not because of the drink, but his bitter expression. "Hold your nose and just chug it down. Linda just wants you healthy Bob," I say, knowing he'll discard it or place it in the company refrigerator until it grows old with mold.

"Or she wants to kill me."

"Shush, I wouldn't voice that so loud," I say with a wink.

Dennis swivels his chair in my direction. His mischievous eyes roam my body then he grins lasciviously. I frown and narrow my eyes in disgust. Blonde-haired, blue-eyed Dennis Fahey has been Wheaton's Bond-Trader for twelve years. Unmarried, he lives a playboy life in Manhattan with days of stressful trading followed by nights of countless women and drinking, some mornings you can still smell nocturnal pursuits on his clothing—heart attack material, perhaps before his 40th birthday. His expression signals crude, provoking remarks forming on his tongue.

"Linda doesn't want to kill you, Bob, she just wants to control you, man," he says with a sneer. "You know how you women are," he says, challenging me with a stare.

His misogynistic ways make me shudder. With too many girlfriends to count; his sexual objectification of women is disturbing. Many times I've heard his sneering contempt for women. His air of superiority is annoying, and I rarely tolerate his sexist jokes, but sometimes it's better to ignore him. However, this morning, I can't help biting back. "Ooh ... And we don't want to do that now do we? We know how all that female power scares you," I say with an eye roll.

Alex, sitting behind Dennis hisses and shakes his head in disgust. "Man, this is why you can't find a wife. You're so disrespectful."

"Uh-huh, well, I only take my cues from them. Disrespect gets them all hot and bothered," Dennis says with a wink in my direction then swivels toward the computer.

"Don't mind the idiot in the room, Vic. We forgot to put him back in his cage," Bob says throwing me a look of compassion.

Alex hisses between his teeth, shaking his head in disbelief. I give him a grateful smile, banish Dennis' remarks, and ask, "How's it going, Alex?"

"Busy day with the ZyTech IPO," he says with a hint of anxiousness.

Straight out of Princeton University, Alex Ferrara is the youngest of the group. He seems misplaced in this room. At five-feet-seven-inches, he appears a boy beside Bob and Dennis's six-feet frames. His raven hair smoothed back with gel makes his aquiline nose more prominent. He's always on edge, and the constant frown will soon remain permanent if he doesn't learn to relax. I sense trading isn't what he'd hoped, and sometimes catch him sneaking out of the office, taking private calls in the stairwell—perhaps headhunters calling, offering him a less stressful position.

"Well, guys, good luck with the IPO," I say and turn to leave.

"Your legs look hot in that dress, Vicky," Dennis yells before I take a step down the hall.

I know what he's doing, trying to get under my skin, the bastard. I imagine a nasty retort, but let it go and continue down the hall toward Andrew Kelly's unusually quiet office. I peek my head inside, surprised the room is empty. As CFO of the firm, Andrew's always in before seven in the morning and never misses a day of work.

A few doors down, an impressive golden-lettered plaque proclaims Kayla's title, Jr. Compliance Analyst. I'm still in awe how far we've come in our short careers. She's in early, and I wonder why. Peeking inside her office, I find her bag and trench coat strewed across her desk. *She must be getting coffee.*

Two doors down, a golden plaque proclaim my role—Victoria A. Powell, Equity Research Analyst. The cream office where I spend most of my waking hours, glows from light off St. Bartholomew's golden dome through the window. I relish the morning serenity before my day commences.

More rituals begin the moment I slide behind my desk and power on the computer. I grab two Zen meditation balls from my desk, exhale deep and open Bloomberg, Wheaton's position screen, and Outlook. Contemplatively, I roll the Zen balls in my palm and scan my daily calendar. Eight o'clock research meeting. Ten o'clock conference call with management. Lunch with analyst Chip Meyers. Two o'clock meeting with Rawlins Corporation. Daily tweaking of financial models and research reports. *When does it end?*

Putting the Zen balls aside, I prop my chin on my hand, gaze at the beach screensaver, and imagine an impromptu island getaway with a willing partner. Chase's sculpted legs and alluring scent come to mind. A voice jars my reverie.

"Uh-oh ... I know that look."

Quickly, I dispel the ambiguous expression and wonder how desire looks on my face. I contain a laugh and lift my gaze to Callum McKenna, a young intern and mathematical genius from Columbia University.

"How's the Queen of Biotech," he asks, running his hand through his sandy brown hair. "Busy day ahead?"

"God, it never ends, Callum."

Grasping the door frame, Callum leans back, stares down the hall, and then swings his body forward with a baffled expression. "Something's going on this morning. Andrew is MIA, and did you see the action in the conference room?" He asks, sitting in the chair facing my desk. "Man ... Bruce is pissed!" He says elongating each word. "I've never seen him so angry. Who's the man with him in the conference room?"

"I don't know, but those were my exact thoughts."

Callum's brows furrow. "I swear I've seen his guest somewhere. Hmm, it'll come to me," he says and twists his lips.

Suddenly, I remember Callum's new status. "I heard you accepted the offer. Congratulations Mr. Junior Quantitative Research Analyst!"

I exclaim and high-five him across the desk. "I'm impressed," I say, admiring his impeccable tailored suit and Rolex watch, ceratainly a present from his father.

"I'm psyched," he says, rolling the research report around his well-manicured hands. "It was a tough decision between Wheaton and JP Morgan Chase. But dad convinced me this is a good place to work."

The spark in his eyes reminds me of the excitement Kayla, and I felt when Wheaton recruited us off campus. We were surprised to be hired by one of the most reputable hedge funds in New York City. "So, will you still commute from Greenwich?"

"I just signed a lease," he says with a tug of his magenta tie. "On Fifty-Second Street."

Smiling into my hand, I jest. "Ooh, look at you, your own place … Mr. All-Grown-Up."

"Hmmm, we're practically neighbors, Vic."

"Yeah, right, with thirty blocks between us," I say with a smirk.

"Well, I'll come by if I need to borrow some beer."

"Ha!" I screech, wondering if he'd just pop by without a warning.

"Anyway, are you excited about the ZyTech IPO?" He asks with eager brown eyes.

"Well, they're expecting a hot market for this one."

"By the way, good research Vic," he exclaims, raising my monthly research report. "You mentioned ZyTech. So the FDA gave the green light on the clinical trials. I know how important given your mom's…"

"Cancer," I say, noticing his unease. "It's okay, Callum; I've been fine with Judith's death for a while," I say, turning my gaze toward the computer. After a year of assuring others I'm fine, my reply feels rote. Callum's unease is one I recognized when people wield uneasy condolences, a look that causes me to smile reassuringly or look away as I had just now. "Anyhow, ZyTech's drugs been in the pipeline a long time and the IND has only just been approved. It could take years before the drug makes it to market."

"Let's hope this one makes it through trials swiftly," he says with earnest intent. "Wow, I can't believe the number of drugs these companies bring to market," he states, staring at the research report.

"It's called competition, Callum. Novelty is the name of the game. If they're not continuously developing drugs—"

"Then they're acquiring smaller-cap companies," he says abruptly finishing my words.

"Exactly!" I exclaim with a smile.

"By the way, I heard you have a meeting with Rawlins' management today. That should be interesting."

"Well, if you consider listening to medical terminology, and clinical trial results interesting, well then, I guess so," I say, glancing at my wristwatch. Turning my attention back to Callum; I notice his eyes have left my face. I follow his gaze to my nipples protruding like two pebbles through my dress—hardened by the air-conditioner.

Nervously, shifting in his seat; he lifts his gaze back to my face while lowering the research pamphlet in his lap.

God, Callum, I thought with a silent chuckle, *they're only nipples.* Casually, I reach for the cardigan on the back of my chair, wrap it around my shoulders, and feign a shiver. "Is it cool in here?" I ask, all the while wondering what Judith would have done—throw the young man a smile while teasing him with her assets. I suppress a laugh at his obvious embarrassment but wonder what he was thinking the moment he noticed my hardened nipples.

He clears his throat to conceal discomfort. Silence spills across the room, but only for a moment when Chris Brannon appears in the doorway.

"Excuse me," Chris says, clearing his throat to catch Callum's attention. "Good morning, Vicky. Can I pull this young man away for a while?"

"Morning, Chris. He's all yours," I say with deference and a smile. My mentor, Chris Brannon, is a well-respected Analysts and Economists on the street. As a regular speaker on CNN Finance, he's unaffected by his status, maintaining a humbleness I've always admired.

"Callum, I'll be in my office," Chris says as he turns to leave.

"There in a second, Chris," Callum replies and rises from the chair nervously. "Well, Vic, I better get going; wouldn't want the boss screaming at me the first day on the job."

Screamed at? I doubt management will yell at their latest acquisition, not at a wealthy kid whose family is as well-connected as his. I've heard his family is old friends of the Wheaton's, and probably have a financial interest in the firm. "Oh, don't forget the Goldman Sachs' healthcare conference at noon tomorrow."

"I haven't forgotten," he says, pausing for thought. "Now, I remember where I've seen Bruce's guest. His brother was three grades ahead of me at Brunswick in Greenwich."

"Ah! Then maybe he's a friend of Bruce."

"Or adversary," he whispers. "From what I remember of that family, they were a strange lot. They keep their distance from many of the locals, but he could be Bruce's client. I doubt he's a friend."

"Hmmm..." Remembering Bruce's angry scowl, Callum might have a point.

"Well, see you at the morning meeting," he says, winking with a boyish grin.

He's cute, but I would never acknowledge his crush or lead him on. I return to Outlook, skim thirty new emails, delete office junk, and highlight current biotech research from sell-side analysts and Bloomberg alerts. Inhaling deeply, I glance at my research notes for the morning meeting, realizing Kayla hasn't made her usual morning coffee visit. Unable to start my day without our morning chat, I leave my office, searching for her whereabouts.

* * *

Past the cafeteria and mailroom, I find Kayla stretched over the middle drawer in the file room—fingers moving across files frenziedly.

"Hey, there you are."

Startled, she jumps, banging her head on the upper drawer. "Ow! Vic, you scared the crap out of me," she howls, pushing the top drawer closed with a bang while rubbing the top of her head. "I was coming by in a few minutes, but I'm having trouble finding a file," she explains and pushes a folder back in its cramped space. Reddish tresses fall into her eyes as she rummages through the drawer. Her skin is paler than usual, making her signature freckles appear darker. She's wearing a conservative tan pantsuit and simple flats—not her usual designer dress, high heels, and pearls. It seems she dressed in a rush—no jewelry or makeup, only a slight hint of gloss on her lips.

"Kayla, why don't you let your assistant pull the file?"

"I can't wait till nine when he arrives. I need it now," she says with a sigh of exasperation. "Darn ... I just had it last night," she says while thumping her hand on the center of the files. "I put it right here in the fifth drawer. I even put a yellow sticky on it so I could eye it easier." With scrutinizing eyes, she stares at the drawer as if willing the folder to materialize. Flabbergasted, she sweeps falling strands from her mouth and stands akimbo with shifting hips. "Okay ... It's gotta be somewhere; it can't just disappear into thin air."

"Maybe someone else pulled it," I say with an allusive raise of my brows. I remember the thick file Bruce held in the conference room and wonder if it's the file she's searching for.

"No, can't be," she states with an elevating voice, her pale skin now a crimson shade. "I was the last to leave the office yesterday and the first to arrive this morning. No one else could have the file."

"Okay, calm down Kayla. You're going to burst a blood vessel," I say with a smile, but realize she's not finding the statement funny. "Anyway, what's so important about this file?"

Her eyes meet mine as if deciding to let me in on the cause of her angst. With narrowed eyes and tight lips, she fans her hand and shakes her head. "It's nothing. I just hate misplacing stuff."

Concerned by the dark circles under her emerald green eyes, I wonder if she's been sleeping. "Kayla, you look exhausted. What's going on? Is everything okay in the office?"

"I…well…You know, with law school and work, I'm just not sleeping enough lately. It's tough."

I detect a lie, but let it slide, concerned more about her agitation than her elusive demeanor. I've known Kayla since freshman year of college, and nothing has ever gotten her this riled up. A behavior I don't recognize replaces the composed exterior she always exudes as she searches through the files. "Let's get some coffee. Maybe getting some air and caffeine will clear your head."

With a peculiar squint and rub of her forehead, she closes the file drawer. "Alright, let's go."

Whatever's in that file must be important. But her manner tells me more is going on than the missing folder.

In the conference room, Bruce Wheaton and his anonymous guest are now standing. I assume they're wrapping up their heated meeting. As we pass the conference room, Bruce peers at Kayla and the strange man cast a furtive eye, sending shivers down my spine. I glance back just as the man passes Bruce a file. He extends his hand, but Bruce rudely declines a handshake. *What's that about?*

Chapter 3

Leaving Kayla at the register, I claim two seats in front of the window between two oblivious men engrossed in their laptops. A familiar blend of eclectic-Indie music, common at Starbucks, stream through speakers, diluting Barista's voices and patron's quiet chatter.

Outside the window, Lexington Avenue's rush hour congestion whirls about the coffee shop. I glance across the street and study the GE building's art deco façade from top to bottom, stopping on the entrance as Bruce Wheaton's anonymous guest exits the revolving door. He peers up and down the avenue, pulls a cell phone from his pocket, makes a quick phone call, then walks north toward the Citicorp building. At the corner of Fifty-Second Street, he enters a black Lincoln Town car.

"What's so captivating, Vic?"

I turn toward Kayla, and rescue an apple rolling from hands filled with coffee, bottled water, and a dangling banana. "I just saw the man from the conference room."

"What man?"

"The man meeting with Bruce. Didn't you see him?"

Easing onto the stool gracefully, she places the coffee on the counter without a spill. "No, I wouldn't have noticed if the office was on fire because of that darn file," she says with a scowl. "I didn't even know Bruce was in the office. He's usually in the Greenwich office on Tuesday? Is there something going on today?"

I'm amazed she hadn't notice Bruce or his mysterious guest. I suspect she arrived at work before the crack-of-dawn, hours before other employees, and long before night and daytime security switched places in the lobby, all because of that file. *It must be important.* "Not that I'm aware of. Bruce's presence stunned me, especially so early in the morning," I say, watching the Lincoln Town car disappear around the corner. "I wonder who his guest was. Their meeting was tense."

"Maybe it's one of his clients," Kayla says, peeling the plastic cap from the coffee and acknowledging the attractive hunk next to her with a frisky grin.

"No," I argue, pondering the confrontational scene. "I don't think so. Bruce would never raise his voice at a client," I say, and wince from the hot coffee scorching my tongue. "Do you want to sit a while before heading back?" I ask, hoping to get Kayla to relax.

"Sure." She places her purse beside the stool and looks out the window. "Next week, Bruce is holding his infamous company dinner in Greenwich. Are you going?"

"Do we have a choice?" I ask with a frown.

"I wish we did. I never liked being stuck with the guys for an entire weekend. But I do love Bruce's gorgeous home, and spending time with my best friend," she says with a playful nudge.

Remembering Dennis' vulgar remarks earlier, I scowl disgustedly. "The weekend would be perfect without Dennis' constant sexual innuendos."

"He's horrible!"

"Isn't he!" We both laugh; disturbing the man beside Kayla who lifts his tenacious gaze from the laptop finally. His face gleams interest, not annoyance as he eyes the redhead at his side.

"Oops!" Kayla places her fingers on her lips, smiles ruefully, and says, "Sorry," to the riveted man. With lifted brows, she smiles an impish grin and resumes our conversation in a lower voice. "Dennis believes his good looks works on every woman." With an empathetic head shake, she digresses. "I bleed for those poor girls always showing up at the office. I just want to scream run for your life!"

I chuckle at the image of Kayla chasing the women away like a herd of deer targeted by seasonal hunters. "It's so disturbing. They keep coming back knowing he's noncommittal and dating more than one woman. Remember the fiasco from last year's company weekend when two women showed up and fought in Wheaton's driveway like two cats in heat. Dennis dragged them to their cars so nonchalantly. How tasteless. The entire image makes me angry. He has no remorse for those poor girls."

"He must be wicked-delicious in bed. You see the look in their eyes, it's like they can't get enough of him. I swear Vic it's the sex."

"Uggg ... don't go there, Kayla?"

"Oh, Vic, come on, I'm sure you've thought about it once or twice. What if you didn't work with him every day and weren't privy to his misogynistic ways, would you turn him down?"

Shuddering at the idea, coffee goes down the wrong windpipe, and I choke, coughing and protesting at the same time. "God, no Kayla. Besides, blondes aren't my type." Noticing Kayla's twisted grin, I hope Dennis hasn't lured her into his lair.

"Kayla, you wouldn't; I hope?"

"Well—"

"No, you didn't!"

"Hold on. I'm not finished. I was going to say he'd attract me if I was oblivious of his misogynistic ways like most of his girlfriends."

I gag, feign disgust, and throw her a disapproving frown.

"Uh-huh. Don't give me that face Victoria Powell. Honestly, we're just as susceptible as other women to a piece of eye candy. Besides, women fall for men like Dennis every day. With a bad Forrest Gump imitation, she says, "Like a box of chocolate, you never know what you're going to get."

"That was horrible," I say with a guffaw, "but an excellent metaphor. The perfect man does he exist?"

"Perfect ... I don't think so. Anyway, perfect is boring. I have too many flaws to require perfection of any man," Kayla says.

I imagine a chocolate high and the resulting guilt. "Maybe Dennis is that sinful blend you can't get enough of and consume until you're sick."

"Heart-sick, heartbreak … poor things," Kayla says, feigning a tear. "If only men came with a warning … death-by-chocolate"

The man next to Kayla chuckles quietly, his eyes never leaving his laptop. Chagrined, Kayla and I grin.

"Well," I say in a low voice, "when I see a man as good-looking as Dennis, I run the other way. I don't want the competition."

"I'll take the traditional dark chocolate any day," Kayla says licking her lips. "All kidding aside, men like rocky-road Dennis should be the least of our concerns with all the maniacs roaming the streets. You gotta be cautious forgo that first bite on the first night."

I laugh at rocky-road, reckoning death-by-chocolate the possible result of Dennis' charms. "You really believe women are in Dennis' bed the first date?"

"You kidding, I've seen Dennis in action. Remember the pretty auditor last year?"

"Which one?"

"The little brunette with the big chest and annoying voice…"

"Oh no, did she?"

"Yep, I caught them exiting the stairwell. She was so embarrassed she rushed past me hanging her head. That was her first-day auditing, and Dennis didn't do anything but flash a sexy grin. He sauntered out of the stairwell like it was nothing to take a woman in a public place. I wanted to wipe that smug look off his face."

"Wow, I'm shocked. She seemed so professional."

"Well, she wasn't professional enough. Anyhow, Dennis knows he has no effect on us, and possibly why he's always throwing those sexist remarks around."

"Well, Ms. Junior Compliance Officer, you can end those sexist remarks. You should draft a memo about sexual harassment and disseminate it throughout the office. Ooh, better yet," I intoned with mischief, "you should tape it to Dennis' computer." I imagine him scornfully ripping the note from the console, and blithely tossing it in the trash. "As the first female associates Wheaton's hired, well besides Amber, they've probably never worried about sexist remarks before our arrival."

"Uh-huh, well, I've already gone to Bruce. One day Dennis pissed me off so badly, I marched straight to Bruce's office and reported him. Bruce said he would have a talk with Dennis, but I haven't seen a change in his behavior."

Kayla lifts her coffee with narrowed eyes and pursed lips. I assume she's piecing together some current news or office gossip. I can almost hear her synapsis click.

"Are you aware of their relationship?"

"Who? Dennis and Bruce?" I recognize the fascinated tone and perceive she'll enlighten me with some new headline as she'd often done in our seven-year friendship.

"Dennis is related to Bruce you know. I believe they're third cousins or something like that."

"Really, I had no idea. You can't tell by their features. They're so different."

"Ha! They're different in appearances, but in temperament they're the same. Bruce is a sweetheart until he's pushed the wrong way. I've seen his temper in compliance," Kayla says.

"Bruce might have a temper, but he's nothing like Dennis. He treats women with more respect," I retort with no evidence other than personal observation.

"That's for sure," she mumbles with a wicked grin.

Hmmm ... She's still fascinated with Bruce. I see his appeal. I've often found myself lost in his stormy eyes, which warm whenever I catch his stare. Every ounce of him exudes sophistication and wealth—from his salt-and-pepper hair to his muscular physique. His chiseled features are enough to turn any woman's head. I've often seen his female clients lose composure like some mesmerized schoolgirl. Why would Kayla be any different, but I hope it's merely girlish fantasies and nothing more. He's old enough to be her father.

Fathers ... I wonder if Dennis Fahey's misogyny is a product of his upbringing. *The hand that rocks the cradle rules the world*—words of Dorothy Dinnerstein from *The Mermaid and the Minotaur*. A book Judith stashed among countless books on her bookshelves. Oddly, I remember those enlightening words—*the mother is the first to form a child's attitude toward the human flesh.* I wonder if Dinnerstein's psychoanalysis would explain Dennis Fahey's behavior. I'm sure it would.

"What's going on in that brain, Vic?"

"Oh, just thinking about the Mermaid and the Minotaur. Have you ever read it?"

Kayla's eyes narrow. "Hmm, I haven't read the entire book but skimmed a few pages years ago. Why?"

"Dinnerstein's analysis could explain Dennis' behavior. Perhaps his mother treated him poorly and now he's rebelling against women in his life."

"Or," Kayla says with emphasis, "his father treated his mother with such contempt; Dennis grew up just like him."

"That's a good point. Have you ever met his parents?"

"No, but one of our theories is right," she says, and blows steam from her coffee. "I feel sorry for the unfortunate woman who marries him."

"Maybe he'll find someone to tame that bad-boy image," I say dubiously and ponder Dennis Fahey and Wheaton's employee's upbringing in affluent Greenwich Connecticut. "Do you realize everyone in the office is from Greenwich? It seems all their families are old friends, even the new kid Callum."

"Hmmm," Kayla mumbles. "It's peculiar. Maybe Bruce is doing all his friends a favor hiring their children, keeping a watch over their fortunes."

"So, why did he hire us? Our families aren't connected to the Wheatons."

"Vic, I've always wondered about that. You didn't apply to the firm, right?"

"No."

"Neither did I, so, how did they find us?"

"Maybe with recent pressure for corporate diversity, Wheaton was compelled to enhance the sex and ethnicity of his staff. And he killed two birds with one stone by hiring me," I say with a wry grin.

"No, I don't buy that. Our recruitment has always struck me strange. We never applied to the company. It's as if Wheaton beamed in and plucked us out of Wellesley. If we weren't such good friends, I wouldn't give it a second thought. But what's the chance of a top New York City hedge firm choosing two close friends from a non-ivy-league college," Kayla says rolling her lips sideways.

"Wellesley is a well-respected school. And we were top-ten in our class. Maybe that's what Wheaton was looking for."

Kayla purses her lips and stares out the window. "Hmmm, well, perhaps."

I detect an attitude change and study her profile for a despondent look that mars her face now and then. I suspect she's having second thoughts about Wheaton. Is she regretting her career choice and her indebtedness to the company for paying her tuition? With one semester of law school, she'll soon be Kayla Collins, Esquire. I wonder if that same expression ever crosses my face. Does my own dissatisfaction mimic Kayla's? "Do you ever regret accepting the position at Wheaton?"

Her deep sigh ruffles napkins on the counter. "Yes, I do ... God, Vic; I just wish I wasn't beholden to Wheaton. I can't see spending ten more years with the firm, and if I decide to leave, I'll have to pay back all that tuition." Regret swiftly reflects alarm. "Vic, sometimes I sense something's wrong at Wheaton."

Her expression triggers automatic humor that occurs when I sense trouble. "Are you going to tell me Wheaton's a coven of warlocks?"

"Vic, seriously, something just doesn't add up. You know Andrew quit last night."

"No way! Are you serious?"

She turns and examines the room quickly. Facing me, she narrows her eyes and says in a low voice, "Yep, I was there last night and witnessed the whole blowup. Bob and Andrew had a disagreement.

I heard all this shouting down the hallway and went to see what it was about. When I realized it was coming from Bruce's office, I turned back, but the anger in Andrew's voice made me stop and listen. He was upset about reporting of inaccurate account activity."

Here we go again. Kayla's expression means trouble. When something piques her interest, she'll snoop until she has answers, even at the risk of her safety.

"You know, I wouldn't be so concern about simple record keeping and reporting, but it was what Andrew said before he stormed out of the office."

"What did he say?"

"He said, 'When the shit hits the fan, I want no part of this mess or any blame for your transgressions.' And then he just quit. Vic, you should have seen his face. He wasn't just angry; he was scared."

"Scared of Bruce and Bob?"

"No, no, I believe it was fear from whatever he'd discovered. They didn't even stop him when he stormed out of the office. And they froze in shock when they saw me. I guess they assumed everyone had gone home. I was so uncomfortable standing there, so I acted nonchalantly, smiled, and walked back to my office."

"Wow! Well, that explains Andrew's absence this morning."

"But Vic, something's wrong. It's been coming for days. Andrew has been back and forth in compliance questioning trades and accounts. I saw him in the file room pulling records from seven years ago. By accident, he left one on my desk. That was what I was searching for in the file cabinet."

"What do you think he found?"

"Hey, ladies."

Startled, we both turn simultaneously. Bob stands behind us grinning and holding a monstrous pumpkin Moccachino with whip cream.

"Bob, Linda would have a heart attack if she knew you were drinking that mess."

"What she doesn't know won't hurt her," he says with a wink.

I wonder if he uses that reasoning for everything he does behind his wife's back. "But it might hurt you. What happened to the veggie drink?"

"I took two sips couldn't stand it. Are you two heading back to the office?" He asks, glancing at me and then Kayla.

Kayla grows silent and retrieves her purse from the floor.

"I guess we are," I say, collecting my coffee.

"Ladies, after you," he says, politely holding the door as we exit onto Lexington Avenue.

* * *

Back at the office, Amber, the receptionist, has just arrived. She turns with a smile and "Good morning."

Strangely, Kayla hasn't said a word since Bob appeared in the coffee shop, except a good morning to Amber. Quickly, she heads to her office, avoiding Bob's inquisitive stare.

"Someone woke on a thorny bed this morning. Or did my presence offend her?" Bob asks.

"No, she's just got a lot on her mind," I say to allay his suspicions, even though I thought the same.

"I hope that's all. I wouldn't want to make an enemy in compliance," he says with a wink and a smile. "Well, ladies enjoy your day. The market awaits me." With a little jig, he sautés down the hall.

I laugh at his playfulness and wonder how such a sweetheart can cause Kayla unease. Amber, unaware of Bob's little jig, searches her desk frantically. "You misplace something?"

Crouching under her desk, a muffled voice replies, "I can't find the guestbook." Standing straight, she adjusts her tight skirt's rising hem and pushes flat-ironed, chestnut-brown hair behind her ears. "It's usually right here," she says, pointing at the corner of her desk. "Did you see it earlier?"

"No, sorry, but Bruce was in the office with a client earlier. Maybe he moved it and forgot to return it."

Amber turns with her hands on her narrow hips and an inquisitive glare. "That's odd. He usually tells me when he's expecting a client so I can have coffee and tea prepared. You sure it was a client?"

"They were in the conference room. I just assumed he was a client."

With suspicious brown eyes, she deliberates Bruce's anonymous guest. "Hmmm ... well, maybe it's in Bruce's office."

I detect concern in Amber's eyes. *Maybe my instinct about Bruce's morning visitor was right.* And the glare he gave Kayla was peculiar.

As Bruce's assistant, I realized Amber is aware of Andrew's sudden departure. Not only the receptionist, but also Bruce's personal assistant, and office administrator, Amber runs the office as an extension of Bruce's hands. She's the go-to person for office gossip; an undercover sleuth who ferrets and discovers information so effortlessly. She knows everything about everyone at Wheaton and I often wonder how. Does she solicit information, or is she so good at engaging people, they don't realize they've told her their entire history? I'm sure the latter, as I've stopped myself many occasions from divulging information for her query. I'm certain she's aware of Andrew's resignation.

"Do you know Andrew quit last night?"

"I heard ... so sad. I saw it coming weeks ago," she says without a blink. "He's just been on edge the last month or so. I wasn't surprised when Bruce called last night and asked me to pack and mail his stuff."

Bruce's precipitous demands to box and mail Andrew's possessions, swiftly discarding a trusted colleague's remains, appear insensitive. I pry subtly. "I guess they'll find someone to replace him soon?"

"No, there won't be a rush right away. Bob will assume the role again."

"Bob, Bob O'Connor?"

"Yes, he was CFO before he became Head Trader?"

"Oh, I didn't know." I wonder if Kayla's aware of that fact. And why was she so quiet when Bob showed up? *What was she going to tell me before he interrupted our conversation?* I stare at the small cup and wish I'd bought a larger coffee. I'll need the caffeine to help me through the morning. "Well, it's time for the meeting." Before I make it down the hall, Amber calls my name.

"Vic, I haven't received your RSVP for the company dinner. You're coming, I hope."

"Didn't I give it to you last week?"

"No."

"It's probably in my office. I'll give it to you after the meeting."

"Don't forget," she says and resumes her desperate search for the guestbook.

Inside the trade room, Bob's consumed by the market ticker crossing his screen. I know there's something Kayla wanted to tell me in the coffee shop. She'd never be so blatantly rude. Has she discovered something about Bob? Is that what she wanted to tell me before Bob interrupted our conversation?

Chapter 4

Morning dew mists my face as I increase my pace and leap over puddles. With a splatter, I disturb a large white bird, sending it soaring to a boulder ahead. On the reservoir water, a sord of mallards glide through cold water with a deep grunt to crude for the graceful creatures. Perhaps it's a mating call or just a morning ritual. Behind me, slapping feet approach swiftly. I glance back, and it's him smiling and waving. Finally, Chase catches up, slowing his pace to my stride. My freedom dance subsides.

"Hey," he says winded. "I was hoping to see you. I didn't expect to find you on the reservoir. I thought you ran the loop mostly."

"No, I run both." His panting tells me he must have sprinted to catch up. In response, I slow my pace, giving him time to catch his breath, and just as I do, I land in a puddle, splashing Chase's legs with muddy water. "Yikes! Sorry," I squeal, looking down at his muddy legs.

"It's okay. I like getting dirty," he says in a suggestive way.

Dirty, sounds so appealing coming from his lips. My heart does an unexpected leap with the thought of him muddy from head to toe. Quickly, I pull my mind from the gutter, back to the sound of our breathing. It's been months hearing the breath of another person running beside me.

"Are you on your last round?"

"Yes. I'm done after this."

"Darn, I was hoping to run with you a little longer."

Why's he so anxious to run with me. I suspect it's not my pace, but an attempt to talk to me. Increasing my stride, as I always do the final quarter mile, I test his stamina and leave him behind, but only for a moment, as he catches up and surpasses me. I'm not surprised, but curious why he's been toying with me. I knew a body like that could surely outrun me. Ahead, he stands with a smirk on his face; waiting for me to join him. "Ah-ha! So, you can run faster."

"If I have to," he says with a laugh.

"Well, why were you trailing behind me for several days?" I ask with a curious grin.

"Hmmm ... well, the view from the rear was so pleasing, I decided to stay behind."

I was right. It isn't just my pace he's interested in. For the second time, we stand at the end of a run, basking in a runner's euphoria. Studying him fully, I'm certain he's no more than twenty-eight or twenty-nine. His baseball cap shadows the true color of his smiling eyes. He's undeniably handsome. He's Latino I assume. His well-proportioned body holds me captivated and the scent I noticed during our first meeting lures me again.

"I'm throwing a party at my place next Saturday with a group of friends around eight. I would love for you to come. I live just there," he says, pointing toward a prewar building on Fifth Avenue, a building I've seen movie stars and dignitaries come and go.

"The Rossellini building," I mumble under my breath but realize he's heard my digression.

"Rossellini?" He asks with raised brows.

Chagrined, I stammer. "Oh-I, well, it's just a name I gave the building."

"Why Rossellini?"

"It's silly. I often see Isabela Rossellini entering after walking her dogs, so I named the building Rossellini."

"Oh, I've heard she's a resident, but I've never seen her." His eyebrows arch expectantly.

Considering his address, he probably thinks I'll jump at his invitation. But I don't know him well enough, and money has never impressed me. He tilts his head, waiting for an answer. "I have plans next Saturday, but thank you for the offer," I declined offhandedly. His crestfallen gaze affects a response. "I have to attend a company dinner, but perhaps another time."

He stares beyond my face, and then extracts a leaf from my ponytail. "There we go," he whispers, displaying the burnt-orange leaf between his fingers. "I'll keep this to remind me of this moment." His eyes glint with his smile.

His touch and words send a delicious ripple through my core. Unsure of this new emotion, I stutter, "Thanks, I—Ah, I have to go." I turn and look back, catching an amused grin. Well, that was obvious rushing away so childishly. I wave goodbye and he does the same with a discerning grin. I sense his eyes on my backside as I walk toward the entrance and quicken my stride with a bashful grin.

Chapter 5

Chase's touch disoriented me and I'm certain he noticed my odd behavior when I fled the reservoir. His smirk assures me he knew of my attraction when I turned and waved good-bye. I snicker at my girlish behavior and a young woman standing on the train platform peers quizzically from her iPad.

I exit the subway in the west village and make my way to Buvette's—a small Parisian restaurant—for brunch with the gang. A few feet inside the door, I find the group seated around two tables pushed together to accommodate my six friends, my confidants, my anchor, I couldn't exist without them. I'm the lone wheel unadorned by a male counterpart unlike my friends—one married with twins, the other in an exclusive relationship for several years. Hannah and Paul, Michelle and Taylor sit watching as I enter the restaurant. Their greetings a simultaneous dissonance of words—"Vicky, hey, hi, there she is."

"Hey all," I reply, realizing the group is missing one.

"Where's Kayla?"

"She had to pick up a file from the office," Michelle reveals in an unusually bubbly manner. "She'll be here soon."

They all seem so happy, but I know all their problems. Like their therapist, I've witnessed years of growth and compromises. Hannah and Paul married two years; sit like Siamese twins staring at one menu. Hannah is choosing, and Paul consents to every choice. I know the boss in this family. Hannah looks more tired than usual. A new mom to twins, I'm sure her schedule is full. Hannah's not the girl I remember from college—so carefree and full of promise. She's slid down that rabbit hole and emerged on the other side of carefree—whatever that may be—but the youth is draining from her eyes and she's just twenty-five. Once the fashion plate, she no longer cares. Maybe being a mom has created this other half.

In school, Hannah was the ambitious one with plans to conquer the field of journalism. A brief stint of writing for the New York Times, and the promise of a burgeoning career, halted when she met charismatic Paul. TV Executive, Paul Wentworth of the Scarsdale Wentworths, comes from old money, but you can hardly tell by his mannerisms. He's the generation of bleeding-heart liberals who hate his family's wealth and defies them at every turn. He married an African-American, surely defiance. They're two extreme opposites, Hannah extroverted and outgoing, Paul introverted, solemn, Hannah's shadow, allows her to run the show. I've heard people can resemble their pets, but can people resemble their mates? Maybe too much time together, couples adopt each other's attitudes, mannerisms, and diction. I study the two, remembering horrific arguments a week ago. I guess most couples have fights, but Hannah and Paul's was over-the-top. Are issues brewing, promises made not fulfilled and regrets developing? Here they sit so affectionately. *Is it an act?*

Michelle, the other half of the Bella Sorelle, as we called ourselves in college, still appears the same. Of course, she does, money has a way of doing that. With no financial worries or responsibilities, she floats through life without aspirations or directions. She's still daddy's girl. I wonder when that will change. On campus, Michelle was envied by all. Her dorm room decorated like some plush hotel suite—closets overflowing with designer clothes. Every year she'd arrive with a new BMW. I often wondered if her parents bought her degree. Her family's wealth, I can't comprehend, comes from thriving global businesses. I assumed Michelle would work with her father one day, but she always protests. *"I could never work with my dad."* Perhaps it's too much work for her. Michelle was the Asian beauty on campus. In a minuscule world of minorities, we became inseparable. Outside campus grounds, I don't believe we would have been such good friends. Now and then, prejudices ingrained from her upbringing rears its nasty head—racial biases, contempt for immigrants, the poor, and the list goes on—but she's trying to reform. Her political persuasion is not mine, but I'm open-minded. Most of the time her childish ideas infuriates me, but I'm sympathetic. No matter how different our backgrounds and beliefs, Michelle is a devoted friend—always there in my time of grief.

Who knew Michelle would be attracted to blondes. In school, she dated strictly Asian men. Taylor was a total surprise. He's the rock that holds her down and centers her. The group welcomed him wholeheartedly, a present from the heavens made just for Michelle. Of course, her parents are angry, preferring she dates her own kind, but they'll never disown her. Taylor, a self-made man with a middle-class upbringing, works hard for his money. A doctor, after all, no one can accuse him of being a gold digger. He's way too independent and caring for that.

Michelle wiggles a finger with a glistening diamond and exclaims, "We're engaged!" At once, I'm happy and sad—another wedding, more kids, Auntie Victoria again. I smile and rush to their side with a huge hug. "Have you chosen a date," I ask, choking back tears, which always appear at births, weddings, and now engagements.

"November 22," Taylor says. Michelle snuggles close.

"We wanted a summer wedding, but there wasn't enough time to coordinate everything."

"Hmmm, are you two hiding something?" Hannah asks twirling her finger at Michelle's belly like a magic wand.

"Hannah, for God's sake no," Michelle protests. Even if I were, it's not why we're planning a November wedding. Taylor's hospital schedule is so crazy; November is the only month that works. Oh, you two are my Maid of Honors."

Oh good, I thought, remembering Hannah and Paul's wedding. The emotional roller coaster lasted weeks. Finally, happy when it was over, I vowed never to walk down the aisle. Perhaps a leap from a plane, or a walk on the beach, but never will I walk down the aisle in a ceremonial gown.

"You only have a month to go guys. I hope you've found a church for your ceremony," Paul says.

"We have..." Michelle says. A distinct 'but' lingered in the air, "...and the rest, well, you know, mom has taken charge. She's already started booking the caterers, musicians, and all that other stuff."

She tries to smile, but I see conflict burning in her eyes.

"If mom had it her way, she'd write our vows."

I laugh, remembering how Michelle's mom planned her birthday parties like some major cultural event—over-the-top with everything. I'm already dreading being a Maid of Honor. Her mom might prove trying.

"Michelle, you can control that. This is your wedding, just take command." Why am I the voice of reason lately? Is it aging, or dwindling tolerance for stupidity? I presume a combination of both as I glance around the group. I sense life has changed everyone. When did I become the voice of reason, Hannah lax, and Michelle conventional? I never pictured her married, and never in a church—perhaps on Machu Picchu mountaintops with a recently found climber. I laugh surreptitiously. Hannah peers and smiles.

"What's so funny?" Hannah asks.

I wave my hand and choke on my words. "Nothing," I say, almost spurting water in her face. It was then I realize I've become rather cynical.

The group laughs at me, but they wouldn't if they knew what I was thinking. I study the group peering at Hannah and Paul, concealing their troubled marriage just for the occasion. I study Michelle and Taylor, glowing with love and wonder if marriage will change them too. On the table, Hannah's cell phone buzzes. Her face lights with alarm before she answers the phone. Quickly, she picks up.

"What's wrong?" The words of an overly concerned mom. "Has she been coughing long?" Hannah asks rising from her chair.

And I already know the group will be less two as she gathers her purse swiftly.

"Guys, I'm so sorry..." she says, kissing everyone on the cheek before she finished her sentence, "...the nanny is frantic."

"Guys, see you soon," Paul says rather peevish, leaving money on the table and following Hannah through the restaurant door.

Outside, Hannah screams, "Taxi!" A car pulls up, they enter and the cab pulls away. Silently, I hope nothing is wrong. Now I know why Hannah appeared haggard—the stresses of children and all that comes with being a new mom. Maybe there's no time to enjoy life's pleasures. She's become the women of Park Avenue wearing a coat over their pajamas, making sure the children are on the school bus, and kissing their husbands as they leave for work. I've often wondered what they do after the kids and husband are gone. Do they shout hooray or saunter back to bed to an empty day, no plans, no life other than their family. I turn to Michelle and Taylor and ask, "Are you ready for that?"

Seconds later, Kayla rushes through the door in an agitated state.

"I just saw Hannah and Paul get into a taxi. Where are they going?"

"Oh, it's the babies again," I explain, noticing worry in her eyes. "Are you okay?"

She sets her bag on the floor and then takes a sip of water from a glass Paul had been sipping moments before. "Thirsty," she says, forcing a smile to hide anxiousness. I can tell because her eyes are not smiling. "So, what did I miss?"

Kayla, the fourth Bella Sorelle, was the last to join our group in college—two African-Americans, an Asian, and Kayla, Irish-American. Our little group is culturally well-rounded. Kayla is the fearless one, all brains, and good looks. Opinionated, she'll fight to her death for a worthy cause. From a well-to-do family and the only daughter of five siblings, she grew up one of the boys. The inquisitive type, she should have been a private detective. In school, she would intrigue us with her sleuthing and stories she'd discover about students and faculty. Forever involved with social and political causes, she wears her heart on her sleeve. Like me, her ethics are way too high for the field we chose as a career. I always believed one day her snooping will get her in trouble.

"You're working hard these days," I say, wondering why she went to the office on a Saturday morning. Something smolders behind her eyes as she stares into space with a tight smile that starts to twitch. Her body is way too tense as she sits upright in the chair. Again, she sips more water as if to calm her nerves.

"Kayla?"

"Oh, sorry, it's that file, Vic. I still can't find it. It's just disappeared, but I found something else," she says lost in thought again.

"What is it?"

She shakes her head and takes another sip of water. "I don't know yet," she mumbles. "I can't figure it out, but it's not right."

Something's up, but I leave it alone. I know she'll tell me in her own time. Across the table, Michelle makes a face, which mimics my own curiosity.

Kayla rubs her fingers demonstrably and asks, "Vic, you have any lotion? My hands are so dry from all the dusty files I went through in the office."

I motion to my tote, but before I can reach for it, she leans underneath the table. There's a long pause, then fumbling noises. "Kayla, what are you doing?" I ask playfully. Just as I'm about to check beneath the table, she emerges with the hand lotion, squeezes it in her palm, and replaces the tube in my bag.

Michelle thumps her fingers on the table, signaling Kayla to notice. Kayla glances at the ring in disbelief then at Taylor. "Did you?" A sharp screech escapes Kayla's mouth, causing my ears to vibrate. With lightning speed, she rushes toward the betrothed couple, kissing them so hard they both grimaced. "Oh my God, when did this happen? When's the wedding date? Are you pregnant?"

Michele fires back in rapid succession, "Last week, November 22, and no, I am not pregnant. As I told Hannah, the engagement is short because of Taylor's schedule and we don't want to wait too long. Oh, you are also a Maid of Honor."

"Vic, it's just us now," Kayla laments with a frown, "single and desperately seeking Mr. Right."

"Speak for yourself, Kayla," I say with a scowl.

"Kayla, I know a few single men who'd love to meet you," Taylor offers.

"I'll think about it, Taylor," Kayla says with a wink. "Let's celebrate. Where's the champagne," she asks, leaning into the table and beaming at the couple. Cheerful exaltations replace anxiousness seen moments before. The engagement has smoothed her edges a bit, but I still sense something brewing.

* * *

Moments later, after several glasses of champagne, I'm startled by Kayla's prying and surprised Michelle is her target. Maybe the alcohol has given her courage to speak her mind. I recognize the subtleness of Kayla's tone, trying to make her inquiries less intrusive.

"Michelle, what's the name of your father's company?"

"That came out of left field," Michelle says glassy-eyed. "Well, dad has more than one business. Which one are you referring to?"

"I believe it starts with a T or TH..."

"Thawone," Michelle says.

"That's it."

I detect a change in Kayla's energy with Michelle's affirmation.

"Thawone is one of dad's manufacturing companies."

"Where did you see the company's name," I ask.

"Oh-ah—on the way here I saw the name in a magazine."

Again, I detect a lie, the second time this week. Is she on another witch-hunt, and why Michelle?

"What products does Thawone make?" Kayla asks.

Michelle swirls ice around the glass of water and squints her slanted eyes, recognizing Kayla's prying. Deadpan she says, "They produce frozen foods and some other culinary items."

Unruffled by the squint in Michelle's eyes, Kayla continues. "Have you ever tried the products?"

Michelle, scrunched in the booth, slowly detaches her shoulders from Taylor's arms and sits straight. From her expression, I can tell she doesn't like being on the receiving end of Kayla's questions. With a steely gaze, she answers her queries. "On occasion, dad would bring home a few samples of the frozen dinners. I didn't care for them. I prefer fresh foods over frozen."

"So, you've never bought them from a store?"

Now a little more annoyed, Michelle leans on the table. "Kayla, what's with the sudden interest in my father's company?"

"No particular reason," Kayla says quickly. "I just realized you never talk about your family's business. I just want to know more about the company, which is doing well. Have you ever visited the offices?"

Michelle glares at Kayla and replies bluntly, "No. You know the company's headquartered in Japan, right?"

"Yep, I just thought maybe you've visited on one of your trips."

Michelle slouches in the booth with a heavy sigh. "No, mom and I rarely get involved in Thawone. And dad has never asked or offered to take us to the company, which is fine with me. Anyway..." she says with a scoff, "... he might try to talk me into working for him. And honestly, I'm just not interested."

"Maybe you should be ... I mean it's your family's business. I know I would be curious to see what my dad does for a living."

With Kayla's condescending tone, I snap my head in her direction, noticing the *are-you-serious* expression on her face. What is she doing?

"Okay, when have you been so interested in my father's business?" Michelle asks, taking offense.

"I'm just saying, you need to take more interest."

Taylor in accord with Kayla reveals, "I've been trying to get her to do the same, but obviously, Michelle has her reasons for keeping her distance. So, I respect her decision."

Realizing her bad timing, Kayla eases off. "Michelle, I'm a total ass. Forgive me for ruining your moment. I don't know what came over me."

Michelle sits with quiet concern on her face. And I perceive Kayla wield her questions for this precise reaction from Michelle.

Chapter 6

"Working on a Saturday Miss Collins?" The security guard at 570 Lexington asks as I enter the office building lobby. "Wheaton got you working hard these days—two weekends in a row," he says.

"Always," I say with a dry grin and hand him my employee I.D. "I left some work behind. I'm just picking it up."

He studies the I. D. and places it in my hand with a grin. "Don't work too hard Miss. You know what they say—"

"Yep, all work and no play makes a dull Kayla," I say ambling toward the elevator and stepping inside. Pushing the button to the thirty-eight floor, and anxiously gnawing on my bottom lip, I pray everyone's left for the company weekend. If I'm caught snooping around Amber's desk, there's no excuse I can give, except I'm looking for a pen. I just hope I don't need a reason.

Two nights ago, Amber's expression was of classic guilt, the look of someone caught with their pants down. She hadn't expected me to be in the office so late. When I turned the corner, I swear the wall behind her desk slid closed. A wall I've never seen open, a wall that had always been just a wall was suddenly a doorway. I held a stone face, pretending I hadn't seen anything. Amber acted nonchalantly, but her coolness belied worry in her eyes. I continued to my office as if nothing happened, waiting for the perfect time to explore behind her desk. And today is that day when everyone's traveling to Bruce's

Greenwich estate. I hate abandoning Vicky at the last minute, but I know there's something Wheaton's hiding behind that wall.

Inside the office, Wheaton hums like an abandoned ship. I check every room, even the utility closets to make sure I'm alone, and then rush back to reception. Remembering Amber surreptitiously placing keys beneath the desk, I fumble underneath for a knob, a latch, or a button. Instantly, my finger hits a switch. I flip it back and a tiny compartment slides forward, with a set of keys. I'm certain one opens the wall, but there's no keyhole anywhere. I run my hands up and down the panel until I graze a slight notch. It's almost invisible but the design around the dent looks like an infinity sign—a perfect disguise. After trying three of the keys, the paneled slides open with the fourth one, revealing a small room.

I step inside and the door swiftly closes. Worried, I search frantically for a latch then notice a flashing console on the adjacent wall. Tapping several buttons, the door opens and shuts twice. Relieved, I continue searching the room. A small, flat-screen television hangs on a wall opposite a beige sofa. In the center of the room, on top of a plain wooden desk, sits a computer and several magazines. A navy cardigan, Amber sometimes wears when the office gets chilly, drapes a chair. A photo of Bruce and Mallory wearing costumes in Saint Mark's Square in Venice is taped to the computer. The light on the monitor signals the computer is asleep, but still on. Pressing the power button the computer awakens, revealing multiple office views. Wide-eyed, I stare in disbelief. Every room at Wheaton has surveillance cameras. Searching for my office, I find a camera positioned directly over my desk. *They can see everything I do.* Doesn't this violate workplace privacy rights? Flipping through other rooms, cameras are angled in a similar fashion—pointed at employee's computer. A sharp buzz emanates from the wall console. On the computer monitor, a man wearing a black, leather jacket enters the reception area. He's not wearing a uniform, so he can't be building security. And how did he get into the office without a key?

The man pauses at reception with his back to the desk and peers left-to-right. He turns facing the wall, pulls a cell phone from his jacket, and makes a call. The room must be soundproof. I can't hear anything on the other side. Talking on his cell phone, he continues toward the back. On the cameras, I watch him roam room-to-room. *What's he searching for?* With mounting fear, I begin to worry someone knows I'm here. Does he know about this room? I watch and wait until he moves further into the office. As soon as he's far enough, I open the door, dash to the desk, and fumble for the switch. I gasp when the keys slip my hands, hitting the floor with a dull jingle. Quickly, crouching to the floor, I grab the keys and return them to the secret compartment.

Nearing the entrance, I glance back, shocked to see the wall door wide open. I listen for approaching feet, but there's none. Rushing to the door, I push hard, but it won't budge. If I go back inside that room, the door will surely close. I can't take the chance of him finding me. I strain, pushing harder, but the stubborn door is fixed. Down the hallway, footsteps approach.

Damn it!

Leaving the wall wide-open, I rush from the office, and flee down the stairwell. The spikey heel of my boot wobbles. I topple forward, catch the guardrail, and slide down several steps with a piercing screech, landing awkwardly on my ankle. Two stories above, a door opens. I ease off my twisted ankle, onto my feet, limp painfully toward the thirty-six-floor exit, and onto the elevator. In the lobby, I straighten my leg, put pressure on my heel, and try to look normal.

"You're done already?" The inquisitive guard asks.

I force a smile. "Yep, all done." With a painful gait, I enter the revolving doors and limp onto the sidewalk.

Chapter 7

Amber, crimson, and gold peaks in Greenwich Connecticut. A sole passenger on this chauffered ride, I rest my head on the limousine seat, take in autumn's brilliant foliage, and ponder Kayla's last minute change of plans. The Wheaton estate comes into view as the company rental winds down the narrow road. Early morning clouds disperse, revealing cerulean blue skies glistening off the Long Island Sound like sapphires through the trees. The estate dubbed the Wheaton compound, and rightly so, sits on 10.8 acres. With three guest homes surrounding a massive Georgian-Colonial, sunken gardens, pool, and tennis courts—the estate appears like a dream by the sea. I read somewhere the Wheaton estate has graced the land since 1918.

Hosted every year by Bruce and Mallory Wheaton, the company weekend is a formal gathering, filled with pomp and circumstance one expects of the wealthy. Servants greet guest and whisk them off to well-prepared rooms long before the main event—a seven-course dinner. Breakfast aromas and cacophonous kitchen noise suffuse the main floor. A young servant reaches for my bag, but I protest.

"Has everyone arrived?"

"No, Miss, they're starting to trickle in." He smiles and leads me to a second-floor guest room where a festive door plaque reads, 'Welcome Lady Victoria.' The servant opens the door and says "Enjoy your stay," leaving me in a room I'd marveled at previous years. Mallory Wheaton remembered my fascination with the high-plated ceilings, reading nook, and fireplace off the private balcony. On the four-poster bed lays a blood-red gown, crimson, velvet wrap, and a gold Columbina mask etched with crystals, lace, and red feathers, chosen by Mallory for the big affair.

I heard years ago, after visiting the Venice Carnival, Wheaton started his own mini-version; throwing parties in the seventies, eighties, and nineties, frequented by the wealthy. Now in their golden years, grand parties no more, they still integrate carnival's mystique in company dinners. At first, I thought it outrageous, but after the first dinner, I've grown to love the occasion. I'm curious what mask she's chosen for the men. Each year they don mask appearing like some mythological creature. It's a comical sight seated around a formal dining table with figures straight out of a Venetian masquerade ball.

Placing my overnight bag on the bed, I immediately withdraw my mobile and call Kayla. I hope she doesn't bail on the weekend, leaving me with the guys and their significant others. Surprisingly, she answers on the first ring. "Kayla, are you still at the office?"

"Hey Vic, I'm sorry about this morning. I had some work to catch up on. I'm in my car on my way. Don't worry; I'll see you in about thirty minutes."

I sigh deeply, collapse on the bed, and stare at the ceiling. A sharp edge scratches my cheek, and I glance sideways at a menu and itinerary. *Mallory has thought of everything this year.* I notice brunch has already begun in the informal dining room and back patio, and chuckle at an Oktoberfest planned in the sunken gardens and waterfront area. *Hmmm, sounds like fun.*

Noise springs from the backyard. Curious, I saunter toward the private balcony overlooking gardens and the Long Island Sound. The yard appears like a carnival, littered with booths and vendors preparing their specialty—food, games, trinkets and more. Brightly carved Jack-o-Lanterns line intricate-brick pathways winding around the property. An attractive woman with wavy, brown hair to her derriere, wearing a gypsy outfit, large hoop earrings, and headband prepares objects around her stall while Dennis Fahey distracts her from her work. I hope she sees through those devilish good looks.

Wondering what's in store for the weekend, I study the gold-embossed itinerary in detail.

Wheaton Asset Management, LLC - Weekend Celebration
Saturday, October 30th
10:00 A.M. - 1:00 P.M. - Brunch
Place: Informal Dining Room extending to Covered Porch
1:00 P.M. - 6:00 P.M. - Oktoberfest
Place: Sunken Gardens and Waterfront Area
3:00 P.M. - 5:00 P.M. - Afternoon Movie
Place: Main House - Theater Room
7:30 P.M. - 8:00 P.M. - Bruce Wheaton's Speech
Place: Great Room
8:00 P.M. - 10:00 P.M. - Seven Course Dinner
Place: Formal Dining Room
10:00 P.M. - 12:00 A.M. - Drinks Served
Place: Great Room
Sunday, October 31st
8:00 A.M. - 10:00 A.M. - Breakfast
Place: Formal Dining Room
10:00 A.M. - 4:00 P.M. - Continuation of Oktoberfest
Place: Backyard and Waterfront Area
12:00 Noon - Lunch
Place: Back Patio
2:00 P.M. - 4:00 P.M. - Halloween Treats
Place: Carriage House
We hope you enjoy the weekend.
Bruce and Mallory Wheaton

Mallory has planned an outrageous seven-course dinner that far exceeds previous years. I can't imagine the formalities involved in serving each course. I close the menu, waltz to the mirror, fix my wind-blown hair, reassess my poncho, dark leggings, riding boots, and then exit the room. Strolling along the corridor, I study names on door plaques, noticing Kayla's room three doors away. When a familiar voice echoes down the hall, I stop and listen.

"I wouldn't put it pass Andrew to take this to FINRA. The man is too ethical. We're stupid to let this slide," Bob O'Connor's angst-ridden voice declares.

Alarmed, I tiptoe closer, chiding myself for eavesdropping. But after Kayla's revelation in Starbucks, my curiosity is piqued. King of Denmark cigars scents the area, signaling Bruce's presence. His fractious voice booms in retort.

"For God's sake man, calm down; I'm sure we can persuade Andrew to let this go, perhaps offer him a package he can't resist … Let me handle this. Just go back outside and enjoy the brunch and wipe that fear off your face. We don't want people thinking something's wrong, especially your busybody wife."

Something brushes against the door, and I jump and rush downstairs. *Kayla's right. Something's happening at Wheaton.* I straighten my face as Linda O'Connor approaches.

"There she is, and more gorgeous than ever," she exclaims with raised arms. Taking my hands, she leans in, kisses my cheek, and examines me with new eyes less a wrinkle or two.

Her blond hair, now streaked lighter blond along the hairline, gives her sixty-five year-old face a more youthful appearance. Her lips are plumper than I remember, but soften her thinning face. The holistic diet of juicing must be working because she's slimmed down a dress size or two since our last meeting.

"You look just like your mother. I should have seen it day one."

I wonder if she'd seen Judith on stage or knew her personally. "How do you know Judith?"

"I met your mom many years ago before you were born. She was popular in her day and a special friend of the Wheatons. Mallory was talking to Bruce, and I overheard you're her daughter. I just couldn't believe they hadn't told me."

Hadn't told you, what about me?

"You know, Bruce was fascinated with your mom." Her eyes crease, the only indication of a frown on her rigid countenance. "Dear, I was so sorry to hear of your mom's passing." She wiggles her head with a troubled frown that barely wrinkles. "She was still in her prime." She stares quizzically. "Why didn't you mention you're Judith Powell's daughter?"

Still stuck on Judith and Bruce's friendship, her words escape unheard. Then I notice her questioning eyes and stammer, "What-oh, I'm sorry Linda; I didn't hear what you said."

"I was wondering why you never mentioned you're Judith's daughter."

Why would I? There was never an indication Judith knew the Wheaton's. Embarrassed Judith hadn't told me, I provide a flimsy excuse. "Well, I try to keep my personal life separate from work."

"Dear, you should be proud of your mother."

Trying to disguise my surprise, I force a stiff smile. "How long did my mom know Mallory and Bruce?"

"Oh, sweetie, many years, but I'm not the person to ask. You should talk to Bruce. He can tell you more than I can." With a squint, she considers my inquiring mind then offers validation. Pointing toward the home's second wing she says, "In the library, family photos hold marvelous photos of your mom. She was close to them at one time. Judith was always at Wheaton parties, held right here in this home. That's how I met your mom." She dissects my face with microscopic eyes. "You have her beautiful brown eyes and wonderful heart-shaped lips." She pauses as if waiting for Judith to materialize. "I adored her work ... such a talented opera singer and a captivating woman," she reveals. "You should be proud."

"I am," I say forcing another smile. An epiphany seizes my mind. My recruitment wasn't a coincidence. *Bruce hired me because of Judith.*

"Are you okay dear?"

Words slip before I can catch them. "Yes, I'm just surprised Bruce was Judith's friend." Then I realized what I'd said. Now Linda is aware I'd never been told.

With a discerning smile, she locks her arm in mine. "The rich and famous sometimes run in the same circles."

She guides me past the dining room, onto the covered porch, and toward a table lined with a substantial feast. The news of my mom and boss' friendship has squelched any hunger, but I grab a bottle of water to suppress unease settling in my stomach. Barely grasping Linda as she gabs on about afternoon festivities, I stare blankly, suspicions forming in my mind. "Linda, I—uh, excuse me." I stammer. "I forgot something in my room." I smile apologetically and rush upstairs to my cell phone.

On the other end of the phone, my father's once rich and hearty voice sound grainy at seventy-three. Perturbed by his frail voice, I stifle the angry voice in my head.

"Vicky, what a surprise sweetheart."

"Dad, did you know Judith was an old friend of Bruce and Mallory Wheaton?"

"Where did you hear that?"

"From Linda O'Connor, my co-worker's wife."

"Linda, yes, well…" Aiden sighs deeply. "I told Judith you'd find out one day," he says and clears hoarseness from his throat. "Well, this is one conversation I promised your mom I'd never broach, but there's no sense in keeping a promise now that you know. Vicky, Judith just wanted you to have the best. And you know Judith had many connections; people who would have done anything for her. Bruce Wheaton is one of those people. He promised when you graduated, he'd offer you a position with his firm. Honey, there's no harm in that. Judith did you a huge favor."

"I just wish I'd known. Why didn't Bruce tell me?"

"She swore Bruce to secrecy. Vic, you're so damn independent. She knew you'd reject Bruce's offer if you knew she'd gotten the position for you."

"Well, she was right about that. You know, even from her grave, she gets her way."

"That's our Judith," he says with a chuckle. "Honey, are you happy with the job?"

Lately, I've asked myself that question often. "I think so, dad." Recalling the conversation overheard between Bruce and Bob, I ponder telling him. But I don't. "Dad, can we talk later? I'm at the Wheaton estate."

"Sure Vic, but just remember, Judith did it out of love."

"As she always had, dad..."

* * *

I walk the backyard oblivious to festivities, stewing over Judith's arrangement with Bruce. Her silence must have been more intricate than my objection. Lost in thought, I'm unaware I've entered the endless garden maze designed out of hedges. A place I once spent thirty minutes trying to find my way out of two years ago. I turn to go back when I'm stopped by low voices a few feet away.

A female voice, obviously in the throes of passion, lets out a moan of pleasure. A male voice asserts in a thick, lusty voice, "You like that don't you."

A jerky, "Yes," escapes her mouth with a plea for more, "Harder."

Suspiciously, the male voice, though huskier, sounds like Dennis Fahey's. Lured by the sensual moans, I inch a little further inside the maze. At the next turn, in a small round alcove carved out of shrubs, Dennis, sexually straddles the woman I saw earlier in the gypsy costume. Standing with one leg on the bench and the other on the ground, his exposed cheeks clench as he guides her backside into his hardness. The long prairie skirt raised over his shoulder reveals her pale bare legs and ankle boots as she leans into the shrubbery. His hands loosen her top and her full breast jiggle and escape. Her passionate moans grow deeper. Surprisingly, I'm fascinated and embarrassed all at once. With the woman's loud squeal, I turn and run toward the house.

On the covered porch, I notice Kayla filling her plate and approach with an impish grin. In less than an hour, I've managed to uncover three secrets—Bob and Bruce's alarming conversation, Judith and Bruce's friendship, and now, Dennis' sexual tryst. Sudden laughter erupts into deep hiccups.

"Vic, what's wrong?" Kayla asks, taking a bite of the crispy bacon. Noticing my hiccups, she hands me bottled water, but water never squelches the annoying spasms.

"Honestly, you won't believe my morning," I say followed by a noisy hiccup. "When did you get here?"

"Just a few minutes ago," Kayla says, filling her plate with a huge croissant.

In the corner of my eye, Mallory approaches. Her long raven hair now a short blunt style, swings above her shoulders. Her pale complexion grows papery with age, but her beauty is still disconcerting. Her dazzling blue eyes, sharp cheekbones, full lips, and a nose appears molded by an artist. Her outfit is simple, but always well put together. I guess a style developed from years of modeling.

In a high voice and almost rising on the tips of her toes, she exclaims, "Ladies, I'm so glad you're here. What do you think about the Oktoberfest? This year, I thought a Halloween theme would be fun and different."

I smile, hiccup, and apologize at once, questioning Mallory's silence about my mom. "Everything's magnificent, Mallory. I can't wait to participate in all the events." I wonder if she and Judith were good friends and *why hasn't she ever mention my mom.*

"Did you girls see the gowns I chose for you this year? I hope you like them. Vicky with your honey-toned skin, you'll look ravishing in red." Touching Kayla's hair, the diamond ring, and tennis bracelet sparkle on her finger and wrist. "And with your fiery hair Kayla, you'll look stunning in emerald green."

I manage through a series of hiccups, "The gown is gorgeous. I can't wait to wear it. Thank you."

"Green is one of my favorite colors," Kayla says, munching hungrily. "Plus, I trust your judgment, Mallory. Thank you." Forever probing for information, Kayla presses on. "I hope you don't mind me asking, but where do the gowns come from? They look expensive."

"A few designers are willing to lend me dresses for the occasion." A loud shatter in the kitchen releases Mallory from Kayla's probing. With a start, she looks around. "Ladies, please eat and have fun, and Vicky try rapid breathing, that will ease the hiccups," she says, rushing toward the kitchen.

* * *

Inside the Wheaton's family library, Kayla listens wide-eyed to my morning discoveries. Bob and Bruce's conversation and Dennis' mid-morning trysts don't faze her, however, Judith and Bruce's friendship piques her interest.

"Now that makes sense! It explains how we got the jobs at Wheaton." Kayla slides on the leather sofa, removes her boot, and examines her ankle with a pained expression.

"It seems Judith was looking out for both of us," I mutter with a wry grin. "Isn't it strange I never met Mallory or Bruce growing up? Judith never mentioned them, and they never visited the house."

Kayla's Sherlock Holmes glare tells me she's deliberating the fact. Straightaway, I notice the purplish bulge sprouting from her ankle. "Kayla, what happened? Why are you walking around on that?"

"I'll be fine. I'll ice it later," she says, pulling the boot over her ankle and placing her foot on the floor with pinched lips. "You need to talk to Bruce."

"I intend to," I mumble imagining the throbbing ankle sweaty and confined in the tight, leather boot.

"Here they are," Kayla squeals, handing me two large black albums embossed with Wheaton.

I search through photos of Wheaton's children and friends, but not one picture of Judith appears.

"Wow ... Look at this Vic."

A young woman dressed in a red gown holds me in captivation. "It's Judith."

"She was beautiful, Vic. She looked just like you."

"Isn't this creepy? Judith is wearing a gown similar to the one Mallory chose for me." Turning the page more pictures of Judith appear at Wheaton parties, reclining on the back patio, sitting in the great room. In every picture, a young Bruce appears enamored with Judith. The photographer captures every riveted gaze.

"Wow, Vic, I don't know, but they seem close. Is this your dad with Mallory? Look at this one."

I'm surprised Mallory is holding my father's hand while Judith sits wrapped in Bruce's arms. "They look like couples."

"I'm glad you said it, Vic. I thought the same."

Pulling the picture from the plastic, I turn it over. June 25th, 1972. "Judith would have been twenty-two in this photo," I mumble, "eighteen years before my birth." The next picture is more telling than the last, an image of masked men and women around a long dining table. Judith and Bruce are seated together, and Mallory next to my dad.

"Why would my dad keep this secret?"

"You should talk to him first before going to Bruce," Kayla says, glued to the photo. "There's more here than friendship. Maybe that's why Bruce and Mallory haven't said anything."

"I have a strange feeling about this. Something's not right."

"Vic, let's just make it through the weekend. Don't let on you've seen the photos. When you get back to the city, you should head straight to your dad's place. Take this picture to Aiden. He can't deny tangible proof."

Chapter 8

After an exhausting day, I slip into the claw foot tub and enjoy a warm bath before the seven-course dinner. Reclining with my head back, the erotic scene in the maze enters my thoughts and quickens my pulse. Did the risk of getting caught make their pleasure greater? Perhaps discovery was part of the thrill. Or was desire so strong, passion unleashed in daylight. Knowing Dennis, he lured the poor girl into the maze with romantic ideas. However, after visiting her booth and seeing her up close, I realize she couldn't be more than eighteen or nineteen-years-old, an impressionable age, but she's no ingénue. Her carriage and mannerisms were of sophistication beyond her years. Perhaps she was the temptress, luring Dennis into the maze.

Ingénue or not, she's an experienced Tarot card reader. The chill I felt earlier from Kayla's reading, eclipses the warm bath. Judith was a true believer in Tarot reading. Her bookshelves overflowed with astrology, palmistry, and tarot books. I was a skeptic many years until one hot Fourth of July in Martha's Vineyard when Judith had a reading at a country fair. Those cards sit as plain as day in my mind—The Tower, Five Swords, Sun, and Death Card foreshadowed approaching death. She knew her time on this earth was short. Soon after the reading, she started arranging her financial affairs—making sure everyone's taken care of before she left this world. A month later, she was diagnosed with breast cancer. Two years later, the fate foretold by the tarot cards came true.

Today, I saw the same cards at Kayla's reading. When the gypsy girl stared with worry, my heart dropped with a nauseating fear. With every try, she produced the same results and demanded Kayla's palm. Her truncated lifeline confirmed the Tarot cards prediction. She peered at me before dispensing a lie to save Kayla worry. But I knew what those cards meant, and was grateful for her fabrication. *"A life-changing event will soon come your way,"* she'd said to Kayla.

A dubious expression crossed Kayla's face as the young woman swept the cards off the table. *"You looked worried,"* she'd said with an inquisitive glare. *"Is it something to do with work? If so, I could have told you that,"* Kayla had quipped. The young woman glanced away and equivocally answered, *"Perhaps."* Her oblique answer evoked memories of Martha's Vineyard when Judith's death showed clearly in my cards. The gypsy girl caught my troubled expression and asked, *"Would you also like a reading?"* And I wondered if Kayla's life-changing prediction would show in my reading. Curious, I said, *"Yes."* When she spread the Nine of Swords, Queen of Swords, the Tower, and Death Card, I remained impassive for Kayla's sake. But I knew instantly the ill-omened cards meant the tragic death of a loved one.

With a slight head shake, the gypsy dismissed the cards, but a sparkle in her eyes heralded better news. *"Ah! The love of your life will appear soon."* She spread the Lovers, Four Wands, and Hierophant. *"Aww ... Do you see the Six Cups of Justice? This card suggests a new man entering your life is from a past life."*

I scoffed. Although I'd become a believer soon after Judith's death. But no good news after Kayla's grave cards can ease my strife.

Slipping lower into the tub, I ponder a faceless, fated love. Swiftly Chase assumes his place. I dismiss the thought, exit the tub, and towel off. Eyeing the red gown, I wonder if it will look as good on me as it had on Judith. With difficulty, I button the dress from the back and stand in the mirror, admiring its perfect fit. The deep neckline reveals more cleavage than I like, but I love how sexy it makes me feel. Remembering Judith's French twist in the photo, I try to emulate her style. Examining the back with a hand mirror, I examine my hair, inadvertently glimpsing the port-wine birthmark on my neck, a small figure-eight; Judith called the perfect infinity sign. Self-conscious of the mark, I pull a strand of hair from the French twist, letting it dangle over the purplish mark. Adorning the Columbina mask, and red satin heels Mallory provided, I study my image one last time before heading to the big event.

I open the door at an inopportune time, coming face-to-face with Dennis passing my room. I stifled a laugh at his mask—a black and silver wolf mask. How appropriate, a wolf in disguise no more. Tonight, he wears his true nature for everyone to see. *Good job Mallory*. Dennis halts on his heels and leans in with one hand on the door. Alcohol-laced breath pollutes my face. With the image of his clenched cheeks in the maze, I flinch uneasily.

"Did you like what you saw today?" He asks.

I scowl surprise. Was he putting on a show while I watched?

"Would you like to give it a try?" He asks in a huskier voice.

I'm fuming inwardly, but calm outwardly, ready to give him a piece of my mind. Contrarily, I muster a voice huskier than his and state, "I bet you'd like that wouldn't you?" And run my fingers down his shirt. His breath quickens, and I realize I've aroused him. I laugh, slip under his arm, and head down the stairs with a big smirk.

In the great room, Stanley Kubrick's movie, *Eyes Wide Shut* comes to mind. I giggle; picturing everyone undressed wearing only a mask. Then I shiver at the thought and continue into the room. Looks like Kayla was inspired by Judith's photo as well. Similarly, she wears her hair in a French twist with tendrils escaping about her face. She's captivating in the forest-green Columbina mask. Etched with black lace and sequins, iridescent forest-green feathers rise from one side of her head. Mallory was right; the emerald dress was the right choice for Kayla. I edge next to her and observe masked-face guest in the room.

Bob adorns a purple hawk mask with purple feathers—a fitting mask for a man who's always scrutinizing people at great length with hawk-like eyes. Bruce adorns a reddish dragon mask, like that fiery creature he's an imposing figure. The room brims with variations of the

Columbina, Dotore, and Gatta masks. In the corner, a Harlequin Court Jester and a Bird of Phoenix both smile and wave at me, but I'm not sure who they are. With their bodies covered by guests, it's difficult to discern, but I wave back. Other mythical creatures, even the Phantom of the Opera, wait to hear Bruce's annual speech.

Front and center, Bruce pushes the mask atop his head. "Welcome all you wonderful creatures," he says with a chuckle. His eyes scan masked-faced guest, landing and freezing on mine. He appears surprised. His eyes warm. I blush and lower my gaze, realizing my likeness to Judith must have startled him. In that brief moment, I saw an expression of affection that only a man in love would hold. *Was he in love with Judith?*

After a twenty minute speech, Bruce ends with statistics on growing assets under management and praises to his staff. Fraught with suspicions of unethical business, Kayla throws me a dubious glare. At the moment, I'm thankful the mask hides my wary expression. A toast of champagne to another successful year and Bruce leads the group to dinner. When I cross the threshold, I picture Judith with Bruce years ago, walking under the same archway into the massive dining room.

* * *

As usual, the table is immaculate, covered with votive candles, and tall crystal candelabras, spanning the room length table. Above, three large crystal chandeliers provide soft lighting. Candlelight bounces off crystal stemware, casting sparkles along walls. Sequined masks shine like stars in the dim light. Floral centerpieces shadow reddish and purple hues across crisp, white linen. I find my place card, between Callum McKenna and Alex Ferrara, neither of which I'd seen all afternoon. Suddenly, I hear Callum's voice behind me. I turn, and he's wearing a dashing phoenix mask. I realize it had been him waving across the room. I wonder why Mallory chose this particular mask for Callum—a symbol of the Roman Empire's resurrection. Through my reverie, I hear Callum's voice.

"I got lucky. I get to sit next to the beautiful Victoria Powell. I'm glad Mallory didn't place me next to Linda, she'd talk my ear off all night."

I grin and glance over at Linda, who's already gabbing away with two people I don't recognize. She adorns a Gatta mask, a cat, a chatty cat I think. Across the table, Kayla, sits next to, of all people, Dennis Fahey. She throws me a disparaging look. I frown and sit down. "Callum, we both got lucky," I say. Perceiving it could have been me in Kayla's seat, but she can handle him. I've seen her snap at Dennis with steely, green eyes and biting words.

To my right, sits Alex Ferrara in a teal fox mask. Again, Mallory got it right. With Alex's quiet, guarded ways, you can never read his emotions. I sense Mallory placed me among these young, single men for a reason. I glance around and realize she's separated married couples, which I find odd. *Is this some experiment on Mallory's part?* Is this what happened with Judith and dad years ago? Suddenly, I realize Amber is missing. She's here every year. She'd never miss Bruce's party unless something important came up.

Accidentally, I catch Dennis' taunting eyes behind his mask and offer a wicked grimace. Kayla's engrossed in a conversation with one of Wheaton's guest—perhaps a client or family friend. He's out of place wearing a white Bauta mask. While most masks partially conceal guest's faces, his mask hides his entire face. Kayla is leading the conversation—probably more of her snooping.

A servant enters and announces an aperitif of cranberry champagne cocktail. I study the menu, hoping my stomach can handle the large meal. Several servants begin serving the guest, making their way down the table expertly. The young servant, who escorted me to my room earlier, strolls toward Bruce and whispers in his ear.

"Excuse me all, I have to take this call," Bruce explains with a glance at Bob.

A few seconds later, Bob follows, and curiosity burns through Kayla's mask as her head follows him through the archway. I take another sip of intoxicating aperitif and wonder what's taking place between Bruce and Bob.

Alex leans over. "Bruce seemed upset. I wonder what the emergency is," he whispers.

With alcohol loosening my tongue, I could easily blurt suspicions, but reply, "It must be important to leave the table." Through Alex's masked profile, I sense tension, certain underneath frown lines gather between his eyes. "How's trading going?"

Sipping the cocktail, he leans into my ear. "I'm resigning next week," he mummers candidly.

"Oh," I feign surprise, but I've been aware of his dissatisfaction for a while. "Have you found another trading position?"

"God no, I'm leaving the industry."

"What will you do?"

"What I should have done originally. I'm taking a position at a small Tech firm. Technology is my true passion. I only took the job at Wheaton as a favor to my dad. But, it's just not my calling."

"Well, I'm happy you found a position to your liking. Have you told anyone yet?"

"No, and please don't say anything until I give my notice."

"I won't," I promise, realizing the trading area is now less two with Bob assuming CFO again."

"You know Bob is taking over Andrew's position?"

"Yep, I heard. I'll hang around until they find someone to replace me." He glances across the table at Dennis, explaining market trends to the man beside him. "Although I can't stand the bastard, I don't want to leave Dennis straddled with all the trading."

I chuckle and sip more of the aperitif, wondering how Dennis will react to the news.

Alex glances around the table and then leans over. His face is so close his breath tickles my neck and his cologne clutches my nostrils. Turning his face from the table, he whispers, "Vic, you didn't hear this from me. Wheaton's going to be investigated in coming weeks. If I were you, I'd start searching for another position."

"Wh-what—Why?"

"I can't talk here, but it's not good. I don't want you involved in this mess."

Bruce saunters back to the table with a fake grin. A few minutes later, Bob reappears. He slides back into his chair with a sly glance at Bruce and then downs the aperitif in a quick gulp. At the far end of the dining room, I catch the servant eyeing Bruce. With a quick shake of his head, he walks out of the room.

Precipitously, Bruce exclaims, "Let's get this dinner rolling."

Guests clap their hands, unaware of the anguish behind Bruce's eyes. With his request, servants roll the first course into the room—one down, six more to go.

Fifteen minutes into the meal, Kayla excuses herself from the table and the man seated beside her follows soon after. As the man leaves the table, I catch Bruce's look of repulsion. It's the same look he gave his anonymous guest in the conference room. Just as I consider leaving the table in search of Kayla she reenters the room ten minutes later. *What was she doing?* I perceive more of her snooping, as I squint in her direction. She throws a reassuring grin. At the end of the table, Mallory's eyes Kayla with interest. Maybe I'm wrong, but I perceive she's annoyed. The man seated next to Kayla returns. I notice the furtive glance beneath Bruce's dragon mask, thrown at Kayla and the man beside her. With secrets uncovered this weekend, I wonder if other mysteries exist at this table.

* * *

Several hours after the company dinner, way past midnight, Kayla slips out of bed and places her ear to the door. There's no sound, and she's sure everyone is asleep. She limps down the hall toward Bruce's office. Moonlight gleams through the window, casting a milky sheen across the room. Pulling the door halfway closed, she makes her way toward Bruce's desk and turns on the computer. Anxiously strumming her fingers while the computer boots; she peers back and forth between the computer and the door, fearing someone entering. She scans Bruce's spotless desk. At one end stands a picture of Mallory and the children, a clean ashtray, and tawny-leather, cigar box sit in the center. A framed photo of Bruce accepting an award, and a cover photo on Money Magazine rests at the opposite end.

While the computer powers on, she takes the key Alex gave her earlier, opens the drawers, and searches for the missing file. Inside Bruce's meticulous top drawer, odds-and-ends rest in separate compartments—a silver business cardholder embossed with BW, a box of unopened business cards, personally embossed stationery, a silver flask, and pens—nothing unusual. She searches the neatly kept bottom drawer, noticing a separate folder toward the back. From its thickness, she's certain it's the elusive file.

Tugging at the binder, the folder slips forward, revealing a brown leather box underneath. Inside lays several postcards from Venice—one with a picture of Venetian canals, and several of La Fenice Opera House. A framed photo hidden under several postcards contains a picture of a man, woman, and child on the beach.

Kayla aims the photo toward the window. Moonlight reveals a young Bruce and a woman with a child no more than three-years-old. In the photo, Bruce chases after the child while the woman sits with outstretched arms, laughing. "Oh my God…" *It's Judith and Vicky."*

Writing, dated from 1970 to the 80s, have faded over the years on the postcards, but the salutations reads legibly, *My Sweetheart and Love Judith.*

Kayla places the box in its hidden spot, and returns to the computer, clicking the Outlook icon. With unblinking eyes, she stares at what she'd suspected and now knows for sure. A shadow moves past the door. Swiftly turning off the computer, she slides beneath the desk, listening for noise. Peeking around the edge, she stares at the door, and waits a few seconds before rising with a grimace on her swollen ankle. She pokes her head out the door, staring left to right and then limps down the hall with the file hidden beneath her robe. Just as she enters her room, a figure peers from the other end of the hall as the door closes behind her.

Chapter 9

My morning run subdues lingering unease from Wheaton's company weekend only temporarily. To avoid glum, Monday morning faces, I hail a taxi and bury my face in the newspaper until the cab arrives at the office. Immediately, I sense doom when I enter Wheaton's reception room, not even the picturesque view window view calms my nerves. I continue toward the ladies' room when sniffling from a stall halts me at the door. I waver to leave, then stand frozen when the cubicle door swings open, and Kayla exits with red-rimmed eyes. Never have I seen her cry. It takes a lot to crack Kayla's shell, so whatever's wrong, it must be serious. "Kayla? Why are you crying?" My words cause more tears. I reach for a tissue and wipe dark mascara rolling down her cheeks.

"I'm sorry. I'm a mess," she mumbles.

"Don't be silly. What happened?"

"Oh, Vic, you haven't heard. It's horrible!" She says, blowing her nose into the tissue.

I brace for dire news and ask warily, "What's going on?"

"These people are dangerous, Vic. If I'd known the measures they'd take to protect themselves," she says, stopping abruptly.

"Kayla, what are you talking about?"

"It's Alex Ferrara."

"Alex? Is he okay?"

"No."

"No? What happened?"

She blows her nose again and mumbles,"He's dead."

"What? Did you just say he's dead?"

She shakes her head.

I grasp my chest and stare into her swollen eyes. "No, he can't be. We just saw him yesterday."

Kayla glances up; her green eyes a shimmering pool. "It's my fault. I should never have involved him."

"Involved him? Involved him in what?"

Quietly, she walks toward the door, listens a few seconds, and then walks to my side. She stares up at the ceiling and then wrenches her hands. "Alex was helping me," she whispers.

"Helping you with what?"

"God, I wish I hadn't involved him. All of this is my fault."

"Whatever's going on, I'm sure his death is not your fault."

"Yes, it is Vic," she says abruptly. "If it weren't for me, he wouldn't have gotten involved."

"Kayla, please just tell me what's going on. You're scaring me.

"Remember…" she starts then shakes her head, uncertain of her words. "There was some strange coding on the computer I couldn't understand. I figured with Alex's programming background, he would be able to decode the accounts." She stamps her feet sharply, controlling tears garbling her words. "If I'd known, I wouldn't have asked for his help."

Taking her lead, I lower my voice, aware someone could be listening on the other side of the door. "Do you think he's dead because of what he discovered?"

"I'm certain of it."

"If that's true Kayla, you need to go to the police."

"I don't have enough proof."

A greater fear creeps into my mind. "What's so important it would get Alex killed?"

She sighs deeply and leans on the counter. "You know, all Bruce talks about is business transparency. Well, that's a bunch of bull," she sneers. "Nothing's transparent in this firm. A week ago, Alex figured out the coding used to disguise client trades. Vic, you won't believe the sums of money wired offshore in Bruce's client's accounts."

"Which account?"

"Thawone, the Japanese business account."

"But what's the big deal? Everyone knows offshore banking is a tax haven for the wealthy—"

"Vic, just listen ... Alex said it's a layering scheme. The account coding prevents anyone from detecting the origins of wired funds."

"A layering scheme? As in money laundering? Are you sure?"

"Uh-huh. Thawone has been laundering millions through Wheaton for years. Vic, that's the reason I was searching for that file. With the coding deciphered, Alex and I discovered accounts with similar money wiring, and internal journals moving funds between non-related accounts."

"Money laundering ... At Wheaton ... I can't believe that."

"Well, it's true." Kayla shakes her head, blows her nose, and continues with weeks of discoveries sorely needing a release. "After Alex figured out the coding, he grew more suspicious and started digging for more information on Thawone. Right before the company dinner, he discovered Thawone is a fictitious business entity."

"Fictitious?"

"Uh-huh ... Thawone is an illegal shell company. Alex said its sole purpose is money laundering. Vic, these transactions go back twenty years, maybe farther. I believe this is why Andrew Kelly quit."

"How did Alex figure out Thawone is fictitious?"

"He couldn't find information about the firm, other than a suspect website. When he told me what he'd found, I made some calls. Then I realized Thawone's address doesn't correspond to the telephone number and email address on file. I knew something was wrong. There's no telephone listed in Japan, only a contact here in the U.S. I realize multinational companies have many locations, but something isn't right, Vic. I never got anyone on the phone, only a recording. And strangely, the person responds to my emails, but never my calls. I went through ten years of files, and my suspicions were confirmed when I noticed the unusual trading pattern. These are million dollar accounts and over ten years, there's been no purchase or sale of securities, just cash. It appears they're just letting money earn interest."

"Kayla, I'm confused. With the Patriot Act's stringent anti-money laundering laws, how's this possible? Don't we have preventive measures in place?"

"Remember, we're not held to anti-money laundering rules of other financial institutions."

"Even if we aren't, wouldn't deposits greater than $10,000 create a red-flag?"

"It would if we were a bank or a brokerage firm. As a hedge fund, our minimum opening deposit is one million. A person could deposit several million and not create an exception report."

"Hmm, wouldn't intermediaries, banks, generate red flags when funds are wired into Wheaton's accounts?"

"That's what I thought until Alex explained how money launderers operate. These people are clever, Vic. They probably have hundreds of accounts in the U.S. and consolidate the funds into offshore banks. Anyway, it's so intricate; you couldn't possibly tell where the money originated from. Alex said hedge funds are an ideal haven for these people. They just let their money sit for years before withdrawing the funds."

Suddenly, the room vibrates fear. "Poor Alex … I just can't wrap my mind around this. He was talking to me last night and now he's gone."

"Vic, I swear we were so careful. No one could have known what we were doing."

I imagine Kayla and Alex's secret collaboration, and someone stumbling on their conversations. "Well, clearly someone overheard you in the office."

"No. That's impossible," she says quickly. "We never spoke about this in the office, only outside." She wrenches her hands again. "I was, we were so careful. Somehow, someone figured out what we were doing. I replayed every conversation with Alex, where we met, the day, the time, what we said, our conversations in the office, even our encounters at the company weekend. There's no way anyone could have known," she says low.

"Well, someone knew."

"I swear we never saw this coming, Vic. When he called me last night, he was so scared he didn't go home. He believed someone followed him from the Wheaton estate. He said he drove around his home three times trying to evade them. At first, I thought it was just paranoia, but when he ditched his car, I started to worry. He was so determined to show me what he'd found at Wheaton, he decided to take the train into the city."

"What do you think he found?"

"I don't know, but it was important enough for him to travel to the city at night." With emotion threatening her voice Kayla murmurs, "The last time I spoke to Alex, he was heading toward Metro-North train station. He called me several times from the train, but reception was so bad all I heard was breathing. God, Vic, his last call was so frightening."

I imagine Alex's encounter with death and dread details, but I ask anyway, "What did you hear?"

"At first, I thought we had a bad connection, but then I realized it was Alex breathing. He was running. In the background, someone was chasing him. I wonder if he kept the phone line open intentionally."

"If he was running for his life, hanging up was the furthest thought from his mind."

"Maybe Alex knew he was in trouble and wanted me to hear what was happening. I can't get his winded breath out of my head. He tried so hard to evade them. When he stopped running, I thought, finally, he'd escaped, but then footsteps sounded again. I think they cornered him because he screamed, *'What do you want?'* They didn't respond, but footsteps grew closer. Then I heard a rustling noise and almost jumped when Alex screamed, *'Is this what you want?'* He was so scared, Vic. My heart was racing so fast I almost screamed Run! Get away! I believe Alex gave them what they wanted because I heard a sliding noise. Everything after that happened so fast. Alex screamed, *'Wait ... Stop!'* Then a loud thud and scuffling followed. My heart stopped when a man said my name through the phone. He must have seen my name on the caller I. D."

"What did he say?"

"His voice was cold," she says with a shudder. "I'll never forget it. He said, *'Kayla, I know you're listening. If you don't stop, you're next,'* and the connection dropped."

"Kayla that's a warning; you've got to go to the police."

"No, no!" She says shaking her head. "I thought about it all night. I have to let them believe I've stopped prying. That's what they want," she mutters to confirm her stance. Her shoulders shudder. "That laugh, Vic, he was laughing when he said my name. It gave me the creeps," she says, wrapping her arms around her waist with a shiver stronger than the first. "I paced back and forth all night hoping Alex would call—hoping they'd only roughed him up with a warning, but never this." Kayla exhales deeply. "I wanted so much for Alex to still be alive. So, I called him again two hours later, and a woman answered."

"A woman?"

"It was the nurse at the hospital. She said Alex had passed on. And then I realized I'd heard Alex's murder."

I wrap my arms around Kayla's shoulders to stop the trembling.

"He was right, I should have told him to go to the police ... I didn't believe someone was following him," she garbles into my shoulder.

Anger swells at Alex's heartless murder. I imagine his thin five-feet-seven inch frame outpacing his killers. Did he believe he'd be killed or escape with a warning if he handed over the object they wanted? *What did he discover worth killing for*? "Maybe they found out Alex spoke to FINRA."

"What are you talking about," Kayla says backing away. "He wouldn't have gone to the authorities."

"At dinner, he told me there'd be an investigation soon. I just assumed he'd spoken to authorities. Why do you think he wouldn't?"

She paces in deliberation. "I don't want to get you involved any further, Vic. It's too risky."

"Are you kidding? It's too late for that Kayla. So, just please tell me."

She wrenches her hands for the umpteenth time. "There are so many people involved, Vic."

"What people?"

"Shareholders, clients... Bruce isn't the only one involved in this mess. We uncovered money transfers from the Thawone account into accounts of major stakeholders and some of Bruce's friend's accounts."

"That's even more of a reason for Alex to expose the money laundering."

"He would have if his family wasn't a major stakeholder. If he'd gone to the authorities, not only would it destroy Wheaton, but also his family. I don't believe Alex would bring down his own parents."

"Wow ... He sounded so certain. Are you sure Kayla?"

"I'm positive."

"From the certainty in his voice last night, I believe he spoke with the authorities or someone else has."

"He might have spoken to his parents, but he wouldn't have gone to the authorities."

"Are other people at Wheaton involved?"

"So far it appears Bruce and Bob are the only ones. But I'm not sure of the others ... *The cameras...* Kayla looks at the ceiling certain she hadn't seen a camera in the bathroom. Either way, they couldn't hear their conversation. "You need to leave the firm, Vic," Kayla says commandingly.

"Leave!" Studying her face, I can tell she's withholding information.

"You're not telling me everything ... If there's more, I need to know what's going on."

In the mirror, Kayla wipe smudged mascara from her eyes. Her face is emotionless, an expression I've witnessed many times when she's defiant. She stops and stares blankly at her reflection. Her eyes meet mine in the mirror, and a steely demeanor claims her face again. She shakes her head. "I've told you too much already. I'm not saying any-more; it'll put you in danger."

"I'm already in danger Kayla. Just my association with the firm and you put me at risk. I'd rather know what I'm dealing with than walking around blind."

"Okay, but I don't want you getting involved. Swear you'll leave this alone. Let me handle it."

"Kayla, how can I stand by and do nothing when you're in trouble?"

"Then I'm not telling you anything further."

I sigh and blatantly lie. "Okay, I won't get involved." She scrutinizes me from the mirror. "Kayla?"

She sighs, slaps her hand on the counter, and then faces me. "I didn't take the limo to Wheaton's estate because Alex found more informa-tion on Thawone."

"Well, what did he find out?"

"Alex figured out Thawone is an anagram for Wheaton."

"What!"

"Yep and it gets worst. I pretended I had to use the bathroom during Wheaton's dinner and snuck into Bruce's office to check his email."

"Isn't his computer password protected?"

"Alex had been in the office earlier and figured it out."

"That easily?"

She shakes her head. "He was good at that," she says quietly. "When I left the dinner table, I headed straight to Bruce's office. I almost had a heart attack when Bruce's servant caught me behind the desk. I pre-tended I lost my cell phone and needed to make a phone call. I could see by his wavering stance he didn't believe me. The odd thing is I caught one of Bruce's guests watching me when I came out of the office. He gave me the creeps with that mask covering his entire face. I think he was watching me the whole evening. After dinner when everyone was asleep, I snuck back into Bruce's office."

"Kayla, you could have been caught."

"I know, but I'm glad I did. What I saw confirmed my suspicion. The emails I've been sending to Thawone's contact person were going straight to Bruce. He's the contact person."

How could Alex possibly figure out Bruce's password in such a short time? Is that why I didn't see him at any of the festivities? He was snooping in Bruce's home all afternoon. And when and how did he exchange information with Kayla? "When did Alex give you Bruce's password?"

"He sent it to my cell phone via text message. Do you think..." She pauses with a shake of her head, "No, no I told Alex to delete all his texts."

"Maybe he didn't, and his killer discovered you two were snooping."

I see doubt on Kayla's face and hope for her sake Alex had deleted everything. At once, I worry about Kayla's emails to Thawone. "Kayla, what did you say in the emails to Bruce?"

"I'm not stupid, Vic. I pretended I was sending out account updates and just needed to confirm the address on file, nothing that would cause suspicion."

"Thawone ... Isn't that Michelle's father's business?"

She shakes her head. "Now you understand why I asked Michelle all those questions at brunch? I wanted to see how much she knew about her father's business."

"And that's little," from what you heard," I say.

"If she knows more, she didn't let on."

"I can't believe Michelle would lie, or be a part of something so unethical."

"Vic, the evidence speaks for itself. Michelle's father owns the company."

"But it doesn't mean Michelle is involved, or even aware of her father's corrupt business dealings. You know how Michelle avoids her family's business like the plague."

"Yes, and have you ever wondered why? Maybe Michelle knows and just refuses to acknowledge it. You remember how she acts around her family like she's afraid of them. Vic, Michelle may not be aware of the money laundering, but she suspects something's wrong with her family's business." Kayla stares in thought. "Vic, I wonder if Michelle's father and your mom were the reason you and Michelle met on campus. Your meeting couldn't have been a coincidence. Both your parents have known Bruce and Mallory Wheaton for years."

"Was my mom involved in this?" I ask tentatively.

"I haven't found any evidence that suggests she was," Kayla says.

Kayla's tarot card reading of impending death shakes me again. Was it Alex's death, not Kayla's the gypsy predicted? But those cards predicted a close friend or family member. Suddenly, I'm terrified for Kayla's life and ask, "How did Alex die?" I hold my breath with her pained expression.

"A single gunshot wound to the head."

Chapter 10

A child wearing striped tights and a white down jacket blows warm air into her gloves as she skates across the ice skating rink toward a woman admiring from the side. "Brava! That was wonderful, sweetie. You're getting better every time. Maybe you should be a professional ice skater."

"No mom, I want to be like you, I want to perform at Lincoln Center just like you."

Childhood memories fade with clapping around Rockefeller Plaza's ice-skating rink. The burgeoning crowd applauds a figure skater performing a triple axel ending in a graceful pirouette. I push through throngs of holiday shoppers and head uptown remembering that happy day with Judith. Special occasions with her grew less and less when I learned of her infidelities—her betrayal to my father. Nights when Aiden traveled on business, and Judith thought I was asleep, a strange man would visit, a man I never saw only heard whispering. Afraid of pain Aiden would endure, I never told him. I remained a silent partner to Judith's infidelities.

I inhale deep and thrust old memories and wounds aside, but a new pain fills my mind—Alex's murder. Can I be in danger as well? Suddenly feeling vulnerable, I imagine a stranger flinging me into oncoming traffic or a stab from an unseen hand amid midtown congestion. I quicken my pace, survey surroundings, and hail a taxi, fleeing invisible danger. Fifteen minutes later, I'm outside Hannah and Paul's condo. Walking toward their door, I pictured baby things strewn about their once immaculate apartment. I miss our carefree days, relaxing with a glass of wine and discussing our lives. Conversations now consist of baby things and arguments with Paul. I wonder what's on Hannah's mind today.

The door opens, and I'm surprised to see the nanny. She usually leaves before five P.M.

"She's been crying all afternoon," the nanny says dismayed.

"Where is she?"

"She's in the study."

I drop my bags in the foyer and hurry down the hall. There she sits with vacant, puffy eyes. "Hannah, what's wrong?" And I realize I've asked that question twice today—first Kayla now Hannah. I hope it isn't serious. I've had enough bad news for one day. Maybe she and Paul had another argument.

"I don't know, Vic. I can't stop crying. I just glance at the babies and start bawling."

"Hannah, it's just hormones. After carrying those babies nine months, all that progesterone and estrogen is making you crazy. Now your body is saying, what the hell is happening?" I try to make her laugh but fail miserably. Her lips didn't crack a smile. "Have you been out today?"

"No, not looking like this." Hannah peeps up more emotional than I've ever seen her, in fact, I've never seen her like this in all of our seven years of friendship.

"Look at you, Ms. Wall Street. You look so good. Vicky, don't ever have a baby; it messes with your head, gives you big hips, and sagging breasts."

I laugh, although I shouldn't. But it puts a grin on her face. "Hannah, you've done something amazing. You gave life to two new souls. I can't imagine anything more important."

"No, you can't. It's the worst decision I've ever made. I threw away my entire career when I married Paul, and now I'll never be able to start over."

"Hannah, have you seen all the working moms? You can always go back." I'm ill-suited lecturing Hannah about work and babies. I have no idea what she's going through, but I know it's possible to work and have a family. I see it every day. All of a sudden, this is so unappealing and messing with my desire to ever be a mother.

"Do you want to go out for a walk or drink while the nanny is here?"

She stares at me with swollen eyes and shakes her head. "No."

"Do you want me to stay a while?"

"Please, I can't stand being with myself."

I head to the kitchen for a bottle of wine to calm both our nerves. In the large kitchen, a weekly calendar, scribbled on a chalkboard wall, highlights the babies feeding schedule, Hannah's doctor appointments, and hubby time at 7:00 p.m., circled several times. *Hmmm, the life of new parents.* Walking toward the study, irritable babies on the verge of crying, emanate from the nursery as the nanny coos soothingly. I pad down the hall to the study and deliberate telling Hannah about Kayla and Alex. However, in her current state it might be too much to handle.

I pour Hannah a glass of wine and watch her take a huge gulp. I take a seat, and pour myself a glass and then realize Hannah's still breastfeeding. "Should you be drinking while nursing the babies?"

"It's okay; I just pumped a gallon earlier. The rest, I'll just pump and dump."

Immediately, I imagine her with that ridiculous contraption, pumping until purple streams of milk turn pure and white. I take a sip of wine to conceal my grin and then relax in the armless chair. Unable to contain my concern, words slip from my mouth. "Hannah, I'm worried about Kayla."

"Why? What's up with Kayla?"

"Well, she's snooping again. And I'm afraid she's in trouble."

"So what else is new?"

"Hannah, this is different. She's dealing with dangerous people. It's not like her college snooping. She could get herself killed. Remember Judith's Tarot reading in Martha's Vineyard?"

"How can I forget? I was there. I remember your mom's expression like it was yesterday."

"Well, at Wheaton's company weekend, I saw the same cards in Kayla's reading. My cards also confirmed the approaching death of a loved one."

"Vic, now you're scaring me."

I hope this news doesn't cause Hannah undue stress in her already fragile state. But I've already spilled the beans and Hannah will hound me until I tell her everything. "A co-worker died yesterday."

"What? How? Is it anyone I know?"

"It was Alex. He was murdered, and the scary part is he was helping Kayla."

Hannah stares without blinking. Seconds later, she's blaming Kayla. "What the hell did Kayla get Alex involved in?"

"Money laundering..."

"What!"

"Alex and Kayla stumbled on evidence of money laundering."

Now concerned, Hannah straightens in the chaise. "Vic, you have to stop her. I've seen horrendous things happened in my journalistic days. You two need to alert the authorities or get out of that firm."

"Hannah, there's so much more to this."

"Vic, this money laundering could be tied to terrorist or drug smugglers. You guys have no idea what you're dealing with. And if I know Kayla, she's going to piss these people off. You have to stop her."

"I can't! You know what she's like."

"I remember all right," she states with a snarl. "She almost got us kicked out of Wellesley with her snooping. Why does she do this?"

I realize it's a rhetorical question, but reply, "It's in her genes." *In her genes ... Hmmm,* recalling the Collins family involvement in political and social causes and Kayla's forever-inquisitive mother, I'm sure Kayla's genetic disposition for snooping stems from her mom.

"Remember every time we tried to stop her in college how defiant she'd become? I warned her today, but I don't believe she'll stop. You know that look she always gets when she's determined to uncover the truth, that expression of defiance and determination, well, I saw it on her face earlier. I don't believe we can stop her."

Hannah pours a second glass of wine, but I don't protest, realizing it's probably much needed. With a deep gulp, she asks, "Do you have enough evidence to go to the FBI?"

"I believe that's why Alex was killed. He told me the firm would be investigated soon. Maybe his killers found out."

Pushing the wool throw to the side, Hannah slides to the edge of the chaise and cups her chin in contemplation. "Vic, if they have any suspicions about you and Kayla, your lives might already be in danger. You need to call the FBI or the police. For your own protection, let them handle this."

With another sip of wine, I start to see the old Hannah resurfacing—the one I used to admire, the Hannah, who could dig her way out of any problem with that ingenious mind. A sudden surge of energy lifts her from the chaise, and she scampers down the hallway yelling, "Vic, I think I know who can help. I have a contact at the newspaper who's handled cases like this. He knows people who can protect you." She returns in her baggy, elasticized mommy pants and an oversized T-shirt, holding a business card and cell phone.

"I haven't spoken to him in a year..." she mumbles while searching through her list of contacts, "... but I know I still have his number." Scribbling a number on the tattered business card; she states sternly, "Call Frank. Tell him you're my friend. He will know what to do."

"What does Frank do?"

"He's a reporter who's handled cases like this in the past. Recently, he reported a story about a whistleblower at one of the major banks. I think it was Chase, maybe Morgan Stanley, or Lehman. Well, one of those top banks," she says with a hand dismissal. "Poor woman not only lost her job, but also received death threats, and was blackballed by colleagues. She went to the papers and the police. That's how she met Frank. He helped her blow the lid off the case. And I believe she received a million dollar settlement for reporting the money laundering. Unfortunately, she'll never get a job in the industry again."

Surprised by the settlement, I speculate, "Well that's probably why the reward is so high; they realized her career is finished."

Hannah narrows her eyes. "Vic, promise me you will call Frank tomorrow."

"I will."

"This is not to be taken lightly. Do I have to call him myself. You know I will? I'm not going to lose my best friends."

Hannah's threats are always real, and she will follow through if circumstances are dire. "Don't worry. I'll call him as soon as I can."

She throws me a sterner look.

"Okay, okay, I will tomorrow. I take another sip ready to reveal another piece of information. "Have you ever noticed anything suspicious about Michelle's family?"

"Other than the fact her mother always looks frighten in her husband's presence," she says with a smirk. "Now if that's not strange, I don't know what is. Why do you ask?"

Hannah's observation is intriguing. I ponder Mrs. Kimura's behavior, wondering if fear is from her husband's transgressions.

"Vic?"

"I was just wondering about Mrs. Kimura. I've always thought her behavior cultural, you know, the submissive wife thing. But now that you've mentioned it, she did appear afraid."

"Is there a reason for the sudden interest in the Kimura family?"

"Well, Kayla found information that proves Mr. Kimura is the money launderer at Wheaton. It appears he using a shell company to cover up his misdeeds."

"What! Have you said anything to Michelle?"

"No, I just found out today. Kayla said I shouldn't mention anything to Michelle. She may be involved."

"That's absurd. Michelle would never participate in illicit business. Hmm, this might explain her refusal to work with her father."

Remembering Michelle's expression at brunch, and how upset she became, I wonder if she's trying to protect her family.

"Wow, Vic, remember Michelle's birthday party at her family's home in Greenwich? You made a joke about the place appearing like Fort Knox?"

"Yep, but I was joking. I just assumed Mr. Kimura is an important man, who needs considerable protection. But with all this new information, it's suspect."

"Well, I always thought it suspicious. Michelle gets so agitated whenever she's in that house. She's ready to bolt the moment she arrives."

"I noticed … I believe she despises her brothers. She said they never got along."

"They give me the creeps as well. Come to think of it, I've never seen Michelle show any affection toward them. But, she loves her mom. They're the only affectionate members of the family. Vic, if they're involved in some seedy business, this could have severe consequences for Michelle. Wow … Regardless, you and Kayla need to go to the authorities."

* * *

After several glasses of wine, Hannah falls asleep. Just as I prepare to leave, Paul's keys jiggle in the door. I cover Hannah with the throw, turn off the light, and slowly walk toward the foyer.

"Hi, Paul, Hannah's sleeping. When I arrived she was in bad shape."

"What else is new?" he grumbles and sighs at once. He places his keys on the console and scrubs his face wearily. "She's been in a foul mood for weeks." Noticing the concern on my face, his scowl slackens. "She'll be okay once she gets some rest. We were up all night; I almost didn't make it to work this morning."

Studying his face, there's not a dark circle in sight. I smell liquor on his breath and stare at my watch, wondering if he always comes home at ten at night. Remembering the scribbled appointment with hubby at seven on the kitchen chalkboard, I realize Hannah may have been upset because he broke their date. But it's not my place to interrogate him. So, I leave it alone. "If I were you, I wouldn't take her state so lightly. I believe she might need to talk to someone, maybe a therapist who deals with new moms."

He shakes his head in approval, "I've already tried, but I'll talk to Hannah tomorrow."

"Well, I've had a long day. Hannah is asleep in the study." Before I exit the door, I glimpse a new expression on his face. *Is it resentment? When did their romance die?*

Chapter 11

Bruce makes his way through a masked crowd, his eyes never leave my face. His features vacillate young and old, stopping at a youthful countenance. He grows closer and whispers, "Judith, I've missed you." His lips meet mine and I scream, "I'm not Judith!" Walls vanish. I'm in the park with Chase. Burnt-orange leaves fall and form a maze of leaves. Chase's face distorts, changing to Dennis Fahey's. With a devilish grin, he makes lustful demands and pushes me into the shrubbery. I protest, trying to escape his hands. He lifts my skirt, pulling my hips from behind. Pounding my fist on the burnt-orange wall, I push through a maze of leaves; tumble and fall through empty space, landing on my bed.

Waking with a jolt, my heart races with images my subconscious conceived disturbingly. I lie back and roll over in bed. Again, sleep comes fast.

A loud thunder crash and boom, lightning flashes, shifting mythical yellow-eyed creatures across the wall. I jump out of bed, running down the hall toward Judith's room. Whispers and moans seep under the door. I pause before turning the knob. Two figures lay entwined. Lightning flashes through

the room irradiating a dragon masked man. Frightened, I
dash back to my room, jumping under the covers.

Sweat drenched, I throw the blanket off and sit up in bed. Childhood memories of Judith's late night visitor have reemerged, wearing
Bruce Wheaton's dragon mask. Was it Bruce all those years ago in Judith's room, or is my mind assimilating information from the company
weekend? Again, I lie back, roll over, and try to sleep, but I can't. I toss
and turn, unable to quiet thoughts of Judith and Bruce, Alex's murder, Wheaton's money laundering, and Michelle's father. My thoughts
wander again to Kayla's predicament. There's nothing I can do. If I
go to the authorities, I'll put both Kayla and myself in danger. And if
Wheaton knows Kayla's snooping, she's already under their scrutiny.
Are they watching me too? Restlessly I toss for another hour until the
alarm signals it's time for a run. I jump out of bed, dress, and head out
the door, hoping a workout will clear my head.

* * *

I enter the dimly lit park and notice several runners ahead. One glances
around and separates from the group. He doubles back in my direction.
His features are imperceptible in dawn's light, but I recognize Chase's
athletic build and smooth stride.

"Victoria?"

My heart leaps. I wave and continue toward him.

"Can I join you?"

My mind screams yes! Tired of worried thoughts, I welcome his
distracting presence. "Of course," I say. "I'm doing the full loop this
morning."

"So am I," he says assuming my pace. It's only our second run together, but I feel we've run together many times. I stare at the waning
full moon on the western horizon, when his voice intrudes.

"Victoria, who are you? What do you do? Where are you from?"

"Whoa," I say with a laugh, "You ask many questions."

"I know so little about you, other than you love to run," Chase says.

"Hmmm," I wonder where to start. "Well, my full name is Victoria Angelica Powell. I'm all of twenty-five; born in Martha's Vineyard, raised in New York City and I graduated magnum cum laude from Wellesley College."

"Come on you can do better," he says with a chuckle.

"Boy, you're demanding." I inhale deeply and continue. "I graduated with honors from NYU's Business School. I'm a Research Analyst."

"Come on ... more."

"Well, you know I like to run."

"Uh-huh ... more ... favorite color, food, and hobbies?"

"Blue. Strawberries. I love the ocean, reading, and old black and white movies."

"Brothers, sisters?"

"Nope, only child..."

"Single, dating, married, children..."

"You want my entire life story in one run?"

"Uh-huh."

I chuckle. "I'm single with no children. Now that you know my story, it's your turn. Who are you? What do you do?" I ask, deftly turning attention to him.

"Well, my full name is Chase Matthew Dillon. I'm all of twenty-eight, born and raised in Maine."

We laugh in sync as he mimics my tone.

"I graduated with honors from Columbia University, and I'm an Orthopedic Surgeon at Mt. Sinai Hospital. I come from a long line of doctors. I love food, sports, and running. I'm an only child, single, and no kids to mention. I have a Golden Retriever named Milo. Oh, and I love ultra-sports."

"Nice, a doctor," I say with surprise.

"You know ... I almost chose a Wall Street career."

"Really, so why'd you change your mind, Doctor Dillon?"

"Coming from a family of doctors, I wanted a different life. I'd always been interested in finance. So, during my junior year, I accepted an internship at an investment firm. After a summer staring at a computer screen, I knew I wouldn't last in an office environment. So, I heeded my calling, packed my bags, and off to medical school with no regrets," he says with a strong exhale.

"You're lucky, most people don't realize they're calling until it's too late," I say, alluding to my own career choice. Like you, I wanted a different life, a career my family hadn't planned."

"And what's that?"

"Well, my mom had this idea I would follow in her steps as an opera singer."

"Opera, wow! That's exciting."

"Well, my mom was gifted. My talent paled in comparison. After years of music, voice, and drama lessons, I just didn't see life onstage. I lacked my mom's passion, thus, my venture into my father's world of finance."

"But you're not happy?" He asks.

"No, I'm just bored. I feel something's missing. Don't get me wrong, I'm good at what I do, but I feel unchallenged."

"Well, you're still young enough to pursue a different career. Maybe you haven't found your calling yet."

"Maybe ... So, Chase, what else should I know about you?" Silence ensues, our pounding feet and breath the only noise as we approach the steep hills on the western side of the park. Our breath comes fast with the steep ascent and slows with our quick descent.

With winded breath, Chase states in stacatto words, "Well, Ms. Powell, you'll have to have coffee with me if you want to know more. You do like coffee?"

"Is that the moon above?" I ask, pondering his offer. "Do you mean after the run or some other time?"

"How about after we're done?"

"I don't believe there's a place open this early."

"There's a place that makes great coffee all the time," he says mischievously.

"Oh? And where may that be so early in the morning?" I ask, already aware he's alluding to his apartment.

"1120 Fifth Avenue … My place … I'm only two blocks away," he says as if this would influence my decision.

I pause, consider the fact I've only known him a short time and ponder the danger of going to a strange man's apartment.

"Come on Victoria… If you're afraid, I assure you my doorman will know you're in the apartment."

He read my mind. I'm wary but accept his offer. "Okay." I concede not so much for the coffee, but for novelty, something more exciting than ritual four and five, and someone to take my mind off Kayla and Wheaton. We run the last three miles in silence. Somehow the park appears magical with moonlight shimmering on the Great Lawn's ice-laced grounds. Suddenly, I'm thankful for Chase's presence.

Chapter 12

The doorman at 1120 Fifth Avenue, adorned in full regalia—a dark-blue-double-breasted jacket with golden lapels, a black bowtie, and trousers striped with gold piping—steps aside and opens the door with white-gloved hands. "Good morning," he greets us formally as we enter the building. I detect a hint of surprise disguised beneath his cap. Is he in awe of my running clothes or my early morning visit? Or maybe he assumes I'm headed to Chase's bed for *an early morning quickie*? "Good morning," I say with an assertive air, ignoring the curious stare.

In the elevator's close confinement, Chase's presence is disarming. He must be at least six-feet-one or two. I shiver quietly in my sweat-soaked running attire, questioning my impulsive behavior. Just as I'm about to change my mind, the private elevator opens into his apartment. Beyond the foyer, windows frame dawn over Central Park's reservoir bound by bright lanterns and autumn trees.

"Are you going to stay in the elevator?" Chase asks with a grin.

"Oh…" Awestricken I exit the elevator with a nervous grin and remove my running shoes as he has. A Golden Retriever jumps from his spot; running toward me then Chase.

"Milo, this is our new friend Victoria. Victoria this is Milo."

Milo rushes toward me, excitedly rubbing his nose into my legs. "Hey, boy," I say friskily while stooping to my knees. "He's gorgeous. I've always loved Golden Retrievers. Do you run with him?"

"Occasionally I do, but he slows me down. He's a scavenger, aren't you buddy?" He says, ruffling Milo's reddish mane. He's always chasing after squirrels and other dogs. It's a little frustrating when I'm trying to put in a long run. So, I take him on shorter treks after work."

Milo licks my hand and wags his tail with glee. Like most people who have adopted the common vernacular of pet owners, and for lack of better words, "Good boy," slips from my mouth. I pet his reddish mane, and his tail wags back and forth enthusiastically. When I stop, his tail freezes in disappointment. Losing interest, Milo turns, finding his space, his eyes remain fixed on my face. I follow Chase toward the kitchen and watch as he makes coffee in an expensive, stainless steel coffee machine built into rich espresso cabinets, hovering above Carrera-marble countertops. I survey his surroundings, which is missing a butler or a maid or two. I'm sure they're hiding somewhere down the long corridor.

"Wow, what a fantastic apartment." The spacious living room appears to meld both masculine and feminine touches. I wonder how many women he's lured with this impressive space. How many have dropped their panties conquered by his charm? Did he invite me for coffee or to lure me into his bed? "Do you live alone?"

"The apartment belongs to my parents, but they're rarely in New York." He turns and pulls a glass container from the cabinet, measures the beans methodically, then pours them into the coffee machine—I'm sure an action performed many mornings. He turns and faces me with a riveted gaze and boyish grin. Staring longer than appropriate, his intense, brown eyes drink me in.

I smile awkwardly.

Aware his stare has caused discomfort; he turns toward the coffee machine and adds water. "My parents make their home in Maine. I use the apartment because of its convenience to the hospital."

"So, Dr. Dillon, your specialty is orthopedic surgery?"

"Yes, sports medicine; it's the family trade."

"Family trade, I'm impressed. That seems like you, the athletic doctor."

The machine begins to swirl and grind, quickly releasing coffee grinds into the filter. "Isn't that amazing? Technology … Just one touch of a button, and voila!—A grinder and coffee machine in one," he says feigning intrigue.

I laugh inwardly, wondering if he also dreads banal chatter. Small talk compels me to skip social decorum and dive into a juicier conversation. But I respond in jest, "All this automation is making us such a lazy culture. Soon they'll design machines to dress us."

He chuckles. "Now that would be a bit much." He opens the refrigerator, removes a chocolate rectangular box and gestures me behind the island with a wave of his hand.

I obey like a summoned pet. On closer approach his body heat pierces my aura, quickening my pulse.

"Close your eyes," he says.

"Why?"

"Just close your eyes and open your mouth," he says alluringly.

"Yes, Doctor," I say. I'm brave this morning. Two follies I don't make often are visiting a strange man's apartments and obeying blindly. But, I close my eyes, part my lips, and hope I won't regret it. Something cold touches my mouth. He teases; brushing it along the bottom then upper lip.

"Open wider…"

I obey. Something hard and cold frosts my tongue.

"Bite," he says.

I do. A burst of chocolate and strawberries awaken my senses. Chase's finger skims my bottom lip. Warmth replaces cold. Startled, I open my eyes, staring wide-eyed into his brown eyes. Butterflies fill my stomach.

He backs away and whispers, "Scrumptious."

Dazed, speechless, and suddenly, miffed I question his impropriety. Did he think he could just kiss me? I haven't shown any interest! *How bold!* Subtly, I challenge his actions, "That was brave of you. I could have protested or bitten your lip?"

"Then I would have apologized for my bad manners," he says with a wink.

I frown. That wasn't the response I expected.

"You're cockier than I thought."

"That's one of my least favorite words. Conceit, arrogance, smugness, I'm neither of those. I just believe in going after what I want."

"So, you just believe in taking it without asking?"

"No, no. I believe you wanted it as much as I did. You could have backed away, right away. But you didn't."

"I was surprised."

"In a good way, I hope."

I don't know what I felt, but I know I didn't want him to stop. I glance away, hoping the truth isn't on my face. "As I said, I was surprised, nothing more." Studying his space, I wonder how often he uses the chocolate strawberry approach and how many women buy it.

"Can you turn around?" He asks.

A sudden fight-or-flight response hits me. "I'm sorry. I think I should leave." I back toward the door, feeling silly as I had the morning I ran away from him in the park. It was only a little kiss.

"Hey—hold on."

Now both concerned master and pet move toward me with caution. Milo licks my hands with canine affection as if to assuage my worry.

"I didn't mean to offend you. If I made you uncomfortable I apologize," he says.

His obvious concern quells my anxiousness as I stand self-consciously pondering my next move.

"Can we start over?" He asks with raised brows and an outstretched hand, a motion too compelling to resist. Lured back to his lair, I relent and take his hand.

"Was my kiss that bad?" He asks playfully to ease tension. "Forgive my bad manners. I couldn't resist your heart-shaped lips."

"You're forgiven; I just wasn't ready for that."

"I'm not going to do anything you don't want. I thought I sensed your interest."

I can't remember a word or action that suggested interest. "How did you determine that?"

"Victoria, come on we're adults..."

The sound of my name on his tongue pricks lusty desires, but I refuse to abandon control.

"I felt it when I kissed you just now and the first day we met in the park. I was attracted to you the moment I saw you."

His admission causes me to look away. "Well, I was shocked. You were feeding me and then you were kissing me. I didn't know what I was feeling. You misinterpreted shock for interest and there's a big difference." I'm protesting too hard because he's right. I was attracted to him the first time we stretched together that foggy morning, but how did he interpret aloofness as interest?

A brisk laugh echoes across the kitchen and I'm irked once more.

"You're in denial. If you weren't, you wouldn't be so upset right now. Victoria, it's okay; you caught my attention the first moment I saw you. I'm brutally honest when it comes to my wants. I sense you're not so forthcoming with your own," he says astutely. "I'm attracted to you. But if you don't want anything physical, I won't pressure you ... I promise ... Hands-off ... I won't tease you again with my treats," he says backing off, feigning a pout, and extending his hands in the air.

His playfulness is alluring. And I'm stunned by his perception.

"Will you please stay for coffee ... please ... I'd like to talk to you ... Get to know you better."

Although nonplused by his observation, I'm intrigued. So, again, I concede. "Okay, but no more surprises."

"I promise." Taking my hand, he leads me toward the window boasting spectacular views of sunrise exploding across Central Park's skyline. "I love this time of the morning," he says.

"I do, too." The coffeepot beeps in the kitchen as I stand shivering in my sweat-soaked running clothes.

Noticing my quivering shoulders, he says, "Come with me."

And again, I'm compelled to follow down a long hallway into the master suite. Chase disappears into a walk-in closet. I wait in the bedroom, examining the king-sized sleigh bed. The only items out of place in the spotless room are a white T-shirt and boxer shorts crumpled in a chair near the window. I assume he'd thrown there as he prepared for his morning run. An iPhone and iPad lie atop various medical journals on the nightstand. A tall chest stands in an opposite corner. A huge flatscreen hangs on a wall opposite the bed. His neat apartment tells me he likes a well-organized space. *Is the rest of his life flawless?* Chase reappears from the closet holding a fleece hoodie. He approaches with a disarming smile and reaches for my zipper. I flinch then stiffen.

"Calm down," he says, unzipping my jacket like I'm a child. He smiles a smile which probably causes many women to abandoned respectability.

As the zipper glides down my chest, I smile nervously. His fingers brush my abdomen, causing a trickle of arousal and cascading warmth from my head to my toes, weakening every limb. I stand like an idiot hypnotized by his touch. He grins, and I believe he knows what I'm feeling. Finally, the zipper slips from the retainer. He slides my jacket from my shoulders like no one's ever done, except my parents. Embarrassed, I stumble on my tongue, "Oh, um, thanks." *Did I expect him to take my top off too?*

"I'll put your jacket in the foyer closet. You can change in there," he says pointing toward the master bath.

Are emotions written all over my face? His smug grin tells me yes.

I enter a large master bath facing a small private courtyard garden with table and chairs scattered about a small waterfall. In front of the window sits a free-standing tub and an adjacent glass-enclosed shower, made of marble and some unidentifiable stone. I wonder how ritual four would feel soaking in his tub. Turning toward the vanity, the mirror reveals a healthy glow and sparkling eyes I haven't seen in a while. And it's all because of Chase.

Chapter 13

A few feet from the kitchen, I find Chase changed into a gray T-shirt that hugs his well-defined back. He's changed out of the running tights which revealed splendid glutes and calves, now hidden inside midnight blue sweatpants. Quietly and admiringly, I study muscles rippling from wrist to elbow as he stirs cream into the coffee. Without warning, he turns, and again, catches me ogling as I had the hairs on his leg that foggy morning. I offer a nervous grin and manage, "Mmmm that smells good." He grins at my obvious embarrassment. Had he sensed my presence before he turned around?

"That looks good on you. Maybe I should let you keep it."

I adjust the hoodie falling around my hips like a fleece nightshirt. "It's a little big, but smells good," I say taking a whiff of the sleeve which smells like nature from a bottle.

Lifting two mugs from the counter, he cocks his head toward a cozy alcove off the living room displaying picturesque views of the park.

"Wow, awesome ... You can see the entire reservoir." Lost in the view, I trip and stumble, catching my fall on an auburn leather sectional.

"Be careful," he warned too late.

I laugh at my clumsy fall and straighten my body on the sofa. Chase places the cups on the coffee table and sits beside me. I survey the room, taking in Chase's world. Bookshelves filled with medical books line an entire wall and an impressive chunky desk angles the window.

I picture Chase, lost in medical journals, forgetting the beauty outside the window. On an opposite wall are pieces of his history. A picture of a boy alludes to the handsome man Chase becomes.

"How long have your parents had this apartment?"

"Wow, years before I was born. This was a sublet when my parents were in medical school. After graduation, they bought it from the owner."

"So, they're both doctors?"

He nods his head. "Yep." Taking a sip of coffee, and settling into the sofa, his shoulders bump mine with a sting.

"Ouch!" We both yelp simultaneously and then laugh.

"It's the fleece," I say rubbing my shoulder.

Still laughing, he turns his face toward mine. "I hate static electricity."

Our eyes lock for a moment.

I glance away nervously and reach for the coffee. "Are your parents still practicing doctors?"

"Well, mom retired early, but when she has energy, she helps dad at the clinic."

"Clinic?"

"It's a family practice my father expects me to carry on, but I just can't see living in Maine all of my life. I prefer the city mostly ... There's so much to do and see, so much culture and life, not that I have time to do everything. My hours at the hospital are insane. I can barely stay awake after a shift."

"The life of a doctor," I say with admiration, imagining him dressed in scrubs, examining a patient's broken bones, or a torn ligament and rendering his diagnosis and treatment expertly. "I'm sure you get much satisfaction from your work."

"Believe me, I do, but I can't wait to make my own hours and enjoy some personal time. Perhaps find a love life," he suggested, lifting his brow and draping his arm on the couch behind me.

"Are you dating anyone?" He asks.

"No. There's no time for that."

"Oh come on, Victoria. That's a horrible excuse, and you know it. There's always time for a little fun, even if it's just a few hours a day. You keep telling yourself that and you'll never find the time," he says judiciously."

Will he challenge everything I say? I worry those x-ray eyes will pierce my steel walls, analyzing every word. But I agree that sounded absurd. "Okay, it's a bad excuse. I guess my priorities lie elsewhere."

"Such as the career you hate?"

"Yes, that and other things..."

"Such as?"

"Well..." and strangely I can't think of another reason.

"Okay, so it's an excuse," he teases.

"No, no, I work long hours and rarely make it home before nine in the evening. And most days, I'm in the office before seven. My spare time is so scarce."

Feigning a violinist, he retorts, "Excuses, excuses ... I'm a doctor remember. I put in close to a hundred hours a week, and I've always found time for a little pleasure."

He smiles that charming grin that makes me want to consume every inch of him. "Okay, I see your point, Dr. Dillon."

"Maybe it's not your job but your life that leaves you unchallenged. You just need more fun."

"Perhaps," I say, deflecting the topic. "So Chase, what's the next step in your career."

"Come on, don't change the topic," he presses with fortitude. "Your avoidance only makes me more curious. So..." he says mischievously "...if it's not a boyfriend, your obvious discomfort with my kiss means either one or two things. You're not attracted to me. Or someone's hurt you," he says without blinking.

He's already pegged me a wounded dove, a scarred soul sullied and heartbroken by a wayward lover. However, my wounds aren't male inflicted, but impressions left by my wanton mother. If only he knew of my growing attraction and how his kiss came close to loosening my restraints. But I feign humor with a twisted face, as I've always done with unease. "Hmm, that kiss just didn't do it for me." On the contrary, it stirred my core.

"Maybe you'll give me another chance to redeem myself."

"You work fast. I'm a nice and slow type of gal," I lie, wishing at that moment to bury my face in his. "But I did enjoy the chocolate strawberry."

"Nice and slow … It might be difficult." Taking another sip of coffee, his eyes dissect mine over the rim. Setting the cup on the table again, he sighs deeply. "I'm not the nice and slow type. When I want something, I act fast. But I can try. Honestly, I'm so attracted to you I'm having trouble just sitting next to you."

His candor is alluring and alarming at the same time, causing two opposing reactions—desire and distrust. I wish I could be more open but I'm wary of his true intent. To be open means revealing my growing attraction and letting go of control upheld so long it's become my nature. Unsure how to respond, I smile, take a sip of coffee, and stare at Milo lying at my feet. Wasn't it me who wanted to dispel small talk for a deeper conversation? But that was before the kiss, before the confusion, before my awkward attempt to disguise my true nature.

I sense he's diagnosing me with his surgeon's mind. For the first time, the room is silent. Sensing my discomfort, Chase doubles back to my earlier question, the question he had ignored. "So, you want to know what's next in my career," he says with a tinge of disappointment. "Well, there're two possibilities; opening my own clinic in the city or taking over my family's practice in Maine. Dad would prefer the latter, his only son continuing the family business."

"I'm sure taking over a well-established practice is easier," I say, detecting subtle changes in his face. The analyst in me emerges, examining every facial detail. Like a swift passing shadow darkening his eyes, a hint of sadness appears then fades.

"I've weighed the pros and cons, but I'm still undecided," he says tilting his head and staring into my eyes. The motion seems familiar, a movement similar to a sigh of remorse. I believe so because I've performed the same motion many times. With the discovery of Judith's cancer, I bottled up my emotions, remained brave, never showing fear or sadness. I wonder if I'm reading Chase correctly, but something's there.

His eyes peruse my face, from my forehead to my chin, settling again on my lips. Before I lose myself in those wonderful brown eyes, I glance at a photo, I assume taken in Maine, of a large backyard and a pier leading to the water. A younger Chase poses with a man and woman beside a boat. "Who are they?"

A sunny smile sweeps his face. "That's mom and dad." He rises from the sofa, grabs the photo, and brings it back. "Wow, feels like I took this picture yesterday. I was seventeen in this photo. We were preparing for a sail—one of my dad's favorite pastimes." He motions to the picture and mumbles wistfully, "That was one of our better days."

Again, the sadness I saw a few moments ago creeps into his eyes. I wonder what he meant by better days. "You look just like your father, except for the hair."

"Well, you can thank my mom for that."

"She's beautiful. Is she Latino?"

"Yes, Puerto-Rican and dad's Irish."

"Well, I see where you got the massive curls from." My constraints loosen for a moment, as I ruffle his hair like a pup.

"That felt good ... Do it again," he says.

His husky voice stirs my core once more. Friskily, I run my fingers through his hair. He closes his eyes like a cat enjoying a rub. I snicker.

"Aww, that's better," he whispers. "I like when you're playful and unguarded."

My shield is still firmly in place. Maybe he thinks I'll drop my guard with words of appeal.

Leaning closer, he brings the cup to my lip. "Take a sip."

And again like a child, I obey. As he takes a sip, I notice his well-manicured hands. I've held a fascination for men's hands since I was a child. There's a particular memory of a man's strong protective hands securing me on his shoulder. I assume it was my father, but I've never grasped his face with the memory. I examine Chase's hands, the shape of his fingers. Chase brings his eyes to where my eyes linger. He twiddles his fingers and stares curiously.

"I was just admiring your surgeon's hands. They look so strong. You must take special precautions to protect them?"

Slowly, he runs his hand along my arm. Warm tingles elicite a soothing effect.

"They're the tools of my trade. So, I've had them insured."

"That's good ... I mean insuring them ... Makes sense."

He holds his hands out, studying his splayed fingers. "Yep, these babies will have to serve me well in my career," he says placing his hand on his thigh.

"Hmmm, a high testosterone level," I say noticing his ring finger.

Taken aback, he peers at me with arched brows and grins.

"I heard a man's testosterone level determines the ring finger's length. Is there any validity in that doctor?"

He places his hand alongside mine. "Well, it explains why men's fingers are longer than women's." He scoops my hand up, slides his underneath, and examines both sides in detail. "Perfect," he murmurs.

My pulse triples with his touch.

"Hmmm, you know what they say about men with high testosterone?"

"Yea, all that stuff about being great baby makers," I say flippant to skirt the topic, especially after witnessing Hannah's condition the last month.

He takes my hand and tickles my palm as if he knew that small action would relax me, and it did. He interlaces his fingers with mine. I tense, then relax, surprised I didn't pull away. The soothing-intimacy of his touch feels right as if we've held hands many times. His fingers tighten and releases around mine, finding the right tension. I relax just a little, but my guard is still high.

"You know, when I first saw you running, I was so impressed with your form. You're in another world when you are running."

"I am usually..." The small motion of his hand is so quick; I wince when he wipes the foam from my lip and licks it from his fingers. I catch my breath and take a sip of coffee to quiet arousal.

He slides lower on the sofa and rolls his head toward my shoulder. "So, I have you all to myself, but I wish you would relax a little. Loosen up, I won't bite. Well, I'll try not to," he says with a grin. "In the park, you seem so comfortable in your body but here you're so stiff."

"I'm prepared if you try to steal another kiss." We both laugh. Milo's head pops up with a dangling tongue as he pants.

Bemused, Chase rubs his face and grins. "Damn, you're so evasive," he murmurs. "But I'll pierce that wall soon," he says confidently.

I grin, imagining him chipping at an unyielding wall, barely making a dent, and finally conceding defeat.

Chase runs his finger across my lip. "You're beautiful when you smile."

That sounds like all the pick up lines I've heard in the past. My mind starts to question his sincerity. I straighten and slide off the sofa. With fading dawn, I realize I should leave. Unaware of Chase behind me, I turn, colliding with his chest. His hands circle my waist. I stiffen.

"Stop fighting it. Just let go," he whispers.

Let go, rings in my ear, and I'm afraid of falling down that slippery slope. *Let go ...* Two opposing actions take over. My mind tries to control my actions, but my body has already surrendered to his touch. *Don't do it,* resounds in my head but my resistance is gone.

His lips part slowly. His tongue summons mine. Bittersweet chocolate strawberries and coffee linger on his tongue. His hands, now more insistent around my waist, pull me closer. In Chase's arms, I've discovered what's been missing the last two years—total abandonment, fearlessly yielding to my desires. Ritual four, five, six, and seven, suddenly, are unimportant.

Chapter 14

In Greenwich Connecticut, menacing clouds loom above Putnam Cemetery while white plumes rise from shivering mourners into November's chilly air. Mr. Ferrara, standing with his grieving wife and oldest son, turns his head, and swiftly, anger replaces grief. He marches toward two approaching men who stop as he advances closer. Alex's father continues behind a large white mausoleum, the men follow. With their obstructed view, I turn my gaze to Alex's family, pondering their rage when they discover Alex's death wasn't a random act, but murder orchestrated by friends in their midst. Beside me, Kayla stands stonefaced, disguising anger and fear. If Bob and Bruce have any inkling, our lives could be in danger as well.

Finally, mushrooming clouds burst open with torrential rain, sleeting in the frigid air, and frosting burial grounds icy white. Mourners hasten, dropping a single rose on the casket, and then scurry to waiting cars. Alex's distraught mother sways on unsteady feet as her eldest son leads her toward the car. Several headstones away, near the massive mausoleum; Alex's father howls inaudible angry words at the two Asian men. Instantly, Alex's father throws a powerful fist to the Asian's face, sending him staggering back to the ground. With fury, Mr. Ferrara continues pummeling the man with several brutal blows until restrained by Bob and Bruce.

From the car, Alex's mother screams words lost in the downpour. Her son forces her into the car and rushes toward his father. With a hand clasped around my mouth, I watch the Asian withdraw a gun, pointing it at Alex's father. Swiftly, the other Asian rips it from his hand pushing him forcibly toward a car.

Bruce and Bob loosen their grip as Mr. Ferrara protest, shoving his way toward his son's casket. Oblivious to sleeting rain, his coat sags miserably as his shoulders heave up and down with inconsolable tears. Bruce and Bob remain close, giving him space to grieve. In their faces, I see genuine sadness, their pain as visible as the family. *Could Kayla be wrong about Bruce and Bob?* Maybe they played no part in Alex's murder.

In the Lincoln Town car, the battered man examines his bruised face, while the other talks on his mobile. The license plate and Greenwich Little League Baseball sticker identify their Greenwich residency. Coincidently, as the car pulls away, I catch the man's profile behind the wheel. At once, I recall Bruce's anonymous guest in the conference room two weeks ago. It's him. His furtive glance at Kayla had roused my curiosity. Now with Mr. Ferrara's angry display, my curiosity heightens. Are they part of Wheaton's money laundering?

Turning to my side, I find Kayla missing. A few feet away, under a large umbrella, Amber and Dennis stand in conversation. Amber notices my glance in their direction and waves with downturned lips and pained eyes. Dennis, who always has some lewd expression or comment purses his lips and acknowledges me with a nod. I manage a grin, wave back, and shudder when my rain-drenched heels sink into the ground. I imagine bodies buried beneath and hurry off burial grounds.

Inside the car, I swiftly turn on the heater to melt chill from my body. For a moment, I stare at Alex's grave, suddenly gripped with his loss. The excitement he exuded when he spoke of his new position saddens me. He'll never have the chance to pursue his passion or marry and have children. With that thought, my eyes are misty.

The scene evokes images of Judith's funeral seventeen months ago in Martha's Vineyard. Mourners overwhelmed the small church, spilling onto church grounds. In contrast, Judith's burial was on a sunny spring day in New West Side Cemetery in Edgartown. I cried hard, realizing for the first time how many lives Judith touched. Mourners spoke of her charitable deeds. Friends she helped, in their time of need, praised her virtues. Fans venerated her work. I wonder if I'd truly known my mom. Maybe if I hadn't been privy to her betrayal of Aiden, I would have seen her differently, adored her like her friends.

I hadn't shed a tear when learning of Judith's cancer. I tucked away emotions, assumed a supportive role, and helped her through two years of pain. All the fear and anguish I contained just for Judith, burst forth at her funeral. I thought I'd die when they lowered her casket into the ground. Much like Alex's mother, Aiden pulled me from the grave.

Eager to leave, I search for Kayla through car windows finding her two cars ahead, talking to Andrew Kelly. She's on an unrelenting mission. Car heat collides with cold windows clouding my view. Just as I wipe the windshield, Andrew slides something into Kayla's hands. She places it in her handbag and walks toward the car. *Is she working with Andrew Kelly?*

She slides behind the wheel without a word. I sit quiet, too tired and sad to argue with Kayla. We decide to skip Alex's repast because Bob and Bruce's presence would be overwhelming. The car glides down rolling hills onto Parsonage Road and headstones weave in and out of trees as Putnam Cemetery recedes in the background.

Kayla and I barely utter a word on the trip back to the city. I recognize her silent brewing and save my questions for another time. Resting my head on the seat, I watch cars through rain-dribbled windows speed past on the New England Throughway. The gray day swirls about me, lulling me to sleep.

* * *

"Vic." Kayla says shaking me awake.

Confused, I open my eyes and glance around, noticing we're parked in front of my condo. "We're here already?"

"Yep, you must be tired. You were out like a light."

The much-needed nap must have reassembled pieces of information in my brain; because I awake angry with Kayla's evasiveness.

"Kayla, is there anything you want to tell me?" I ask with a glare. "I saw Andrew Kelly slip something in your hand. That was foolish. Anyone from Wheaton could have seen you two." I appear as a mother scolding a misbehaving child while Kayla sits stiff and unresponsive like the rebellious teenager. My tone assumes a much-needed urgency—emotions I've withheld for days. Anger and fear push words from my mouth. "I'm scared shitless you're going to get yourself in trouble. You can't mess with these people, Kayla. You saw what happen to Alex; they could do the same to you."

She sits silent.

Irritated, I sigh. "Okay, just promise me you won't do anything stupid."

Taking her eyes from the windshield she says quietly. "I realized you're scared. So am I. I won't do anything stupid. I know what I'm doing."

"I hope so." Reaching over, I give her a hug. "I just don't know what I'd do if I lose you, Kayla."

"You're overly dramatic, Vic. You're not going to lose me. So stop squeezing me like you'll never see me again."

I release my hold and force a grin.

Kayla squashes her lips and squeezes her eyes, a silly frown she feigns when I stress too much. "Stop worrying, I'll see you tomorrow."

I exit the car, stand under the canopy, and watch her car drive off. A sliver of doom shiver down my spine as her car disappears from view.

Chapter 15

Desperate to eradicate gloom enveloping my mind, in one unbroken procession, I race to my apartment, slip off mud-caked shoes, damp clothing, step into a soothing shower, and linger 'til gloom withers. My stomach rumbles, eliciting another yearning. Exiting the shower, and toweling off, I saunter naked from the steamy bath toward the kitchen, when the photo, I place on the refrigerator several days ago, cause more angst. With growing suspicions of Bruce and Judith's friendship, I telephone my father instantly.

"Aiden Powell," my father answers. I miss the old greeting, 'Powell residence,' but now that dad's widowed and living alone, the old greeting seems unsuitable.

"Dad, can I drop by tonight?"

"Sure, hon. You called just in time. Dinner's in the oven."

"Yum, can I pick up anything from the store?"

"No, just bring your appetite, sweetie."

"See you in a few minutes."

Quickly, I throw on jeans, a turtleneck sweater, boots, and head toward the front door. Remembering the photo, I doubled back to the kitchen when the landline rings. I don't answer, but wait for the answering machine to pick up.

"Victoria, Victoria, Victoria," Chase asserts through the phone. "I can't get that kiss off my mind. Well, I'm on my last round at the hospital. I'm hoping to see you soon. I'll wait patiently for your call."

His voice transports me to a kiss that unraveled but hadn't broken my restraints. With the immediate concern, I squelch thoughts of Chase, grab the photo from the fridge, and continue out the door.

* * *

Heavy sleet, now a misty shower, hovers around Manhattan's darkening skies. Heading south on FDR Drive, I ponder dad's reaction when he sees the photo. I hope it doesn't upset him too much. Entering the West Village, I slow the car in search of parking on congested Grove Street. After circling the block several times, finally, a car exits a spot several feet from my family's townhouse—a red four-story Italianate brick townhouse. I imagine Judith waiting at the door, light shining from the interior, motioning me out of the rain.

With keys never surrendered when I found my own apartment, I open the front door. Garlic, onions, oregano, and tomatoes permeate the home, arousing childhood memories. Dad hasn't changed one item since Judith's death. The Venetian décor reminiscent of homes she'd seen while on tour in Italy remains. Curvilinear furniture, teardrop chandeliers, gold, and silver-accented crown molding are present throughout the home. Adjacent to the staircase, a fire burns in the library. I imagine Judith sprawled on the sofa wearing her favorite silk robe, reading a recently discovered author's novel. Down the hall, in the living room, a ghostly Judith hums to the Baby Grand piano.

"Vic, is that you?" dad yells from the kitchen.

"It's me, dad." I continue past framed magazine photos of Judith's performances at La Fenice, La Scala, the Metropolitan Opera House, down the stairs into the large chef kitchen. Outside French doors, leading to the garden, a deluge of rain obscures the patio. As always, dad plays a piece of Judith's music. Today, it's her Violetta Aria from La Traviata.

Wearing a red apron covered in a dozen chef hats, a present from Judith years ago, dad stands over the stove stirring a delicious smelling soup. His passion for cooking hasn't waned but grown in old age. Judith, lacking culinary skills, delegated dad the family cook. He should have been a chef, but he'd always protest, "Cooking for hundreds of people wouldn't be much fun. I prefer cooking just for my darlings."

In his youth, Aiden was a striking broad-shouldered man. Now seventy, dad's six-foot frame is still brawny. He hasn't assumed the characteristic elderly hunch. I presume a result of ritualistic morning treks to the gym. With Judith's constant travels, Aiden was my security, always present, the protective dad.

Aiden turns, wipes his hands on his apron and examines me astutely. Finding the remote control, he lowers the volume on Judith's aria. "What's up kiddo?"

I smile. Even at the age of twenty-five, he continues to call me kiddo, which I don't mind; it makes me special in his eyes. I kiss him on the cheek and plop on a stool around the kitchen island. "You still listen to Judith when you cook?"

"Religiously ... You know your mom's voice always soothes me when I'm cooking."

It's sad watching dad cook. A duty he used to perform for three, he now prepares for one.

He eyes me closely, "Are you hungry?"

"Famished, I haven't eaten a morsel all day."

"Well, you've come to the right place." Turning the heat on low, bringing the soup to a simmer, he stares at me with concern. "Why haven't you eaten today?"

"I was at a colleague's funeral in Greenwich Connecticut. I just didn't have an appetite."

"Funeral, who died?" He asks, sitting at the island with his dear old friend, Johnny Walker.

"Dad, it was so sad. Alex Ferrara, one of the traders at Wheaton, was ki—died," I stammer with a lie. I spare him suspicions of money laundering and murder, knowing such news will cause great concern. "I feel so bad for his family."

"They must be distraught after losing a child," he says, taking a sip of scotch. "Losing a spouse is tough, but a child..." He shakes his head sadly "... I can't imagine the pain."

I study dad for signs of grief and wonder how he's coping without Judith. Except for a few wrinkles and graying hair, his face hasn't changed much. His eyes, which always contained so much life, have dimmed somewhat. Is it sadness or just aging? And his thick eyebrows, once intense with expressiveness, now conveys wisdom tinged with gray. Frown lines are now forever engraved across his forehead. After many years of assiduous trims, the small mustache looks sculpted. Aiden has assumed that distinguished look handsome men grow into with age. "Dad, how're you doing?" I ask, hoping his life's resumed some form of normalcy without Judith.

He sighs and places dinnerware on the island. "Vic, don't worry about me. Your mom's death was tough at first, but I'm managing. Judith wouldn't want me sulking around grieving her loss." He pauses and looks at me with furrowed brows. "What about you sweetie, how are you coping?"

It's just like dad to put my needs before his own, the forever, selfless father figure. "I'm hanging in there." Although I was a mess for several months, I've somewhat overcome grief, but feign normalcy, not wanting to burden him with worry.

Walking to the cabinet, he takes two plates and bowls and signals with his eyes and head, "The dining table or the island?"

"The island is fine," I say, heading toward the wine cooler, retrieving a bottle of courage—red wine. I hope the conversation I'm about to broach doesn't cause too much discomfort. I hesitate and pull the photo from my purse, placing it upside down on the counter.

"Have you decided what to do with the house in Martha's Vineyard?" He asks with a curious glare. "Judith knew how much you enjoyed the island and the home. It would be a shame to sell it. And you don't have to worry about the cost of maintenance. Judith's trust should take care of all the expenses."

"Yep ... I know. I've given it much thought the last year. It's a piece of mom I refuse to discard."

"I'm glad, Vic. By the way, I was at the house a week ago just checking to make sure everything's okay. I gave Mrs. Greene, our next door neighbor, a set of keys a year ago to keep an eye on the property. You know how close she and Judith were."

"I remember. How are the Greene's?"

"They're still going strong. Such good people Anne and Gerald. Oh, Anne asked me to give you her love. She's asked about you often, and always wonders when you'll return. I believe she's missing Judith a great deal." He digresses as he's done a lot in the past year. "I don't think they'll ever leave the island."

"Why would they? They've been on the island all their lives." I inhale, push the photo to the center of the island, and exhale before losing my nerve. "Dad, this is why I stop by."

His brows arch swiftly. "Where did you get this?" He asks picking up the photo.

"At the Wheaton estate."

Pulling his reading glasses from his shirt pocket; he studies the photo closer. "Wow, this was so long ago," he says, glancing at me, "This was the night I met your mom."

"Dad, please be honest. Were Bruce and Judith involved?"

He stares with tight lips and one brow askew, an expression he wears when he's about to part bad news. His silence answers my question.

"Victoria..."

It must be serious. He only calls me Victoria when he's about to correct or scold me, or when he's about to part some grave news.

He exhales a slow breath and states, "It's complicated. Yes, your mom and Bruce dated for a while." Shaking the photo in his hand, he explains, "When this picture was taken, I had just been introduced to your mom. Thanks to Mallory ... You know Mallory, and I became friends before I met Judith. We met at a charity dinner for the arts here in the city. She told me she'd met Judith in Venice at La Fenice. I'd been following your mom's career since I heard her perform a rendition of Verdi's La Traviata. I was smitten the moment I saw Judith and asked Mallory to introduce us."

The word smitten makes me smile; conjuring decades past when old fashioned values and courting a woman respectfully was expected before any physical act transpired. I wonder if dad was that respectful of Judith. *How long did they wait to have sex?* Suddenly, the overwhelming arousal I felt on Chase's sofa comes to mind. "Was it Judith's talent or beauty that attracted you?"

"Oh, Vic, there's so much about your mom that attracted me. Well, besides her beauty and immense talent, there was an immediate recognition."

Is that what I felt when I first met Chase in the park? There was something I couldn't explain when we spoke the first time, a feeling we'd spoken many times before.

"Your mom's wit matched her talent as a singer. I could talk to her about anything. She was so well-read and traveled," he says, pausing in thought.

I picture the two talking all night, surprised to find daybreak's arrived.

"She was just the most interesting person I'd ever met. I admired her determination to succeed in her art. She never let her ethnicity prevent her from pursuing the opera. You know, many of the roles she acquired were performed by Caucasian women, but composer's and producers loved her the moment she was on stage."

"With her honey-colored skin, producers probably ignored her nationality because, on stage, she could assume many ethnicities," I remember how makeup artist transformed Judith from an African-American into a Japanese Geisha, French seamstress, and an Italian courtesan as Cio-Cio San in Madame Butterfly, Mimi in La Boheme, and Violetta in La Traviata. No one would have guessed her nationality if they hadn't known.

"In my book, your mom is one of the greats. I place her up there with the likes of Marian Anderson, Leontyne Price, and Jessye Norman, such amazing talents."

Judith's greatest fan. I remember dad's persistent management of Judith's career. His passion equally matched hers for the opera. "Besides her talent, what else attracted you to mom?"

"Everything," he says with a faraway gaze. "When Mallory introduced us at Wheaton's infamous party, it was kismet."

Unable to reveal his friendship with the Wheatons until this point, I'm intrigued by the fondness in dad's voice as he reveals their first meeting.

"I noticed the tension between Judith and Bruce." Staring at the picture again, he shakes his head. "Whew! Bruce's reaction every time I stared at your mom was like a dagger in my back," he says with a shake of his head. "That man was a force to reckon with when it came to your mom. But I didn't back down," he says with bravado. "The night we met, I perceived Judith's annoyance with Bruce. She didn't tolerate his behavior that evening. See how Bruce is sitting with your mom..." he says, pointing to the photo, "...with his arms around her shoulder. He kept her on a short leash the entire night until she protested."

I give the photo back to dad, visualizing Judith's tight leash and Bruce following every move.

"I perceived Judith had doubts about Bruce. I knew she was still involved with him when we started seeing each other, but I didn't care. I just wanted to be near her. We became instant friends for years. I realized she was confused and torn between her friendship with me and her love for Bruce. You may be shocked to know this Vic, but your mom and I maintained a platonic affair for years until we married. I didn't want to make advances on her until she was ready."

Aiden's face changes with a sudden recollection. Wrinkles deepen on his café-au-lait complexion. Weathered hands, once virile and strong, hold fast to the photo as if trying to recapture the past. "You know Vic, at one time; Mallory was one of your mom's closest friends."

"They were? That's a surprise," I say wide-eyed. "How did they meet?"

"Well, Judith performed in Venice for several years," he says, tugging his mustache, as he often does in deep thought. "She was very popular in Italy. She met Mallory backstage after a performance at La Fenice. Judith said they were instant friends. Remember how your mom disappeared every January? Well, every year those two headed to that wild and crazy carnival in Venice." Aiden lifts his gaze from the swirling liquor and squints his eyes in thought. "You know, it was Judith's idea to enhance Wheaton's dinner parties with costumes and masks."

"Really, I thought it was Mallory's idea. How did Judith meet Bruce?"

"You can thank Mallory for that."

"If Judith and Bruce were dating, how did Mallory end up his wife?"

"Well, Bruce and Mallory were high school sweethearts. They both grew up in Greenwich. I believe when Mallory left for Europe to pursue modeling, the relationship ended."

"That's odd. Why would she fix Judith up with her high school sweetheart?"

"She didn't. She only introduced them, and well, the rest is history. A few years later, I believe your mom realized Mallory was still in love with Bruce. She was uneasy knowing her friend still held deep affections for her high school sweetheart."

Placing his reading glasses and the photo on the island, he walks to the stove and stirs the soup. "I could never figure out Bruce and Mallory. One moment they were together, the next they were seeing other people, even when they were married." Returning to the island, he sits with a heavy sigh. "Judith informed me they had an open clause agreement."

"Huh! Well..." I sneer, "that explains their dinner party seating arrangements."

"They were an unconventional couple."

"Why didn't I meet Bruce and Mallory growing up?"

He takes the last sip of Scotch, then refills the glass. "There was too much tension between Judith and Mallory."

"Why?"

"Well, years later, after Mallory and Bruce married, Mallory became suspicious and jealous of Judith and Bruce. She suspected Bruce was still in love with Judith."

"And...was he?"

"Yes, I believe he loved your mom until the day she died."

"Did mom ... did she love Bruce?"

An expression I haven't seen since I was a child colors his face. I believe its pain he's held for some time.

"Honey, your mom and I loved each other dearly. In life, people can love many people, but not every love survives a marriage. I was aware of Judith's affections for Bruce from the beginning. Your mom's love for Bruce was toxic. Judith said his controlling ways made her claustrophobic. And she always doubted herself around him. Years later, I realized it was their passion, their sex life that scared her the most."

I wince and glance away uneasily at the mention of Bruce and Judith's sex life. "Dad, I'm sorry. I hope talking about this doesn't cause you pain."

"No, I've been fine with this for years. Judith and I were truly happy," he assures.

If they were truly happy Judith wouldn't have seen other men. I want to dispel suspicions about Judith's late-night visitors, but I'm afraid I'll cause dad pain. I ask cautiously, "So, did Bruce and Judith remain friends after your marriage?"

Rising from the stool; he turns the stove off and removes the apron. He doesn't answer which is curious. I recall Judith's evening visitor—always when dad was traveling. He couldn't have known. Now that Judith's gone, should I let her secret rest as well? Why inflict dad with more pain. But he said he was aware of their affections. I need to know what I heard those nights long ago. I could be wrong. Unable to hold Judith's secret any longer, words fly from my mouth. "Dad, I know Judith saw other men when you were married." Instantly, relief floods over me and remorse for the pain I've caused dad.

Chapter 16

Without an ounce of surprise or upset on his face, Aiden turns from the stove, strolls to the island, and takes a seat. Catching my troubled gaze his eyebrows furrow and his face tense contritely. He exhales through his mouth. "I thought you might have remembered, Vic. I just wasn't sure how much," he says as if he were the adulterer.

"All this time, you've known about the affairs?"

"Affair honey, there was only one man ... Bruce Wheaton."

Suddenly, I'm mute with astonishment. For years, I believed Judith had many men, but it was one, Bruce Wheaton. But one affair is still wrong. *Why did he allow it?* "You were okay with that?" I ask with a grimace and disbelieving head shake.

Aiden takes a sip of scotch and leans into the island. "Well, this is one conversation I wasn't prepared for. Judith thought one day you might find out about Bruce. On her deathbed, I told her I wouldn't lie if you asked. She didn't protest. I believe being so close to death she wanted you to know as well."

"Know ... About her affair with Bruce?"

"Not just the affair," he says, holding my gaze. "Your mom and I tried many years to conceive a baby. Her biological clock was ticking, and she was determined to give birth before it was too late. After months of trying and no success, we sought a specialist. Many tests revealed Judith ovaries were fine." He looks at the scotch and twirls the glass in his hand. With a lowered gaze, he continues. "The issue was me. I'm sterile and can never father a child. Your mom was devastated." He lifts his eyes toward me, holding my gaze. "We thought about adoption, but Judith wanted a biological child."

All my senses numb. Aiden isn't my biological father! I should be screaming, but my voice comes out flat. "So, if you're not my father, who is?"

"Vic, listen; you have always been my daughter. Understand Judith wanted you more than anything, and so did I. We would have done anything to have a child of our own. Your mom and I made an unconventional agreement, a viable choice. At thirty-nine, Judith's childbearing years were waning. She said if she couldn't have a child with her husband, it would have to be with the second-best, someone she knew and trusted."

No further explanations are needed. My gut tells me the second best is the man who visited Judith often at night when I was a child. "Bruce Wheaton!"

Aiden nods his head.

My exterior is calm, but inside anger boils. "My boss ... I'm Bruce Wheaton's daughter!"

"Vic, look at me ... You're my daughter and always will be."

"Does Bruce know?" I ask with venom.

"Yes, he was more than willing to give Judith what she wanted. But there was one stipulation, I'm recognized as your father," he says so emphatically it conjures a categorical stance with Judith.

Now I understand why Bruce's expression changes whenever he sees me. He's my father. I'm Bruce's daughter. "Did you or Judith ever consider the possibility I'd look like Bruce?"

"Well, Vic, it's a blessing you got all your mother's qualities."

I catch dad's eyes, and anger subsides, considering the pain he endured with Judith's decision. I take several breaths. Questions swirl in my mind. *Did he allow Bruce's visits to the vineyard after my birth?* "Dad, did the affair end after Judith's pregnancy?"

"If you're asking if they remained lovers, yes, I knew about that Vic. I realized your mom had affections for both of us, but she'd never leave me for Bruce."

How trusting of him. "Dad, why would you put yourself through the pain? Why didn't you end it?"

"I don't expect you to understand, but I loved your mom more than life itself. I just wanted her to be happy."

"Did you ever consider leaving her?"

"No, I loved her too much. You might not understand, but we were happy. I placed no limits on your mom. I knew before we married, Judith was a free spirit, and traditional marriages weren't to her liking. I accepted that fact."

Did they have an open clause arrangement as well? "Did you have other women?"

With a reassuring smile, he says, "No. I had eyes only for your mom."

"Well, you should have given her a taste of her own medicine," I say with rising resentment. Rubbing my temples to prevent a headache threatening to appear; I stifle angry words and stare dumbfounded into the face of the man I've always known as my father. I can't be upset with him for all the pain he'd suffered from Judith's infidelity. I take his hand across the island. "Dad, obviously I'm shocked and angry. I understand Judith's need to have a child, but I'll never be okay with her affair and hurting you." *Is there something I'm not seeing?* It doesn't make sense for such an accomplished man to accept half a marriage—to share his wife with another man. I release his hand, rise from the stool, and walk toward the patio doors, staring blindly into the garden. "Dad, I'll need some time to wrap my mind around this. God, this is so bizarre."

"I understand how disturbing this must be, hon."

"Disturbing ... How about devastating," I murmur, given what's unfolding at Wheaton. Suddenly, I wonder about Mallory. "Is Mallory aware I'm Bruce's daughter?"

"Dear Lord, no! That was part of the agreement; not to tell her. Whew! That would've been a mess. Mallory wouldn't have been as understanding," he exclaims with a convincing breath.

Remembering the conversation Linda O'Connor overheard between Bruce and Mallory, how she'd learned I'm Judith's daughter, I wonder if Bruce decided to tell her finally? "I have a feeling Mallory knows."

"No, I doubt it. With Mallory's jealous nature, I believe this is a secret Bruce will take to his grave. Vic, there's something I've been saving just for this moment. Judith said if you ever found out about Bruce to give it to you."

Aiden climbs the stairs and reappears with a beautifully decorated box painted with Baroque artwork I'd seen in one of Judith's book. A golden lock fastens the box, perhaps protecting valuable items worth guarding, some precious secret of Judith's. He hands me the key and places the box on the island.

"Judith kept diaries for years. She wanted you to know who she was and not judge her for her actions. She knew you might hold some grudge toward her affair with Bruce. These will explain a lot," he says patting the box.

"Have you read them?"

"No, there was no need or desire to do so. Your mom and I talked about every aspect of her life. I'm certain there's nothing she hasn't told me contained within those pages. Besides, I don't want to dredge up old memories."

"How trusting of you," I mumble while running my hand over the box.

"That's what marriage is about Victoria. This might sound ridiculous given your mom's affair with Bruce, but we trusted each other. We were honest about everything. Your mom and I unveiled all our secret demons, no matter how horrible they were." He pauses and stares at the box. "I trust you're grown enough to read what's in the diaries. If I had any doubt you couldn't handle it, I would have kept the journals a secret. Vic, love comes in many degrees and varieties."

News of my biological father leaves me numb. I've gotten the information I wanted, but not what I'd expected. The revelation is too much to digest in one night. I'll wait to tell dad about the money laundering. Although I'm the one needing consoling, I'm the dispenser of comfort, assuring him I'll never blame him for Judith's action.

"Vic, I understand if you need to speak with Bruce ... I'm okay with it," he says considerately.

With suspicions of unethical conduct looming over Wheaton and Alex's death, the last person in the world I wish to speak with is Bruce Wheaton.

Chapter 17

Earlier, I walked into my family's home, Victoria Anjelica Powell and walked out with a new identity. The realization Bruce Wheaton's blood courses through my veins, rock me to the core. The twenty-five-year-old secret festers like a slow-moving virus, nauseatingly infecting every pore. I leave the townhouse with tranquil steps and Judith's prized diaries, arriving at my car indescribably numb. For ten minutes, I stare past the windshield into oblivion, fearing emotions beneath the surface. Is this some cruel cosmic joke? Beliefs I've held so long, that Aiden and I shared similar characteristics was untrue. He's not my father, but another man I've admired until news of his corrupt behavior. All these years, I believed Judith had many lovers, but Aiden dispelled that belief.

"Her affair honey, there was only one man ... Bruce Wheaton."

Her love for two men defined her behavior. My false perception of her wantonness was misgivings of a child turned inward. I've controlled all my wants for fear of being just like Judith.

I ponder my numb reaction to my parents' deceit. Is my apathy normal? Shouldn't I be screaming applicable oaths? I suspect the stupor will dissolve into crushing tears. Frozen behind the wheel, I wait several minutes then start the car and drive aimlessly around the city, avoiding my quiet condo. It's too late to bother Hannah. And Kayla's obsession with Wheaton's money laundering might irritate me further. Inundated with wedding plans my news might overwhelm

Michelle. I double park on Third Avenue and dial the one person who can alleviate my worries.

"Chase Dillon…"

"Chase, can I see you tonight." I hope my words didn't sound desperate. But his message did say he'd wait for my call.

"You sound strange. Are you okay?"

"I just need someone to talk to." A few months ago, I would never have admitted I needed a shoulder to cry on. I've always been strong enough to deal with problems on my own. I remember the sagacious words my father dispensed before I left the townhouse, *"No one is an island, Vic. I'm always here if you want to talk."*

"I'm off in an hour. Where do you want to meet?"

"My place."

* * *

The buzzer rings, doubling my anxiousness. I take the receiver from the wall and hesitate before answering, "Yes?"

"Chase is here to see you," the doorman announces.

"Please, send him up."

I begin to worry I'd called Chase too soon after tonight's big blow. Maybe I should have waited longer before seeing him. In the mirror, I glimpse the short skirt I'd changed into then rush to change into my jeans just as the doorbell rings. Slowly, I walk toward the foyer and take a deep breath. When I open the door, the sight of Chase surprisingly blindsides me. Moments ago, my intentions were purely virtuous, but not anymore. Before the door closes, we're fumbling and kissing. Our swift actions leave me wondering who made the first move. One item of clothing at a time, Chase undresses me. I don't protest but do the same. Every urge I've felt since our first encounter, I indulge. I remove his shirt and inhale the earthy scent that lured me that foggy morning. I bury my nose in dark hairs I'd craved in his kitchen. His surgeon hands, which gently removed a leaf from my hair, now grip firmly, pushing my face toward his lips, a kiss more passionate than the first.

My hands trail dark hair culminating at the v-line above his jeans. I continue unzipping his pants just as he had my jacket in his apartment. All the while, my eyes never leave his brown eyes. I'm amazed at the hardness elicited by my actions. No longer able to control his lust, swiftly and without much effort, he lifts me onto his muscular thighs. His hardness pierces through me, forcing an irrepressible moan. The pain of my parent's deceit doesn't exist at the moment, only pleasure as Chase fills me on my foyer wall.

* * *

Two hours later, the phone rings, pulling me from sleep. I contemplate several rings before answering, and when I finally do, a discordance of rapid breathing, fast footsteps, and city noise sail through the phone with Kayla's muted voice.

" ... Kayla, what's going on?"

"I can't explain on the phone. Did you find the disc I placed in your bag?"

"Disc?"

"Vic, I have to go. Please, wait for me at Engineer's Gate at five o'clock, I'll explain everything."

"Okay. Kayla..."

"That's odd." Worried, I place the cell phone on the nightstand. My body is a contradiction of emotions, lust heightened by Kayla's anxious voice, and stimulated by Chase's mouth and hands on my skin. Before I can express my concern, his lips find mine. No words are necessary as he pivots my compliant hips. And thoughts of Kayla suspend for the moment.

Chapter 18

Kayla can't be dead! Nausea rises in my throat with the mental image of Kayla falling into the cold ravine. I cup my mouth and force the acidity down with irrepressible tears. As I cower in the police cruiser's back seat, the killer's callous voice resonates in my ear. *"Ms. Powell, I know who you are and where you live."* Kayla's senseless murder has rendered me angry, fearful, and inconsolable. Yesterday when I exited her car, I had a foreboding sense that would be the last time I'd see her again, confirmed by the ambulance ahead.

The cruiser sits in the exact spot I froze in shock, turned and sped uphill away from Kayla and the gun-wielding man. The police inspecting the crime scene seems surreal. Only moments ago, I witnessed a murder unfold, unaware it was Kayla. If only I'd demanded she come straight to my apartment, she'd still be alive. Her tearful conversation in the ladies room echoes repeatedly. I should have marched her straight to the authorities or gone myself. But it's too late. No amount of wishing can bring Kayla back.

Yellow police tape, seen often in the park, borders the wooded ravine, confirming a crime my mind denies. I'm the sole witness, the only one to reconstruct a wicked act the crime tape proclaims. Images of Kayla's final plea silenced by a gunshot enrage me. *What could I have done?* If I'd screamed would the killer have stopped—the fatal shot halted? Would a diversion have given Kayla time to escape? No matter how many scenarios I create, she was too close to the gun to escape. There was nothing I could've done to prevent her murder.

The morning rolls in reverse from the man's callous voice on the phone, the harrowing chase through the park, Kayla falling in the ravine, her final plea, ending at the black Lincoln Town car. Then I remember the Greenwich Little League sticker and Connecticut license plate. It's the same car from Alex's funeral. *The two Asian men killed Kayla.* I jump when the car door opens.

"Miss, you okay?" The officer asks.

I nod my head, but I'm far from okay.

"How's your leg?"

It takes a moment to realize he's referring to the bullet graze. I stare at the bandage and bloodstained running shoes, recalling the rush of adrenaline speeding me faster than I'd ever run. What if that bullet had been fatal not a graze? There'd be no one to demystify two homicides, two close friends murdered in the park. After a few years, our deaths would be a cold case, forgotten and discarded on some warehouse shelf. The policeman waits for my response. I stare stone-faced and respond, "Could have been worse."

* * *

After a trip to the hospital, a bandage for my wound, and drugs to calm my nerves, two officers escort me to the nineteenth precinct for interrogation. Fearing my fate will be the same as Alex and Kayla's, I answer questions circumspectly. I reveal there were two men, but the fog obscured their faces. I described the black Lincoln Town car, but didn't mention the Connecticut license plate or Greenwich Little League Baseball sticker. With difficulty, I describe every detail of Kayla's final moments, kneeling before a murky image, and my desperate flee from the gun-wielding man. I don't mention Wheaton's money laundering, fearing exposure will put me in greater danger. In a matter-of-fact tone, I answer questions about Kayla's personal and professional life.

"Does she have enemies?"

"No, she was loved by family, friends, and colleagues," I state and then recall people Kayla pissed off with her snooping over the years. Until Wheaton, no one ever wanted to kill her.

"Ms. Powell, do you have contact information for Ms. Collin's family? We will need to contact her nearest relatives."

Kayla's poor parents, how am I going to tell Hannah and Michelle? Kevin. How could I forget Kayla's brother? "Her brother Kevin Collins is an NYPD policeman." Surely they will contact him immediately and expedite the procedure for one of their own.

The officer's dispassionate expression swiftly changes to alarm. One officer leaves the room at once, I assume, to tell Kevin of his sister's murder. Kevin will be distraught. I can't imagine his pain and anger, but he'll doggedly hunt Kayla's killers.

I protest when the police offer to drive me home, imagining the black Lincoln Town car parked in front of my apartment and the two Asian men watching as I exit the police car. "I would rather not go home. I'd rather be with friends," I explain.

The police car drops me off at Hannah's, but I don't go upstairs. I enter the lobby and wait for the police car to leave. As soon as the car rounds the corner, I summon a taxi and exit a block from my condo. I enter through the building's rear entrance, hoping no one sees me. Before I rush inside the elevator, the doorman calls my name.

"Ms. Powell, a FedEx package arrived for you."

"Thank you." I take the envelope and hurry into the elevator. My heart sinks when I read the sender's name. Kayla Collins.

Inside the apartment, I examine the FedEx slip, noticing yesterday's date. Kayla must have mailed it before Alex's funeral or shortly after she dropped me off. Slowly, I remove the contents, a handwritten letter from Kayla and a file labeled Thawone, LLC. The file she was searching for. The penmanship is shaky, not her usual elegant loops. She must have written it in haste. The Thawone file lies on the dining table, thick and worn with lethal information. My eyes begin to water as I read Kala's letter.

Vic,

I've never been so scared in my life. For days, I've noticed a black Lincoln Town car in front of my apartment. I saw the same car at Alex's funeral. Every move I make they're watching. I want to go to the police, but fear these people will kill me just as Alex. I haven't told Kevin because it would put him and my family in danger. Andrew Kelly has been helping me for a while. He told me the money launders are part of a Japanese drug cartel. The two Asian men are employees of Michelle's father and have used Wheaton to hide drug money for years. Vic, don't mention anything to Michelle. I'm uncertain of her knowledge.

I found the missing file during the company dinner in Bruce's office. I also stumbled on a photo of Michelle's father and mother when we were searching through Bruce's family albums, taken at one of Wheaton's dinner parties in the eighties. You will find both the file and the picture in the package. Vic, I don't believe anyone suspects you know about the money laundering. I feel safer with the file in your hands. I hope by now you've found the disc I placed in your bag during brunch. On the disc, Alex copied not only the Thawone account but also other Wheaton files and corresponding wire transfers.

Vic, be careful of what you say or do in the office. The morning of the company weekend, I found a control room concealed behind the reception area. There are hidden cameras all over the office. I sense Amber is also involved. You can't trust anyone at Wheaton. Please be cautious when talking to her, or anyone except Andrew Kelly. If anything happens to me, please mail the file and disc to the FBI. At the funeral, Andrew gave me a contact who handles money laundering. His name is Mark Ames. That's what you saw Andrew place in my hand at the funeral. Mark Ames business card is also in the envelope.

Vic, I love you like my sister. I realize what I'm about to reveal will disturb you, but you need to know the truth. While rummaging through Bruce's desk, I found a box containing postcards from Venice and a picture of you as a child with Judith and Bruce on the beach. I wanted to tell you so badly, but I couldn't. I believe your mom and Bruce were more than just friends. I could be wrong, but you need to find out. And if my other suspicions are correct, you hold the key to this entire mess. Talk to Bruce, I believe he will protect you given his affair with Judith, but please Vic, keep your eyes open.

LYLAS,

Kayla

Love you like a sister, Kayla. My eyes grow misty again. Shaking the envelope, a photo paper-clipped with a business card falls to the table. In bold print, the card reveals Mark Ames—Special Agent of the Federal Bureau of Investigations and the official insignia of the U.S. Department of Justice. Inside the Thawone file are several years of reports and statements. Each marked with a yellow highlighter, disclosing coding and money transfers from various accounts. *This is unbelievable.* Never in my life would I imagine needing FBI protection. And never because of my best friend's murder and drug-related money laundering.

I remove the business card from the photo and scan dozens of guest at the Wheaton estate. Michelle's father and mother, Mr. and Mrs. Kimura, stand amid guest sipping cocktails. Even donning masks, the Kimura's, features are discernable. Mr. Kimura's square jaw and high cheekbones are prominent. Mrs. Kimura's masks make her oval face and pouty lips sharp. In detail, I examine the photo, finding Judith and Mallory standing side-by-side. Mallory is laughing, and Judith wears shock or disgust on her face.

At once, the room spins and my guts wrench with queasiness. Slamming the photo on the table, I rush to the bathroom expelling built-up nerves from the last twenty-four hours. Alex's funeral, news of my biological father, and Kayla's death culminate in a flood of nausea. As I reach for a tissue, I notice Chase's wristwatch on the vanity. Is he still here? Placing his watch on my wrist, I wander into the bedroom, finding the disheveled bed I'd left before the park arranged neatly. Tidy sheets and pillows appear as if last night never happened. On the nightstand lies a note from Chase.

Victoria,

Last night was remarkable. You were amazing. I was hoping to be waiting when you returned from the park with more of my treats, but I had an emergency call from the hospital. Maybe later we can continue where we left off.

See you soon,

Chase

Suddenly, all I want is Chase's arms around me and to forget the mess Kayla's thrust me in. If she'd listened, she wouldn't be dead. Anger, rage, and tears build swiftly. Books, magazines, and a vase fly across the room. The loud glass shattering against the wall snaps my fury. I collapse on the bed, curl into a pillow, and pull the sheets over my head.

* * *

Slowly, fog drifts, revealing the Asian man beside me. A menacing laugh and icy words boom through the air. "Ms. Powell, I know who you are and where you live." My legs won't move. The hill grows steeper, and before I can reach the top, a hands grab me from behind. Through wet leaves, I tumble into the cold ravine; landing in blood and staring into Kayla's petrified eyes.

I wake with a racing heart, stare around the inky room then look toward the dark window. I've slept through the day. My face is taut with dried tears and feels like it's aged ten years. A throbbing calf brings back memories of the harrowing escape. A sour smell eminates from my body. I'm still dressed in my running outfit. Rolling off the bed and switching on the light, evidence of rage lie scattered across the floor. Tiptoeing around the shattered glass, I exit the bedroom to a dark apartment. A green blinking light reveals several messages waiting on the answering machine.

Kayla's mother's heartbreak sails through the phone when her unsteady voice asks beseechingly, "What happened to my girl? The police said you saw the shooting. Vicky, please call me when you get this message. I need to know who did this to my girl." Unable to contain her tears, the call ends.

The next message resounds through the speakers with sniffling and Hannah's muffled voice. "Vicky, what happened? Kayla's mother called. She told me. I can't believe Kayla's dead." Hannah sniffs again and then composes herself. "I'm worried about you. Call me as soon as you get this message." I hit next, and there's more of the same from Hannah, her voice growing more urgent.

The next message is from Chase—sweet and longing. But I can't bear to hear his voice and hit next. Michelle's tearful voice expresses the same questions as Hannah's. Unable to hear the rest; I press stop.

With darker energy, I head toward the hall closet and retrieve the leather tote where Kayla hid the disc. Lodged craftily inside an interior pocket, is a silver, glass-encased disc. A photo, stuck to the glass, falls to the floor. My heart plunges at the sight of Kayla playfully biting into a caramel apple as we posed for Mallory at the Oktoberfest. In the background, sits the tarot reading booth and the gypsy girl staring at Kayla. Her predictions have finally come true.

I lean against the foyer wall, the same wall I experienced pleasure just hours ago. Sinking to the floor and pulling my knees to my chest, I stare bleary-eyed at the photo of Kayla's last carefree moments. The last time we'll ever pose together—a week before her death. I wipe my eyes, suddenly aware of my next step, which Alex and Kayla failed to take.

With clarity, I pull myself from the floor and walk toward the dining table, straight to Mark Ames business card. Just as I pick up the phone, it rings in my hand. A Connecticut area code displays on the caller I. D. My heart thuds faster, remembering the callous man's voice earlier in the park. I lift the receiver from the hook without a word and listen. Then Bruce Wheaton's voice says, "Vicky?"

"Bruce?"

"I'm glad you're okay. Listen to me, we need to talk, and it can't wait. Your life may be in danger. And only I can protect you. I'm sending a car to pick you up."

Chapter 19

For some unfathomable reason, I agreed to meet with Bruce. How gullible am I, believing he won't throw me to the wolves as he'd done with Alex and Kayla. On the phone, Bruce sounded genuinely concerned. Although I realize my decision is unfounded, I have one advantage Kayla and Alex didn't have—I'm Bruce's daughter. If his love for Judith was as strong as Aiden professed, he couldn't possibly harm her daughter, his daughter.

I want to scream *turn back* as the car approaches Wheaton's circular driveway, but the open front door cast interior light on Bruce's dark silhouette waiting at the entrance. I approach Bruce for the first time as his daughter, not an employee. When I catch his eyes, a host of emotions weaken my anger. He ushers me inside and into the library, the place Kayla, and I discovered Judith's secret past. The confident man who leaves one weak with a single glance appears uncertain in my presence. King of Denmark cigars tinges the air, and I imagine intoxicating fumes allaying his worries. He motions me toward two oversized leather sofas placed parallel to the room. Sitting on the opposite sofa, his eyes warm as they had during his annual company speech.

"Vicky, I'm so sorry. Kayla's death," he says, shaking his head, I just, It's unconscionable." Anger tints his grey eyes. "You must know how much I valued Kayla, not just as an employee, but like a member of my family. This is all devastating—unbelievable. I'm just relieved you escaped unharmed."

Escape? "How did you know?" I ask, probing his face for deception.

His eyes narrow. "I have ways. I understand your misgivings, but believe me; I'm just as shocked and angry as you are about Kayla." He pauses with words on his tongue. The young servant, who escorted me to my room a week ago, enters with a tray of drinks, places it on the table, and exits the room.

"Would you like a drink?"

I need one desperately but fear the alchol is tainted with deadly poison. I decline and shake my head. "No, thanks." I imagine him watching me take a sip, waiting till the deadly poison renders me unconscious. And the Asians slipping in, carrying my body from the room to some Godforsaken place—perhaps tossing me into the Long Island Sound. Alarmed, I sit tense, fending off fatigue from the harrowing day. What was I thinking coming here with no protection, except the useless can of pepper spray in my bag?

Bruce takes a swig of bourbon then leans forward with clasped hands. "I couldn't live with myself if you were injured or killed."

I sit unresponsive, unfazed, and angry.

"There's something I've wanted to tell you for a long time. I wish under better circumstances, but it's imperative you know now. Linda told me about your conversation and the pictures in the library. So you know—"

"I'm aware you're my father," I say abruptly. "Aiden told me yesterday about your affair with Judith." Bruce's eyes lock with mine. I'm not here to share sentimental moments with my newly discovered father but to get to the truth. "I know what Kayla discovered got her killed." Swiftly, I take Bruce's glass and gulp a mouth-full of bourbon. Before he can open his mouth to warn me, the alcohol rolls with a sharp bite down my throat, and I shudder sucking air between my lips to cool the sting.

"It's got a bite," he says too late, wincing at my reaction. His keen eyes watch as I replace the glass on the tray. He sighs and shakes his head in disappointment. "You drank from my glass. Did you think I poisoned the liquor?"

"I would be stupid to trust anyone at this point."

"I'm not a murderer Vicky ... I know you're suspicious, but I hope I can earn your trust." To prove the alcohol is harmless, he fills the un-used glass and takes a sip. "Don't be so quick to judge me. There are reasons for everything. I'm aware you know about the money laun-dering, and that Kayla tried to keep you uninvolved."

How could he possibly know Kayla didn't want me involved?

"I'm aware Kayla found the surveillance in the office. One of my men informed me she was snooping the morning of the company weekend. He saw her just before she ran out of the office. She left the surveillance room open. She knew about the cameras, but she was unaware there're both video and audio surveillance in every room," he reveals.

The ladies room. Remembering the tearful conversation as Kayla told me of Alex's death and the money laundering, I realize Bruce is aware of everything. *Has he been watching me the entire time?*

"Vicky, you might find this hard to believe, but I'm not the person you should fear. I've tried to protect you and Kayla as much as I can."

My angry, eager tongue ready to hurl vicious accusations of "mur-derer," stalls.

"Kayla was aware the Asians were following her, but she didn't know my men were trailing her as well. They were behind every move the Asians made. Unfortunately, Kayla evaded my guys last night and fell into their hands."

Given all that's happened, last night seemed so long ago. But I still hear the distinct rustling of movement, creaking doors, and clinking utensils from Kayla's phone call. Was she dodging the two men inside the restaurant? I imagine the black Lincoln Town car following her trail and the men grabbing her minutes before my arrival. She must have been so afraid when they pulled her in the car. Knowing Kayla, she put up a good fight. If only she'd come to my apartment, she'd still be alive. At the moment I was waiting at the park's entrance, Kayla was fighting for her life. *Did anyone notice when they grabbed her?*

"Vicky, I'm so sorry you two got caught up in this mess. If Kayla had stopped snooping, I could have prevented this from happening."

"What about Alex? Why didn't you protect him?"

"Alex ... Well, Kayla managed to hide Alex's involvement. I suspect they spoke only outside the office. I had no idea he was helping her until it was too late. Alex's only mistake was making a phone call from the office to Mr. Kimura's direct line investigating the Thawone account. That was a fatal mistake and one I've been trying to protect my employees from for years."

"How ... How did he find out?"

"Alex met Mr. Kimura at a charity fund-raiser thrown by his family in Greenwich. He and Mr. Kimura had an elaborate conversation from my observation. I believe from that exchange Alex discovered Mr. Kimura owns the Thawone account. Later, Mr. Kimura informed me Alex had been snooping around his property in Greenwich days before his death. Alex's little charade got him killed."

Examining Bruce's face for signs of deceit, all I see is remorse or am I seeing what I want to see—hoping my biological father isn't the corrupt heartless bastard I had presumed. "Bruce, why am I here?"

"Vicky, you are my blood ... My daughter. I want you to know the truth." He takes another gulp of bourbon and settles into the sofa. "I'm an unwilling partner. We're all pawns in Mr. Kimura's treacherous game," he states straightforward. "These people are extortionists and have held my family and business hostage to their corrupt business for years."

Extortion? I hadn't considered Wheaton the victim of extortionist demands. Kayla and I failed to grasp other motives for Wheaton's involvement. "How were you drawn into their business?"

"How does any victim become unwilling participants in crimes? Through deceit, lies, and fear for one's life."

Indeed, I understand how one can become an unwilling partner in unethical matters. After all, I've been a silent partner to Judith's imagined deceit and lies all of my life, trying to protect Aiden from pain.

"Vicky, I'm an honorable man. But when they threatened my loved ones and livelihood, I would do anything to protect their loss." Bruce sighs and shakes his head. "It took one meeting, one introduction for our lives to entangled with Mr. Kimura's." He sips more bourbon and runs his fingers through his salt-and-pepper hair. "Mr. Kimura ingratiated himself into my family through my wife."

"Mallory, but how?"

"Back in the eighties, Mallory met Mr. Kimura at the Venice Carnival. She had no idea the Kimura family were part of a drug cartel. If she'd known, she would have run the other way," he says with certainty. "By accident, she met him again in New York and invited Mr. Kimura and his wife to our dinner party. He seemed respectable and an astute businessman. We talked for hours about his business, investments, and travels. At the time, he was seeking financial counsel, and before the dinner was over, he'd asked me to manage his company's investments. I was thrilled to capture such a lucrative account." He pauses in thought and then shakes his head. "I should have known. No businessman entrusts millions of dollars without due diligence. Well, within a matter of days, he wired millions into the firm. I thought nothing of it and never question his business's legitimacy. There was no reason to suspect they weren't. My greed got the best of me, and it's cost me over the years. When the Kimura family moved to Greenwich, my suspicion grew. He was getting too close to my family, and everything was happening too fast."

"How did their move to Greenwich occur?"

"Again, with the help of my unsuspecting wife," he hissed in disgust. "They solicited her help with their deceit; telling her Greenwich was an ideal place to raise their family. And of course, Mallory graciously helped them find a home."

In retrospect, I remember Michelle mentioning her parent's Greenwich home while in college. At the time, I detected animosity toward her suburban life as well as disdain toward her father and brothers. She said she couldn't wait to turn eighteen and flee her parent's life.

"It's clear to me now, Mr. Kimura wanted to keep a watch over the man managing his drug-infested dollars," Bruce says in an indignant tone.

I picture a young naïve Bruce thrill with such a large acquisition. He must have been furious when he discovered the truth. I imagine Bruce's jaw clenched in outrage, as it is now, at threat forcing him to yield to blackmail. "When did you find out he was laundering drug money?"

Bruce's cell phone rings and he lifts it from the table and turns it off. "Well, I have to thank Bob for the discovery. He was the CFO at the time, and after a year of handling the Kimura investments, he grew suspicious. If he'd known he was dealing with a drug lord, Bob wouldn't have confronted Mr. Kimura. Like Kayla and Alex, he started investigating further and discovered Mr. Kimura's true identity. Mr. Kimura found out and threatened the life of his family if he went to authorities. You see Vicky, we either reported the money laundering and risked our families lives or kept our mouths shut. We couldn't see a way around this mess without bloodshed. Reluctantly, we've allowed them to park their drug-infested money in the firm, and they've promised to leave our families alone."

Remembering Kayla's revelations about the anagram, Thawone's contact person, and the account coding, I shake my head at the treachery tying Bruce's hands. However, my suspicious mind doesn't relent as easily as my heart. "Bruce, I want to believe everything you're saying, but there's something I don't understand."

"Vicky, I realize how all this looks. I brought you here to protect you and to tell you the whole sordid truth."

"Why the anagram ... Why are you listed as the contact person, and why the account coding? It all looks so suspicious."

"As I stated earlier, there are reasons for everything, Vicky. I took measures to protect my employees. Bob and I needed a way to shield others from Mr. Kimura. The anagrams were not my idea. Mr. Kimura is a smart man. For every account he has, he's created anagrams for their fictitious holding companies." He sighs deeply and scrubs his face briskly. "Thanks to Bob's ingenuity, he discovered that many of the anagrams are names of brokerage firms Mr. Kimura used to park his drug proceeds. It appears for every investment bank Mr. Kimura laundered money; they've created corresponding anagrams. You'd be stunned how many brokerage firms hold Kimura's illegal funds. Several of the accounts Bob figured out—the Langdom Chass, Aber Arnesst, Helman, and Cutheeds accounts are all anagrams for Goldman Sachs, Bear Sterns, Lehman, Deutsche Bank, and the list goes on. And of course, the Thawone account is an anagram for Wheaton."

"But it's a bit odd you're listed as the contact person."

"An internal precaution…"

"Internal precaution …?"

"Yes, to protect my employees from contacting Mr. Kimura directly. I changed the email and telephone number to my private ones. Unfortunately, Kayla's persistence told me she wouldn't cease her effort until she spoke to the owner of the account."

My mind shifts between Kayla and Bruce's stories but information overload and overwhelming fatigue threaten rationality. "What about the account coding?"

Again he runs his fingers through his hair. "Protection from the watchdogs of the street … You realize we're audited once a year by the SEC. I took measures to protect the firm. Bob hired a programmer to create codes concealing money transfers to client accounts."

"You mean the journals into your accounts and your friends. Why would they place money in your accounts? It appears you're profiting from their misdeeds as well."

"That's a reasonable conclusion Vicky and just what Mr. Kimura wants others to believe. He figured commingling money in firm accounts we'd appear partners to their crimes. We're not. Bob and I haven't established how funds got into the accounts. But we're certain it was internal, someone inside or they got through office security and obtained client information. That's why we've installed fingerprint controls at the door and cameras for surveillance. The commingling of money was only the beginning of their threats."

Alex's father's confrontation at the funeral tells me he was also threatened by the Kimura family. "Alex's father ..."

Bruce nods his head with a troubled sigh. "Yes."

"And Andrew..."

"No, but with the help of Alex, he uncovered suspicious wires. If Alex hadn't been such a tech wiz, no one would know about the coding."

"And why hasn't Andrew gone to the authorities?"

"Andrew is not stupid or brave enough. When he discovered the Kimura's are part of a drug cartel he decided to sever ties with the firm. It's understandable. He's not willing to put his family at risk. He was paid well for his troubles and agreed to keep quiet. Now Kayla, on the other hand, was brave enough to see the entire operation blown. But she made one fatal mistake. She went searching for the Thawone file during the company dinner. I knew she was up to something when she left the dinner table. Kimura thugs were on her tail the entire night."

Mr. Kimura's men were at the dinner party? I search my memory of the seating and cringe at their proximity. "You invited them to dinner?"

Bruce hisses in repugnance. "My hands were tied, Vicky. Mr. Kimura insisted his men be there, and I'm sure it was because of Alex and Kayla. It was infuriating watching his men at my table."

I remember the occasional scowl sweeping Bruce's face when he eyed the man next to Kayla, a look I had thought strange, now explained.

"When Kayla left the table and didn't return immediately, his man went after her. Kimura's men must have followed her again later that evening when she returned to my office."

I recall the morning in the file room and Kayla's frantic search. I was right. The missing file Kayla sought, Bruce held in the conference room. I remember telling Kayla someone else pulled the file. *Had she put the pieces together*—Bruce's anonymous guest, Bruce's unexpected office visit, the missing dossier. Did I plant the seed for Kayla's investigation of Bruce's office?

Again, I shudder at the Kimura men's proximity. I'd assumed the man next to Kayla were Wheaton friends. The mask they wore, unlike the others, hid their identity. Every instance of the dinner party falls into place. The man who left the table shortly after Kayla. Her troubled state when she returned. Her sly glance across the table at Alex. Bruce's look of concern when the Asian returned. The servant's curious glare at Bruce, and Bruce's second excuse from the table.

Bruce places the glass on the table and sits straighter. "Vicky, I have to ask where the file is. I know you will perceive my interest as deceit. If the Asians find the file in your possession, it could be deadly. You can't evade these men. If you're hiding it, they will find it. For your safety, I'm asking you to trust me and hand that file over to me," he says leaning forward with unwavering eyes.

There's no way the Asians can get through my doorman. I visualize the file on my dining table and want nothing more than it gone from my life. *The disc, n*o one knows it exists with the same information as the file.

"Vicky, if you've thought about going to the FBI, I have to caution it's a grave mistake. Let me and Bob handle this; we know what we're doing. We've been managing for years. I can only protect you if they believe you're not a threat."

"What about office surveillance ... the conversation with Kayla?"

Leaning forward with clasped hands, he throws a convincing stare. "I assure you the tapes no longer exist."

"Did you or someone else delete them? Was it Amber?"

"Yes, she's been valuable over the years. She's a loyal employee. Her job is to make sure my employees stay out of trouble. I asked her to delete the tape of you and Kayla."

"How long has she known about the money-laundering?"

"For a while ... Much like Kayla, she was curious and found out through snooping."

"And she's okay with all of this?"

"Hardly," he says with a guffaw. "Amber was outraged by the black-mail. At first, she was frightened and worried about her family's safety. She threatened to quit several times, but realized, as a single mom, she'd never find a job that paid as well as I have. I've assured her safety, and she's been my eyes and ears in the firm. When Amber informed me about Kayla, I had my men follow her immediately, but unfortunately, it was too late."

Well, that explains Amber's knowledge of employees. I wonder how much she knows about me. I shiver at the breach of privacy and cam-eras recording my every move. "Are other employees aware of the money laundering?"

"No, just Bob and Amber."

"What about Dennis?"

"Ha! Dennis? All he cares about is getting his job done and his nightlife. If he's suspects anything, which I doubt, he hasn't said a word."

The door opens, and the young servant signals. Bruce excuses him-self; closing the door as he exits the room. Voices rise and fall as feet move down the hall. Suddenly, overwhelming fatigue replaces anx-iousness. I take a sip of bourbon and lay my head on the sofa's edge. The alcohol's potency soothes like a sedative. Tension melts into the sofa. With heavy eyes, I fend off sleep, struggling to digest Bruce's revelation, but finally, succumb to sleep.

Chapter 20

Pop! I bolt upright on the sofa, staring around the room and beyond the windows for the sound that pulled me from sleep. Was I dreaming? A thick, wool throw lies on the floor beside the couch. It must have fallen when I sprang from the sofa. Leaning over, I pick it up, and slide back into the sofa, wondering if Bruce covered me as I slept. Strangely muddled with no concept of time, reality seems deceptive, an illusion I've mistakenly stepped into. I close my eyes and will it all a nightmare, hoping I'll wake in my bed days before Kayla's murder, and her frantic phone call. But it's not a dream and my eyes open to Wheaton's library. I stare at the edge of the couch, the spot Kayla sat a week ago, pulling the boot from her swollen ankle. Bruce said she'd been at the office snooping that morning. Now, it all makes sense, her last-minute change of plans to drive to Greenwich. I imagine Bruce's men discovering her and Kayla tripping or falling onto her ankle during the dash to escape. God, Kayla! How stupid!

My eyes catch the gold-embossed family albums, evoking images of Judith's photos, and Kayla's astonished voice. *"Wow, Vic, I don't know, but they seem close. Is this your dad with Mallory? Look at this one."*

Bruce loved her, loved ones. Bruce's words roil in my mind. *"Vicky, I'm an honest man. But when they threatened my loved ones and livelihood, I would have done anything to prevent the loss."* Had Judith's life been in danger as well?

Footsteps and voices grow closer in the corridor. The library door swings open to Bruce's imposing six-foot-two frame.

"Ah, you're awake."

"Was I asleep for long?"

"For about an hour. You must be tired. If you want to sleep, you can use one of the rooms upstairs."

"No, no, I'm fine." I must look a wreck. Self-consciously, I scrub my face, picturing my skin haggard-looking from earlier tears. The wound throbs on my leg, another telltale sign today was not a dream. Again, questions about Judith enter my mind. I envision photos of Bruce's dinner parties and Judith's proximity to Mr. and Mrs. Kimura. *Was she also a pawn in the Kimura's deceit?* Bruce settles on the sofa, and his eyes sweep my face. What took place during the hour I slept? He looks as tired as I feel. I imagine the worry and strain he's assumed to protect his family and business. *Was he also protecting Judith?*

"Did—when..." I stumbled, uncertain of how to phrase my question. "Was Judith close to the Kimura family?" Not exactly the question I wanted to ask but hope his response will guide my next question.

His response is delayed as he studies me with keen eyes. I fidget with the throw as he fills the whiskey glass with bourbon. He scrubs his face as if erasing anguish he's ready to subdue and releases a deep sigh simultaneously with my own.

"Judith met Mr. and Mrs. Kimura several times at my parties, but that's the extent of their acquaintance." He pauses with a realization. "You're probably wondering why I hired you under these circumstances."

"I hadn't thought about it, but yes, why?"

"When Judith asked me to bring you into the firm, she was so insistent I couldn't say no though I should have denied her request. I realized keeping you close, I could better protect you, and I have for the last three years. My mistake was in hiring Kayla. If I'd known Kayla's propensity to snoop, I wouldn't have hired her. Judith wanted the best for both of you," he explains with steadfast eyes. "Every time I look at you, I see Judith," he says without pause.

"You must have loved her a great deal."

"So much so, I asked her to marry me, but she turned me down."

"Then why continue the affair if she refused to marry you?"

"It's complicated."

I grin. Aiden gave me the same response a day ago. "So I've heard..."

"Well, Judith was a complicated woman," he says with a squint as if trying to envision her image. "I'm so proud of you. I've wanted to say that for a while, not as your employer, but as your father."

Unsure of how to react to fatherly sentiments so soon, I smile and shift in my seat.

Noticing my discomfort, he draws a deep breath. "Well, to answer your question about Judith, my love for your mom was like an addiction. I believe it was for her as well. Ending the affair wasn't easy. We tried to stop, but the more we pulled away, the greater the need to be together. So, we decided to let it take its course."

"Did it ever end?"

"No, we just saw less of each other, but we never stopped. She told me I was too controlling. I admit I wanted her to myself most of the time, but I would never control her. Your mom had a profound fear of commitment I never understood. I was thoroughly confused and surprised when she married Aiden. She just wasn't the marrying type," he says with conviction. "I believe my passion overwhelmed and scared her at times. She would pull away for weeks, sometimes months. But eventually, we'd see each other again."

I can't imagine Bruce's pain when Judith wed Aiden. His greatest love relegated him second-best. I wonder if Bruce benefited as much as Judith from having a child. Maybe giving her a piece of him lessened his pain.

Am I naïve to put my trust in his hands so soon? I ponder Bruce's phone call at the exact moment I picked up the phone to call the FBI. Was there some cosmic intervention? The moment of clarity and my resolve to call Mark Ames dashed with Bruce's voice.

I think of Kayla's mother's message earlier with a stab of pain. "How am I supposed to explain Kayla's death to her parents? They won't let this go until they find out what happened to her."

Bruce stands and paces the room. "They mustn't find out. If they do their lives will be in danger as well. There is only so much I can do. Right now, my job is to protect you from danger. Any attempt Kayla's family makes to avenge her death is a death card. Their lives will be in jeopardy."

Death card... An appropriate choice of words I think given Kayla's Tarot reading. Bruce approaches and sits by my side. The imagined wall, dividing us most of the evening, evaporates. I sit stiffly. He's closer than I've ever remembered.

"The FBI has tried to crack the Kimura cartel for years. There's only been bloodshed in their efforts. People like us, caught in the middle, sometimes have to turn a blind eye."

He places his hand on top of mine with a comforting grip. "Vicky, you are my main priority," he says with grave eyes. "I understand your doubt, but I'm asking you to trust and believe I have only your best interest at heart. Let me handle Mr. Kimura as I always have. If you choose to go to the authorities, I fear I can't protect your life."

Chapter 21

Several hours later at dawn, Bruce's security escorts me inside my apartment, examines every room, and questions the disarray on my bedroom floor. I turn away from the fit of anger raged earlier, shrug and assure him, "It's nothing." Following him into the living room, I gasp when he pulls a gun from his jacket and points it toward my sofa. In the dim room, Michelle lays asleep on her side, undisturbed by our presence. "It's okay, she's a friend," I whisper, pushing his raised arm down. I frown, noticing Kayla's letter and the picture of Michelle's parent's in her hand. The truth about her corrupt father must have been horrifying. When I didn't return her call, she probably grew concerned and came searching for me, using the emergency set of keys I'd given her and Hannah. I imagined she's waited all night.

Quickly, I head to the dining table toward the Thawone file. Bruce's words echo in my mind—*people like us sometimes have to turn a blind eye.* On the backside of Mark Ames business card, I write Bruce a note. *Turning a blind eye is a coward's slow death.* Swiftly, and before I change my mind, I pin the card to the file and hand it to Bruce's man. "Please give this to Bruce," I say, and lead him toward the door. I'm certain Bruce has placed several men nearby for protection.

Heading back to the living room, I turn off the light and curl into the armchair across from the sofa. I ponder waking Michelle, but exhaustion overcomes me. I burrow into the seat, tuck my knees into my chest, and watch Michelle until sleep engulfs me.

* * *

Awaken by rustling; I squint at bright sun blackening the motionless figure before me. Michelle sits blank-eyed, an expression I'm sure I wore when Aiden exposed my biological father. Finally, she stares me in the eye, pain swelling from hiding. "Michelle, I'm so sorry you had to find out this way."

Shaking her head and fumbling with the letter, turmoil steals her voice, escaping in staccato breaths. "Is … this," she says, looking down and resting her forehead in her hand, words bursts forth with tears "… what Kayla was trying to tell me at brunch?"

Her pain wrenches my heart. Words fail me, so I nod and lower my head, pounding from the bourbon sedative. "Michelle, Kayla wanted to see if you know about your father."

"Know! No, I didn't!" She screams. The throb intensifies in my skull. I hold my head, alarmed as Michelle's voice grows shriller.

"I would never be a part of something so debased," she says, shaking the letter enraged. "I would never let them hurt Kayla. I called mom when I saw the letter, demanding answers, but all she said was we have to talk. Vicky, she's known about this all along. How can they hide this for so long? Didn't they know I'd find out eventually? Did they expect me to overlook the murder of my best friend?" Forgetting my presence, she paces the room with a frenzy of questions. Indignation mars her face. The same rage I'd experienced hours ago, now grips Michelle.

I stare at the flapping letter in her hand and wonder if she told her mother how she found out. Did she mention she'd found Kayla's letter addressed to me? If she told her parents, she's put me in greater danger. Fearfully, I sit straight in the chair. "Michelle, did you tell your mom about the letter?"

Chapter 22

The silver Mercedes approaches fast, following my car off the freeway onto the Harrison, New York exit. Since my meeting with Bruce, his men have trailed every move I've made. The large Tudor home appears as I turn onto Cricklewood Lane. I've only visited her family twice in the seven years I'd known her. Many cars border the front yard, revealing the repast is replete with Kayla's family and friends, all except Michelle. Guilt-ridden, she couldn't bear to face Kayla's parents. Since the discovery of her family's criminal past, I can't help worrying she'll fail to protect me if provoked by her father. She's already slipped, telling her mom about the letter. If only I'd hidden the note and file before leaving to meet Bruce, but I couldn't have known Michelle would let herself into my condo.

I park down the road, and the Mercedes stop a few feet back. I sit for a moment dreading the Collins family's inquisition. The passenger door swings open, and my heart lurches into my throat. Kevin Collins, Kayla's older brother, quickly slides into the passenger seat. In the rearview mirror, Bruce's man exits the car assessing Kevin. Assured I'm not in danger; he turns and enters the Mercedes.

"Sorry, I didn't mean to startle you," he says, closing the door swiftly.

Over the years, I've grown fond of Kevin as if he were my own brother. The steely expression I witnessed on Kayla's face, merely days ago, dwells on his face. Kevin's green eyes contain immense anger beneath red-rimmed lids, burning fiercer than his red-buzzed haircut. He reaches over and hugs me tightly. "You okay?"

"No," I say, swallowing tears threatening to shake me again.

"What about you?"

His jaw twitches several times with his clenched teeth. "I'm angrier than hell!" He exclaims, staring straight ahead. "Never, ever in a million years would I have imagined attending my sister's funeral. I've always believed I'd die before Kayla." His jaw twitches quicker than before as we sit in silence. "I know who murdered my sister."

Stunned, I sit speechless, waiting to hear the extent of his knowledge.

"You do ... But how?"

"Vic, you don't have to pretend with me." His voice cracks with emotions. "I received Kayla's letter the day she was killed. She told me she sent you a letter along with the file. Vic, I just want you to know, I'm not letting them get away with this."

"Kevin, these are dangerous people."

"I don't give a fuck if they're terrorists, Vicky! They fucking killed her like some dog on the street. What the hell was Kayla thinking!" A tear slips from his eye. "Why didn't she come to me? I could have protected her. Fucking animals! What the hell gives them the right to take her life like that! Fucking slime!" He howls, banging his fist into his thigh.

I remain quiet with Kevin's rage and wait for him to calm down, imagining outbursts are better than unreleased emotions turned inward, silently poisoning every cell. His reaction is just what I expected, and I'm sure I haven't seen the extent of his anger. I glance sideways at his profile, sensing he'll be unrelenting in hunting Kayla's killers.

Kevin and Kayla cherished each other. He'd often call her Kit, a childhood nickname. I remember Kayla's excitement when Kevin was promoted to lieutenant in the organized crime division of the NYPD. They were closer than any siblings I've ever known, calling each other several times a day. Kevin would show up at Kayla's apartment unannounced for dinner many evenings and like two buddies, would share a football game occasionally when Kevin was off duty. When Kayla had a problem, he was the first person she turned to. *Why didn't she go to him for help?* Then I remember her letter. She wanted to protect him, much as she'd tried to keep me uninvolved.

"They're not getting away with this, Vic."

"Kevin, I know I can't stop you. I certainly couldn't stop Kayla, but promise me you'll be careful." I realize his vendetta may involve Bruce. "You need to know Bruce played no part in Kayla's murder. The Kimura cartel has made extortionist demands for years. Bruce was trying to protect Kayla, but she didn't know. The Kimuras are responsible for her murder." I pause, realizing any actions against the Kimura family will involve Michelle. "And Michelle wanted no part of her family's dealings. She had nothing to do with this and just recently learned about her father."

"Don't be so naïve," he said with a scowl. "Over the years, Michelle's seen something in her family's home. She was probably unaware of her father's ties to the cartel, but believe me; she's seen unethical activity in that house." Taking my hand, he squeezes tight. "I don't want either you or Michelle involved. But if Michelle has any information, I'm going to ask for her help. I'll protect both of you the best I can."

Perhaps it's his concern or the reassuring hand clutch that causes words to fly from my mouth. "Bruce is my father."

Kevin's expression changes several times before he replies." What do you mean ... Aiden is your father ... Isn't he?"

"Kevin, the night before Kayla's murder, Aiden told me Bruce is my biological father. I was just as shocked as you are now."

"Wow! I don't know what to say. You must be upset."

"I am ... was ... Well, after speaking to both Aiden and Bruce, I understand why they kept it a secret."

"I see why you're concerned about Wheaton's safety. Are you certain he's innocent in all of this?"

"A few days ago, I would have said no. But after speaking with Bruce, I'm certain he's a victim of blackmail."

"Vic, don't worry. The Kimura's will get what's coming to them. But promise me you won't do what Kayla did. Call me if you're in danger. Promise me."

"I promise." I perceive Kevin is on a dangerous path if he thinks he can bring down an entire cartel. I hope and pray his fate is not the same as Kayla's.

"Are you ready to face my family? They're going to grill you with questions, but for their safety, you need to play dumb. I don't want them getting involved in this."

After Bruce's speech a few days ago, I've already decided to remain quiet about Michelle's family, but playing dumb for the entire family might prove difficult. "Kevin, what will you do? I don't want you getting hurt."

"I have my connections from years on the force ... They messed with the wrong family."

* * *

I leave the repast without telling anyone of my destination. With a packed overnight bag and Judith's diaries, I head north on Interstate I-95 toward Martha's Vineyard. The conversation with Kayla's family left me shaken. I hope they hadn't seen through my dishonesty when they cornered me in the family den, searching for answers about her murder. It appeared Kayla's mother hadn't slept in days. Her beseeching tone was heartbreaking. Devastated, her father, stood with glassy eyes trying to remain stable for his family. Kayla's three angry and heartbroken brothers listened intently, hoping I'd part some news about her killer. With their persistent stares, I'd lowered my eyes and lied to protect them. Kevin guided my responses with yes and no headshakes from the corner of the room whenever his mother asked risky questions. And I'd replied, "I don't know," lying painfully at every turn. Doggedly, Mrs. Collins had asked one question after another until all her questions appeared the same. She knew her daughter's meddlesome tendencies and had already concluded endless prying was the root of Kayla's murder.

"*Was Kayla involved in more of her snooping … Was it work-related?*"

"*No, nothing was going on at the office. Kayla seemed okay until her murder,*" I'd replied, with Bruce's warning strengthening my duplicitous stance. *I can't protect the Collins if they get involved.*

In the family den, a photo of Kayla's infant form cradled by her brother brought tears to my eyes. Images of her posing cross-eyed on a tree in the backyard evoked memories of her playfulness. On the wall, photos of her birthday parties, high school, and college graduation, and various family pictures revealed her short life. A final beach image, her last summer on Martha's Vineyard, concluded her existence. There will never be a picture of Kayla beyond the age of twenty-five. The finality of her existence hit as I studied her photographed history. How could the universe be so cruel? Was she without any cosmic importance? With her life taken so soon, surely my existence is just as insignificant. The Kimura cartel won't pause to deliberate my worth, but kill me in a heartbeat.

Unlike Kayla, I have no illusion of single-handedly bringing down the Kimura cartel unscathed. I'm not brave enough to dive in feet first, as she always had. I think first, deliberate all my options, and then take action. My first course of action was writing the note to Bruce on Mark Ames' business card. Will he find the courage to act? I hope so.

Chapter 23

I arrive in Woods Hole, Massachusetts just in time to board the ten-thirty ferry to Vineyard Haven. The silver Mercedes, which followed me from the Collins' home, ebbs in the distance, and I ponder my hasty decision as the boat glides out to sea. Kayla's fatal mistake was evading Bruce's men. Hopefully, it won't be mine. As the shoreline recedes, I'm certain the Kimura men won't find me, but my confidence wavers like the choppy water.

Eager to dispel nervous energy, I exit the car, wrap my scarf around my neck, and move toward the vehicle deck. A powerful gust waylays me like a feather, shoving me toward the railing. *Another tragic death,* I think. Fearful of tumbling overboard, I turn toward the car, push against a whipping gale, foretelling an impending storm, and hope it stalls until I make it home.

Forty-five minutes later, a nor'easter batters the East Coast. I disembark the ferry, chastising my slapdash escape before checking the weather report. With obstructed views, I sit tense and focused behind the wheel, cautiously steering the car through the raging downpour. I dread nor'easters' havoc and pray it'll bypass the island with little flooding or power outages. Being alone in a dark house is nerve-racking and downright scary.

The twenty-minute ride from Vineyard Haven to Edgartown takes longer than usual. As locals take shelter from the storm, the island appears a ghost town. "Finally," I mumble as the car turns onto Starbuck Neck Road, the house is just around the bend. The car winds an enclave of homes, and headlights tunnel through the rain, illuminating gray-shingled exteriors hidden behind high hedges. The porch light shines like a beacon of comfort on the Greene's porch, our next-door neighbor. I turn the car onto the gravel driveway, and headlights reveal the two-story Cape Cod, enduring the mighty storm. *I can't believe I'm home.*

The heavens rage a heavy hand, slinging rain like rocks against the gray-shingled roof. And perilous winds threaten to crack heavy boughs and crush the garage rooftop below.

Judith's voice resounds from the past, *"That darn door grates like chalk screeching on a chalkboard,"* she'd always say when the garage door lifted.

Safe inside, the gale is merely white noise. It's been seventeen months since I've been home—since Judith's funeral—and nothings changed but me. Aiden's pleas, the Kayla's death and the Kimura's threat have forced me home, but I wish I was returning under happier conditions, not more fear and mourning.

Turning off the ignition, I sit absorbed in happy memories evoked by the garage. The red, blue, and yellow bikes, hoisted to the ceiling, appear in good shape given countless trips around the island. In the corner, oars and the silvery-blue canoe, which trailed island waterways many times, stand as always. On the wall, Aiden's fishing poles and tackles hang from hooks. Clam rakes and aluminum cans for bait and catch sit side-by-side under wooden storage cabinets, stirring phantom taste of buttery lemon fish. Beach chairs and umbrellas, used many hot summers, lie folded under a beautifully painted sunset over South Beach—a plaque Judith chose for the garage. With a mixture of sadness and elation, I gather my bag and Judith's diaries from the backseat. Unlocking the mudroom door, I saunter inside, flooded with childhood memories and phantom images of Judith and Aiden calling me inside.

Aiden was here. I can tell, because fresh sea air, not the stale musk of homes that sit vacant for months, lingers. I picture Aiden roaming room-to-room opening windows, airing the home as he always does on every visit. Dropping Judith's diaries and my bag on the floor, I head toward the family room and open the curtains and shades. Lighthouse Beach and Fulton Street Beach are barely visible in the storm, only the glow of Edgartown Lighthouse. Waves roar and crash onshore simultaneously with my heartbeat.

Shivering from the damp chill, I head to the fireplace and ignite a fire. Facing the room, vestiges of Aiden and Judith sit in front of me. *"Vic, come join us on the sofa,"* echoes from the past. Remnants of their voices fill the room, fading to silence. The quiet space is unbearable, and I yearn for their incessant chatter, which was always present, except when they'd slept. I roam the room filled with beach-chic furnishings Judith adored. The oversized, slip-covered sofa and two matching chairs surround the large fireplace, atop a seagrass rug overlying bamboo floors. Large windows and French doors frame views of the beach ahead. Above, skylights and dormer windows lend sight to the raging storm.

I hear Judith summon, *"Vic, come here,"* as she always had when she needed help in the kitchen, a room she adored. Surrounded by white bead-board walls, glass cabinets, stainless steel appliances, and a lengthy Carrera-marble island, it was the most used room in the home. I stand underneath kitchen skylights with silence exacerbating my sadness. I've never missed Judith more than this moment. A deep growl breaks my thought and I laugh aware I haven't smiled in a while. Heading toward the refrigerator, I realize I haven't eaten all day. When I open the door, I'm relieved Aiden stocked the fridge with some of his favorite staples, saving me a trip to the market, which might prove impossible after the storm's aftermath. On the counter, next to the refrigerator, lies a note from Aiden.

Vic,

I'm glad you've finally made it home. Judith is smiling from the heavens.

Love,

Dad

How long has the note been on the counter? Did Aiden write it during his last visit, perhaps months or even a year ago? No matter how long, he knew I'd find my way back home. With a sudden urge for tea, I fill the kettle and search the cabinets. A carousel, complete with international teas, spins to a squeaky halt, emitting a potpourri of cloves, cardamom, peppercorn, and ginger toward my nostrils. The aroma evokes memories of the ever-present cup in Judith's hand. Finding my favorite navy mug etched with a white anchor and Judith's favorite chai tea, I wait for the water to boil. Outside the home, storm noise grows fearfully loud—crashing waves, whirling gale, creaking beams, and then a loud whistling pierce my ears.

I place the tea on the coffee table and head upstairs with my bag. Pausing outside my bedroom door, I imagine my childhood space. The verdant forest covering four walls vanish with the bright dimmer. Mythical forest creatures and childhood furniture swapped with pastel beach blue walls, a queen-sized four-poster bed, and furnishings Judith thought would suit a young woman.

Plopping on the bed with my bag, I scrutinize the room and pause at a photo on the nightstand. The image of four laughing women, Hannah, Kayla, Michelle, and I on Fuller Street Beach, seems like yesterday, but it was three years ago we were carefree and having fun. That day, I struggled as Kayla pulled me toward the camera. Happy and laughing, we believed we had the rest of our lives ahead. Who knew Kayla's life would be so short. Suppressing more tears, I turn the photo upside down and exit the room. Down the hall, the door to Aiden and Judith's room is wide open, but I'm not ready to visit Judith's space yet. I head back downstairs.

In the gallery, I stand under the skylight and listen to rain pitter-patter on the roof, a sound I loved as a child. Then a loud groan, splinter, crackle, and thump send me racing toward the front door. Cautious of the dangerous storm, slowly, I open the door, and a strong gust snatches the doorknob backward with a bang against the wall. Pushed by the wind, I struggle to close the door, but before I do, a split tree entangled in a sparkling power line sends a flicker through the house. The interior darkens with minuscule firelight. Closing and locking the door, I stumble into the kitchen, searching for the emergency kit in the bottom cabinet. A box filled with items for a stormy night, flashlights, batteries, candles, matches, an old battery-powered radio, and Aiden's favorite scotch.

In four, tall glass hurricanes, I position the candles around the room and head to the telephone. *Dead. What now, Vicky?* A ghostly vestige of Judith emerges, roaming about the candlelit room, thrilled by the dangerous storm, and the darkness inside. *"Vic, this will be fun. How about smores?"* Only Judith could find delight in danger. I wonder if her private stash is still in the pantry. With the flashlight, I find marshmallows, Graham crackers, and her favorite dark chocolate, which have probably grown stale over the year.

With my cup of chai, I wander to the French doors and watch Edgartown lighthouse cast long roving beams into the stormy night. *Okay, Vicky what now*? Dreading sleep and dreams of Kayla's murder, I consider a night by the fire, and drag three, large, floor pillows in front of the sofa. From my purse, I retrieve the key to Judith's diaries and my cell phone. With my back propped against the sofa, legs sprawled toward the fire; I contemplate Judith's life on paper.

I place the gold key into the box's knothole, and the top pops open, releasing vanilla, acidic muskiness—the smell of old books, mixed with a distinct floral essence. Several rows of matching diaries painted with baroque art, begin at 1966 up to seventeen months ago. I run my hand across stiff binders, choose the first journal, and brush my finger across pages aged sepia-brown, imagining Judith's pen unveiling dark, inky words across blank, crisp, white sheets years ago, words of yet another day.

I'm amazed her first diary began at the age of sixteen. I search randomly through years of writing, bypass earlier diaries filled with notes on developing her talent, tutelage under various teachers, and mastering three languages. My eyes stop on February 13, 1972. At the age of twenty-two in Venice, Italy, my mother meets the love of her life, my boss, Bruce Wheaton.

PART TWO

Chapter 24

February 13, 1972

The three-month production of Verdi's Rigoletto ended successfully at La Fenice Opera House. The ending came at a perfect time, three days before Lent when Carnival closes with Notte de la Taranta (fireworks at midnight). Venice is overflowing with zealous tourists eager to consume every exotic experience. At night, magically lit streets and canals come alive with nobles, princesses, duchesses, counts, and sexy servants making their way to various costume balls.

Carnival is one big theatrical stage. Tonight, I celebrated at the Palazzo Pisani Moretta's Tiepolo Ball, one of the many masked balls at Carnival. Guests arrived in their finest costumes, ready to experience live theatrical entertainment, and lavish food and drink by candlelight. The anonymity of masked-disguised tourists loosens their inhibitions. Flirtations and provocative conversation engulf tables. And lewd sexual acts occur in public and hidden spaces. I've often wondered if participants regret their behavior the next morning, or have they played out long-desired fantasies.

I made my way through masked crowds toward the gondola wearing a purple, velvet, strapless gown. The bodice hugged my waist and cradled my breast tightly, forming a deep cleavage covered by a flowing bell cape. I worried Mallory wouldn't recognize me in the headpiece and Columbina mask when I arrived at the hotel. But I recognized Peter, one

E. Denise Billups

of the performers from the opera, standing beside her, wearing the same costume from the previous night.

Introduced to Mallory Highland backstage, we formed an instant bond. Her outgoing personality is contagious, her vivacious smile and beauty captivating, her energy and interest match my own, making her a delight to be with. Tonight, as I approached, Peter flanked her right, and another friend, Bruce Wheaton, stood on her left side. Intriguing in his tricon black hat, veil, and tabarro, I longed to see his face behind the mask. The dashing, deep blue mantle draped around his shoulders, made him appear a genuine eighteenth-century noble. Mallory and I appeared similar wearing strapless gowns, hers an eggshell white laced with a golden design. Her face, veiled with a gold Columbina mask with white plumage, looked stunning.

At our table of eight, I sensed Bruce's eyes on me the entire night. Later in the evening, when the couple next to me failed to return, Bruce sat beside me. We joked and laughed at various costumes and personalities in the room, and enjoyed the live string quartet. Accidentally, his hand brushed mine, and there was a delayed reaction before he laced his fingers with mine. Strangely, the overfamiliar gesture felt right, and I didn't reject his handhold but reciprocated tightly.

Throughout the evening, Bruce astounded me with his knowledge of Baroque artists and Gianbattista Tiepolo artwork, which covers the Palazzo Pisano Moretta's ceiling. Bruce explained details of the painting, Admiral Vettor carried to heaven after excelling on earth, Venus introducing Admiral Pisani to Jupiter and Mars, and Gods of the sea at the lower bottom of the painting. His understanding of period artists was astounding as well as his knowledge of Czars, Emperors, and other historical figures who visited the Palazzo Pisano Moretta.

Our attention soon turned to an affectionate kissing couple across the table. When the man licked spilled wine from her cleavage, I grew uneasy and looked away, finding another couple feeding each other sensually.

Bruce followed my gaze and asked, "Does the scene aroused you?"

Lowering my eyes to disguise my embarrassment, I'd replied, "Aren't you, surrounded by this lavish environment, succulent food and intox-

161

icating alcohol?" Finally, I looked up noticing eyes sparkling behind his mask. Nervously I continued talking. "Their costumes give them anonymity and the courage to act shamelessly."

"But what about you ... Does it arouse you?"

He was searching for a concrete answer, and I weakened under his steady gaze. "Yes, it does."

"You should be. You're a beautiful woman whose passion shines on stage. I imagine your sexual passion is just as intense," he'd said searchingly.

His insinuations made me nervous, and I replied, "Passion? Well, at twenty-two, I haven't had enough experience or time with men to determine that. Besides, the opera consumes most of my day," I'd said staring, at his ample lips and chiseled jaw."

"A beautiful woman like you should explore your sexuality."

I wondered if he was making an offer. The sexuality he exuded, tells me he's a skilled lover. He couldn't be more than twenty-eight but has the sophistication of a much older man. I'm sure he's had many lovers. Uneasily, I'd replied, "I don't have much time for such things ... With rehearsals and training—"

"There's always time for pleasure."

Beneath the table, I felt his hand on my thighs. I tensed, ready to object but hadn't. With his allure and the intoxicating effect of alcohol, my fascination grew. And I became just as wanton as the other guest. His hand tugged the thick material, pulling the costume aside until he found my flesh. His fingers brushed the outline of my panties, stretching the lace until it tightened about my sex. I glanced around certain people saw the surprise on my face. Gently, his fingers stroked and rubbed, inciting moisture. At once aroused and embarrassed, quickly, I removed his hand and almost died when he grinned and inhaled my essence. Stunned by his actions, I rose, ready to bolt from the table, but his hand caught mine and squeezed gently. I sat back in the chair, confused by sudden willingness to stay beside this man who surely is perverse.

Uneasily, I peered around the room, hoping no one had noticed, finding everyone involved in intimate conversation. To my surprise, so were Mallory and Peter.

Bruce leaned over and whispered, "You're embarrassed. Don't be. You should experience pleasure every day," he'd said with intense gray eyes.

Besides discomfort and shame, I felt attraction and desire. But he made it seem normal to touch me in that way as if he knew something about me I didn't. He must have because I warmed to him thoroughly and oddly wanted more. By midnight, after many glasses of champagne, I was eager to see the face behind the mask.

Later, as the others headed to their hotels, Bruce asked if he could escort me back. We walked Venice's narrow streets and witnessed the debauchery inspired by Carnival—the rustling of lovers fumbling in dark spaces, then a gondola ride through Venetian canals to Saint Marks Square. Under the moonlight, the lantern-lit space glowed beautifully. Between Caffe Florian columns, Bruce's handsome face appeared as he removed his mask. His eyes, I'd only seen slivers of, appeared dark, intense, and mesmerizing. Gently, he untied my mask and ran his thumb across my bottom lip. Perusing my face to the base of my neck, he gently kissed the racing pulse. Finding my mouth, we kissed for an eternity until I sensed his hardness and pulled away.

Back at the hotel, he escorted me to my room; his eyes teased me the entire time. I sensed the desire lurking in his eyes and wanted to taste his lips again. Fearing I'd lose control and later regret my behavior, I said goodnight with much difficulty.

February 14, 1972

The next day, Bruce invited me to the Palazzo Dandolo Ball. I'm not sure how he acquired tickets. Typically, that event is booked months in advance. At my hotel, a package arrived with a note from Bruce that read, "I imagine this will look divine on you." Inside the box were a red gown and a mask. The gown hugged every curve as if made for me, and I wondered how he'd guessed my size.

That evening, Bruce arrived without Mallory. We headed to the Ridotto Ballroom, which was more splendid than last night's ball. I was curious *why Mallory didn't attend. I'd heard from Peter, Bruce and Mallory were together in Venice.*

I didn't want to encroach on her territory and asked, "Where is Mallory?"

"Tagliare la testa al Toro," (I settled things once and for all), he'd said.

"That's a popular Italian saying, but I'm not sure what you mean. Qual è il problema?" (What is the problem?)

"I like your Italian, such a beautiful language. I'm afraid mine isn't as good as yours."

"Thank you," I'd said, wondering why he hadn't answered my question. "Why is Mallory a problem?" I'd persisted.

"She gets in the way of the one thing I want tonight."

"Instantly, I knew what he meant, but self-consciously avoided his intimation with another question.

"And how did you solve your problem with her?"

"I asked her to give me some space. There was no blood or tears shed. She and Peter are out together tonight … She understood."

I was relieved and hoped I hadn't ruined Mallory's evening. I'd assumed they were seeing each other and wanted to make sure they weren't a couple. "Is there anything between you and Mallory?"

He sighed. "No. Mallory is a good friend, nothing more," he'd said with a forced grin.

I was happy to hear this after what took place the previous evening. I'd chastised myself all day, feeling guilty for betraying Mallory's friendship.

I knew I wouldn't be able to resist any advances Bruce made tonight. Several hours later, after much flirtation and alcohol, we arrived upstairs at his suite. I didn't resist as he undressed me. Uneasily, I watched as his eyes took in my naked form and his body emerged from beneath his clothing. His well-defined torso and toned limbs awed and thrilled me simultaneously. I hadn't mentioned my virginity, fearing his reluctance. But, mostly, I was embarrassed that at the age of twenty-two I had upheld my virginity on purpose. I'd never found anyone worthy of losing it to—until now.

No man has ever explored every inch of my flesh as he did. He held my nude body; cupping my breast as he inhaled my skin. Picking me up, he placed me on the bed. With his eyes and hands, he took me in. Those simple actions excited me before sex began. I could see his excitement and wondered how he restrained his desire so long. His hands explored my breast; circling my nipples several times as they harden. His finger traveled past my navel to my thighs, then unexpectedly, inside me. His pause told me he'd discovered what I'd failed to mention, my virginity. His expression froze then warmed. For a while, without words, he teased with his hands, and then finally, entered me cautiously. Momentarily, I felt pain and then yielded to his pleasure.

February 15, 1972

Today is the last day of Carnival. Mallory and Bruce will return to the states tomorrow. After spending two days with Bruce, my heart sinks at the thought of his absence. Tonight, Bruce, Mallory, and I watched the Candlelight Water Parade from the Rialto Bridge as gondolas sailed through the canals lit with many candles. Bruce took my hand, and I sensed his sadness. Later, we attended the Notte de la Taranta (fireworks at midnight), then quickly, rushed back to his hotel to take advantage of the dwindling hours. My body has never experienced the sensations Bruce created.

"I'm glad I am your first," he'd told me. "I can teach you the proper art of sex." And I wanted him to teach me more. He cupped my sex with his hand and said, "I want to give you a memory to treasure until you return to the states." Opening the curtains, the view of the canals and the shimmer of water danced across ceilings and walls. He called me to the window and asked me to face the view. Like a model, he positioned my body, placing one bent leg on the windowsill with my buttock extended in the air. He'd said, "Watch the water and the gondolas and remember the view and sensations."

His tongue slid down my back, teasing my flesh. When my entire body quivered, he slid inside my slippery walls. His passion engorged me as he tensed to control his climax. Carrying me back to the bed, quickly, he opened me again. Our passion exploded more powerful than the last.

* * *

A powerful whoosh and shrill whistle shake the walls and rattle the windows, wrenching me from Judith's diaries. The home's base quivers under the mighty nor'easter leaving me fearful.

Bang! Bang! Screech! Thump! Thump!

I rise from the floor, waiting for the storm to tear the roof off. The walls creak in protest but cleave to its base. I walk to the window and peer outside. Visibility is nil, except wind-whipped rain pushing patio chairs with a bang into the back wall. I close the curtains and rush back to the sofa, praying the storm's ends soon.

I glance at Judith's diaries; ashamed at reading such personal stuff. I hadn't expected a foray into my mother's sex life, and not with Bruce. I'm reluctant to read further, but oddly, my aversion doesn't stop me from picking up the diary and turning the page. I return to where I left off—the day of Lent, the day after their last encounter. Bruce and Mallory leave for the states. Judith spends several months in Venice with the Opera; then traveled to the Italian Riviera. With a longing, she wrote of Bruce for several months, anticipating their next meeting. Four months later, she's back home in New York City.

On the coffee table, my cell phone chimes Aiden's ringtone. Several tweets signal a text from Michelle. Ignoring the phone, I settle into the sofa and continue with Judith and Bruce's affair.

Chapter 25

June 14, 1972

Finally, I've returned to New York after an extended stay in Italy. I'm finding much difficult filling idle hours after such an exciting tour. Thrilled to receive an invite from Mallory to Bruce's dinner party in Greenwich, Connecticut, and eager to see Bruce, I accepted immediately. Although, after four months, I'd worried Bruce's interest had waned. Mallory explained it's a small gathering of close friends, and to dress casually. I found a simple black dress easily worn for any occasion. I'd wanted to look my best for Bruce.

My mouth fell agape as the car approached the Wheaton estate. Neither Mallory nor Bruce spoke of the Wheaton's wealth. Greeted by a servant, I stepped wide-eyed into the foyer, astounded by architectural details. With a piercing scream, Mallory ran down the hall, kissed me on the cheek, and guided me toward guest in the great room.

"Everyone this is the beautiful opera singer I've told you about."

I blushed at Mallory's introduction and bashfully greeted everyone. The intimate party consisted of two couples, Bob and Linda, Caitlin and Jay and Mallory. Enthusiastically, they all bombarded me with questions about opera and travels abroad. I guess, with traditional careers in finance, law, and architecture, my life seemed more thrilling except for Mallory's modeling career. Uninspired by her degree, she eschewed an attorney's life, chased her dream, and became a successful runway model. Gleefully, she spoke of a coming assignment to the city of lights—Paris.

*The overwhelming fascination with my career swiftly turned to poli-
tics and Nixon's new agenda. I assumed they're all Republicans. I detest
politics and would rather avoid the topic altogether, so I found myself
engrossed in conversation with Linda, an old friend of Bruce and Mallory's. She was talkative. At one point, I wanted to walk away but put
up with her endless banter. She'd expressed sympathy for Martin Luther
King Jr. and sorrow for his untimely death. I wondered if she was a true
supporter or just felt compelled to embrace my ethnicity. She bragged ad
nauseam about philanthropic causes she supports. I couldn't determine
after one meeting whether she's braggadocio or just gabby. I coughed to
stifle a guffaw when she spoke of her Woodstock, black lover. She said,
"He was the best she'd ever had."*

*I caught Mallory mouthing a silent apology across the room. I frowned
and immediately changed the topic to the home's architecture. Linda was
full of information about the Wheaton estate, built 1918, Bruce inherited
the estate when his parents died several years ago. Shocked he'd lost both
his parents, I asked how they'd died. Linda explained they were in a car
crash. How the car ran off the road, no one could ever explain.*

"Bruce must have been distraught," I'd said.

"He was; we were," Linda had expressed.

*I asked Mallory why Bruce wasn't at the party. She'd said he sometimes
shows up late for his gatherings, given everyone's old friends. "He always
pops up right before dinner is served," she'd said.*

*Just as we moved toward the dining room, Bruce's voice resounded
from the front, directing servants in the foyer. I'd held my breath, and
he appeared more attractive than I'd remembered. He caught my eyes,
smiled, crossed the room, and kissed me softly on the cheek. "Welcome
back," he'd said. Mallory's eyes lit in his presence. At that moment, I'd
wondered if she felt affections for Bruce as well.*

*Bruce's aloof behavior, as we proceeded to the dining table, made me
wonder if earlier concerns about Mallory were valid. I quickly dispelled
that thought when Bruce caught my eyes several times during dinner. His
intense gaze was hard to ignore. I stole a peek occasionally and noticed his
lips curl a grin. I took a sip of wine to steady my emotions, barely eating*

under his watchful gaze. At one point, Mallory caught Bruce's stare. Her cheerful demeanor and spirit dwindled as the evening progressed. In the great room, after dinner, coffee and drinks were served. I declined and wandered to the backyard toward an incredible maze lit with lights.

It was a beautiful summer evening, and a warm breeze off the Long Island Sound whirled over the grounds. I strode toward the maze and wandered lost for fifteen minutes. Footsteps approached behind, and I turned quickly, finding Bruce.

"I saw you enter and figured I would have to rescue you."

He drew close affecting memories of our kiss in front of Caffe Florian. And as he'd done that night, he traced my lips with his finger. "I've missed these beautiful lips," he'd said.

His touch and his voice aroused me again. He grinned, took my hand, and led me from the maze. Before we entered the home, he pulled me close with a quick kiss. "You taste better than I remembered." His next words were what I'd hoped for, some hint of interest. "I've wanted nothing more since our last night in Venice ... Do you want me?"

"Yes," I'd replied low.

He led me through the back entrance, upstairs to his room. As I write this, I still feel sensations of our bodies. I don't believe I can capture such feelings in words. His passion was overwhelming, as though thoughts of me consumed him for four months. Worn from our exploits, I lay beside him until our breath subsided, but only a moment before his desire arose again. Remembering his costume at Carnival, it suited his sexually-dominating behavior. With a sudden realization, I understood Bruce had not been acting or playing a role. He was himself. He belongs to that era. It would take the wanton lust of a courtesan to satisfy his needs. His hardness erupted, and again, throbbed inside me. Neither of us cared his guests were downstairs. We remained in his room the rest of the night, exploring ways to satisfy our lust.

* * *

Quickly, I close the diary mortified. Strangely, like a teenager reading an erotic novel, I fear someone catching me red-handed, with shame written over my face. I giggle and dismiss my silly reservations. However, this is not what I expected of Judith's diaries. *Has Aiden read this? He couldn't have.* He would never allow me to read the journals knowing its sexual content. Reading about my mother's sex life is shameless, not to mention disturbing. But why am I compelled to read more?

I force a shameful breath and rise from the sofa. Wandering to the window again, I pull the curtain open to an angry storm, and perceive it will rage all night. I exhale deeply and traipse back to the sofa. Unable to suppress my curiosity, I open the diary, ignoring my reproachful conscience. The next entry is dated June 25, 1972, the same date on the photo Kayla and I stole from Wheaton's library.

June 25, 1972

Before the party, Bruce cornered me in the hallway, accidentally ripping the dress I chose for the occasion. I tried to escape his touch, but he pushed me toward the bedroom, and all control escaped me. His sexual demands are overwhelming, but so are mine lately. If I ignore his needs, Bruce broods like a child until he gets what he wants. But in the end, we're both satisfied. I've never been so hungry for a man in my life. Do other women feel this way? I fear I'll lose my will, lose myself to him, and never be able to find my way back. I'm ashamed his lust satisfied my hunger as well. In those moments of passion, I'm his.

I've never been so embarrassed in my life when Mallory came barging through the door. Stunned and apologetic, she swiftly closed the door. Anxiously, we dressed and headed downstairs.

Despite the earlier embarrassment, the party was a success. Many of Bruce and Mallory's friends, as well as a few I'd invited, were at the party. Bruce kept me in his sight most of the night. I blushed whenever I caught his eyes, remembering the scene upstairs.

Mallory introduced me to an interesting man named Aiden Powell. We talked for a while and could have much longer if Bruce wasn't watching me. Bruce's possessive behavior was appalling, and I apologized to Aiden who seemed unperturbed. Before the evening was over, Aiden and I became immediate friends.

* * *

Ignoring the storm outside, I skip through several months of Judith's rehearsals, a period when her passion for the stage was more important than life or Bruce. Many pages consist of rehearsals, perfecting notes, stage fright remedies which affected her before every performance, and herbal cures to soothe her throat. Judith became her character during months of rehearsals. I believe this is why she forbade distractions. Since her last meeting with Bruce on June 25, 1972, she'd returned to Europe for the opera, spending days in rehearsal, nights on stage, and after-hour parties with performers and patrons. I skip these pages for her next meeting with Bruce on December 10, 1972.

December 10, 1972

I'm back in the states, my European tour finally over. I'm sad and missing the opera. When I'm not performing, I'm lost, finding real-life harder than playing a role, but I'll soon acclimate to life back home. I received a call from the man I met at Bruce's party, Aiden. Again, we talked forever. He asked me if I'm still seeing Bruce. I lied. I don't know why, but I did. I want to know more about Aiden and can't understand my attraction to two men at once. My plan to meet Aiden for dinner has left me guilt-ridden. I've betrayed Bruce's trust.

Today, Bruce surprised me for my birthday. We took a trip by plane to Martha's Vineyard and arrived at a beautiful Cape Cod home. At first, I assumed it was a rental, but it wasn't. A romantic dinner waited inside. We spent the night staring at Fuller Street Beach and Edgartown Harbor. But soon, Bruce's desires took ovr as he swept me upstairs. Our passion culminated in the shower with our bodies glistening like oil against each other.

Later in bed, he'd asked if I like the home. I've always desired a beach home on Martha's Vineyard. With a devilish grin, he ran his hand from my abdomen to my hipbones. With a mischievous glint, he said, "If this were our home, I'd ravish your body every night in this bed."

Aroused by his touch, I failed to catch the insinuation. When I asked who the home belongs to, he pulled a slip of paper from the nightstand.

"Happy birthday, love," he said, handing me a deed with my name. In disbelief, I stared for a minute speechless. Instead of happiness, I felt claustrophobic and rushed to the bathroom to catch my breath.

I've never reacted that way. Moments later, Bruce proposed. I told him I'm not a traditional woman. I've never planned or desired marriage. The confinements of matrimony, the role a wife must assume would be counterintuitive to my career. I told him I couldn't accept his gift. Infuriated, he refused to hear it. Like a petulance child, he brooded the rest of the evening. I feared with my rejection, I'd lose him. I couldn't bear that. Hesitantly, I agreed to keep the home, but with one stipulation—he placed no other demands on me. If he did, I promised I would return the keys and the deed.

My rejection must have riled and aroused him all at once. An hour later, I awoke to Bruce holding something in his hand, his eyes strange as he moved toward me. When he turned me on my stomach, I didn't protest, but a sudden fear rose when he bound my wrist and ankles to the bedpost. I've never been tied up before and pleaded for release. His restraints left me exposed and vulnerable.

Bruce ignored me, and from behind, he took me once again. I couldn't see him but felt his eyes exploring my body. Tired of squirming and pleading, I lay still listening to his breath; wondering what he was thinking. And at that moment, I realized he was punishing me for rejecting his marriage proposal. Maybe he's not used to rejection; not the powerful Bruce Wheaton. Soon something leathery stroked my back. Again, I demanded release. Bruce laughed and said, "Not until I'm ready." There was nothing I could do but close my eyes and anticipate his next action. The leather stroked and then lashed across my buttocks. Instead of pain, I balked in pleasure. Sensing desire each lash awakened, he teased for several minutes. With every pause, I awaited the next stroke. Before the night was over, I begged for more.

Chapter 26

Shame rises again, and oddly, Judith's unease as Bruce's captive is my own. I place the journal on the couch and scrutinize Bruce's gift to Judith. I'd always thought Judith bought the home. Now, for the first time, I understand her extreme love for this place. This was their escape, the place Bruce proposed, a token of his affection. What I once thought Aiden and Judith's haven from the city, I'll never see the same again.

Outside, winds gather force, moaning and wailing around trembling walls. Stormproof windows cave and swell faster than my heart. Wide-awake with no desire to sleep, I curl under the throw and prepare for a long night. Judith's diaries are the only escape from Kayla's death and the storm. I sigh deeply and turn the page.

December 11, 1972

I woke surprised to find an empty bed. My body sore in places I've never been. In one night, Bruce has broken me in. I relented in ways I'd never thought possible. I've surrendered control to this man I'm in love with. I should be angry and appalled at my chastened state. This can't be healthy. I fear yet desire him at the same time. Is this what he wants to elicit, sexual codependency so strong I won't be able to leave him? Suddenly, I don't know who I am.

Constraints, that tethered my ankle and wrists, carved crimson traces of pain and pleasure. I rose from the bed, wrapped the blanket around my body, searched for Bruce, and hoped the leather wielded, appeased the petulant man from last night.

For the first time, I saw the kitchen gleam in morning's pale light. *Topless and wearing only jeans, Bruce stood over the stove cooking. A cinnamon aroma filled the room. He turned with a dispassionate greeting as if last night never happened. Approaching, he unraveled the blanket, exposing my nude body in morning light streaming through the skylights. Brooding eyes I'd witnessed last night, again, left me cautious.*

"Don't move," he'd said.

Again, my broken will had compelled me to obey. He circled my body, sniffed my skin, and examined me like a trophy. He paused at my back and parted my legs while silence blanketed the room, followed by the sound of his zipper and jeans hitting the floor. Again, I weakened in anticipation. I closed my eyes, bit my lip, dug my nails into my palm, braced for his touch, and breathe burnt cinnamon in the crisp air. He lifted my hair and his warm breath on my neck, hardened my nipples. As if he'd felt my need, he bent me over the counter, easing the throb he'd created.

Satisfied again, he wrapped me in the blanket. "Your body knows what it wants, but your mind doesn't," he'd said.

I didn't respond. It was obvious what my body wanted, but am I clueless about my true needs? Quietly, I stewed over his words at the dining table, trying to hide my emotions. I study the skylights above as Bruce prepared two plates with French toast topped with strawberries and maple syrup. Still undressed, Bruce sat at the table and started to feed me. Remembering how couples at the Venice Carnivale fed each other, I do the same. His swift hands pulled me astride his lap. With cinnamon, maple syrup, and strawberries on our tongues, we both came once more.

* * *

This can't be good! I shudder recalling, my kiss with Chase and the taste of chocolate strawberries. However, Judith and Bruce's moment was much more passsionate. I glance at the kitchen's skylight, picturing their images and cinnamon filling the air. Was the steamy moment with Bruce the reason the kitchen was her favorite place? It had to be. Biting my lip and squinting sheepishly, I continue reading.

December 12, 1972

After Martha's Vineyard, I need time away from Bruce. When I'm with him, I can't think clearly. With time apart, I reassess my emotions and Bruce's behavior. He's a formidable force in business and social circles. His financial conquest and business success define him. Are his sexual acquisitions the same, conquering a woman's affections until she relents; changing her to suit his needs? I need a break to figure out what I'm doing. But my attraction is so strong. Do I have the strength to stay away?

I met with Mallory today. Sometimes I believe she's still in love with Bruce. I've noticed her change when we're all together. Has she never gotten over him? Maybe it's just my suspicious mind, and their friendship is nothing more than that. Bruce reassured me she's like a sister and any emotions he had for her faded years ago.

* * *

A loud thump and screech skim the roof, pulling me from the couch straight to the window. Winds must have carried something loose atop the house, hopefully without any damage to shingles. Outside, views are hindered for miles by the downpour. The window vibrates beneath my palm, and I fear exploding shards propelled into my face. I back away, close the curtains, praying this is the tail end of the storm.

Deliberating Judith and Bruce, I saunter toward the fireplace and let the flames warm my legs for a moment. Bruce and Judith's affair strikes me strange, especially given her marriage to Aiden. How did Aiden win Judith's love given her passion for Bruce? Did Judith choose Aiden because of Bruce's controlling ways or something more? Inexperienced at twenty-three, she must have felt overpowered by

Bruce's sexual needs. Was he trying to strip away her parochial beliefs, broaden her sexuality? Sitting on the floor cushions, I grab the
diary and skip through several pages to Judith's dinner with Aiden.

December 19, 1972

Aiden's home has such character. I've always loved historic, Greenwich
Village townhomes. He surprised me with a home-cooked, Italian meal,
and afterward, pleaded for a piece from La Traviata, then flattered me
with praises. For a moment, he stared at me as if I were an angel. Under
his gaze, I was bashful but relaxed as the evening evolved.

As a successful businessman, Aiden travels as much as I do. We have
much in common, losing our parents young, no siblings, and a love for
opera. I learned a wealthy couple, his deceased father's employer, adopted
Aiden who was fortunate to learn his trade from his adoptive parents, as
well as inherit their business.

Before the evening ended, we talked about everything. Unlike Bruce,
Aiden's easier to talk to. Bruce judges everything I say, and I'm constantly
walking on eggshells, but not with Aiden. I can voice my opinions with-
out objection. Aiden allows me to be me, and I've never laughed so hard
in my life. Next week we're meeting again, and he'd promised to cook
an authentic French meal. Before putting me in a taxi, he kissed me on
the cheek. I sensed his hesitancy when his face swerved and brushed the
corner of my lips. I wondered if he thought I'd protest, but I would have
welcomed his kiss.

December 24, 1972

Tonight, a group of friends gathered at my apartment to celebrate
Christmas Eve. I haven't seen Bruce in days. Despite his recent behavior,
I miss and want him all the time. Occupied with the holiday season, I've
managed to ignore his incessant phone calls. As the last guest was leav-
ing, Bruce popped up at my door. Every reservation I'd contained faded
with his presence. Tonight he was different. He explained if he couldn't
have me as his wife, he still wanted me in his life. I do, too.

When Bruce sat on the couch, my eyes followed his eyes to a book on
the coffee table. Immediately, I was horrified. After I mentioned Bruce's
behavior to a friend, she lent me a book titled Parental Influence. She

said most men's behavior toward women stems from their upbringing. I thought it intriguing and found the author's words revealing. Bruce's eyebrows furrowed as he thumbed through pages. I feared he'd surmised my reasons for reading the book. Of course, his sexual inclinations intrigues me, and in that instant, I'd felt guilty for trying to analyze his ways.

He glared and asked, "Are you trying to psychoanalyze me?"

Before I could reply, he spoke again.

"If you want to know about me, all you have to do is ask. I have nothing to hide. Judith, I have a healthy sexual appetite when it comes to women I love. I don't hold back. If anyone needs diagnosing, it's you, love."

His words hit hard. And I believed what he said true or perhaps reverse psychology.

The rest of the night, I strove to disprove his belief and remained open to every sexual act we lost ourselves in that evening. I believe he'd sensed my apprehension with every naughty demand, one more obscene than the last. He was testing my resolve to see how far I would go to prove him wrong. Bruce knew exactly what he was doing, and I'd responded to every challenge.

With a knowing grin, he'd kissed sweat from my skin and asked, "Was it so hard letting your body do what it wants?"

How could such wickedness feel so right? Finally spent, shame rose again. Maybe he's right. I need an analyst.

* * *

At the break of dawn, I fall asleep holding Judith's diary and wake several hours later with a stiff neck and legs. I'm relieved the recurrent dream since Kayla's murder hadn't resurfaced, only dreams of Venetian balls and a faceless lover, a place somewhere shameful, spurred by Judith's diary. Throughout the frightening storm, I've managed to read an entire year of Judith's life.

With dull light shining through the curtains, I'm curious about the hour and drag my cell phone to the edge of the coffee table, discovering it's one in the afternoon. I rise and stumble to the patio, slide the door open to cold mist, and a salty breeze. Menacing clouds threaten another downpour. I shiver, close the door, and head straight to the coffeepot, only to remember the power outage. I recall the instant coffee near the tea carousel and heat the kettle, preferring drip, but instant will have to do.

Above, whirling sleet and rain speckle skylights. *Skylights, morning light*, is this where Bruce took Judith while cinnamon filled the air? Their ghosts will forever remain in this spot, and my mind. Quickly, I dismiss the image. Longing for a sweaty run, I bend and stretch my hamstrings, and slide into a downward dog, upward dog, and a few more stretches to quill inertia's ache, then grab my instant coffee and head back to the sofa.

December 31, 1972

The Wheaton estate appeared like Carnival, a suggestion I'd made to Bruce, and he'd quickly adopted. Guests dressed for New Year's Eve looked exquisite in their masks. Mallory focused on a new love interest, had barely paid me or Bruce attention. Dressed in a dashing black suit and Columbina mask, Bruce appeared mischievous, and I'd wondered what he had up his sleeve.

After dinner, we left for the airport without saying goodbye to his guest. A few hours later, we were back at the Cape Cod home in Martha's Vineyard. With a laugh, he'd assured, "Don't worry; I have no plans to tie you up."

It felt odd without his control. Bruce sensed it too. I have to admit; I've grown used to his demands and craved them at that moment. But he'd said "This time you're in control. Just tell me what you want."

I've never been able to voice my wants to a man and found it incredibly hard to do so. After everything we've done, why couldn't I ask? Failing to find my words, he'd finally expressed my desires. With his articulation, embarrassment followed. His comments affected me as a hand stroke across my body would. He'd demanded I repeat his words. With much difficulty, I'd tried, but graphic words refused to leave my mouth.

"You're not a little girl Judith. Use your words," he'd persuaded.

Ashamed and angered by his patronizing tone, I'd refused and obstinately waited to see what he would do, perhaps whip me again?

But instead, he'd said, "Alright, when you're ready I'll be waiting,"
and he strolled upstairs to bed. He'd sucked all the joy out of New Year's
Eve just like that. How frustrating! His unpredictable behavior left me
appalled. I fumed by the fireplace and refused to follow him. After thirty
minutes, I stomped upstairs and fell asleep in the second bedroom.

* * *

"What!"

Just as appalled as Judith, I close the journal, wondering what
Bruce's intentions were. His demands were so unpredictable. I stare
at flames flickering in the fireplace, as Judith must have that night,
pondering Bruce's behavior. Was he testing her resolve? Will Judith
succumb as she often did?

On the coffee table, the phone buzzes with a text from Hannah. Not
ready to deal with the outside world, I ignore the phone and continue
reading.

* * *

December 31, 1972

I hadn't expected Bruce to come to me. Remorse showed plainly on his
face. He didn't utter a word, but I'd found the courage to repeat words he'd
spoken an hour before, words I cannot bring myself to write even now.
And words he'd often say when I obeyed, "Good girl," told me of pleasure
to come. Bruce rewarded my request with actions I cannot write, not even
in my diary.

January 1, 1973

I woke to the New Year with Bruce asleep beside me. Quietly, I exited
the bed, noting the gift, the home, has already created demands, ones
I've given into uneasily. I dressed, exited the room, threw on a coat, and
wandered out of the house. I kept walking until I was on Fuller Street
Beach, invigorated by crisp, cool wind and sea. Staring into the frigid
water, I pondered marriage to Bruce. Sex would never be boring, but he's
much too controlling. I turned from the water and admired the enclave of
beautiful Cape Cod homes, gleaming with sunlight. At that moment, I'd

thought I could be happy here with Bruce, but wondered why I always feel claustrophobic with his demands. Perhaps the idea of marriage petrifies me or perhaps marrying Bruce.

I stared into the distance until I felt a presence behind me and turned facing Bruce.

"I hope I didn't upset you too much last night. I just want you to express yourself more, tell me everything you think, everything you want. I want you to be as open as I am," he'd said.

At that moment, I believed I would never be the woman Bruce needed. I'm not that open I'd thought but didn't voice my opinion.

We spent the day driving around the island and eating at one of the restaurants in town. I enjoy Bruce's company when he's not making sexual demands. I even see a side of him he rarely shows to others, a softer side, the boy he used to be. What made him this other man? I asked him about his parents' marriage, hoping some clue to his personality would emerge. He'd paused and responded tersely, "My parents had a boring traditional marriage." I'd sensed contempt for his family and dared not press forward.

On the drive back to the house Bruce sat silently. Then after a long spell, he'd asked, "Do you want to know about my parents, Judith?"

Clearly, my earlier question stirred underlying issues. I'd replied, "Only if you want me to know."

"My mom had old-fashion prudish ideals. She was religious and afraid of her own flesh. I was surprised my father tolerated her so long," he'd said.

Stunned, I didn't know how to respond. By his tone, I knew his parent's marriage wasn't happy and perhaps why Bruce demands so much openness. That was all Bruce said about his parents, and it was more than enough.

* * *

A bang sounds in the front yard. Instantly, I assume the tree above the garage has snapped, crushing the roof and car inside. I rush toward the front door and spy through the glass panel at the worrisome tree and sigh relief as it sways wildly in the blustery wind. The bang I heard must have been in the distance in someone else's yard. I head toward the kitchen, refill the tea kettle, and make another cup of instant coffee.

Candlelight dwindles, and the home darkens. I wander into Aiden's study, toward the antique armoire where he keeps a box of long-stemmed candles for special occasions, and arrange them around the family room, hoping they'll last through the storm.

Reclining on the sofa, thoughts of my conversation with Kayla at Starbucks and Dorothy Dinnerstein's words emerge. *The mother is the first to form a child's attitude toward the human flesh.* Kayla was right. Bruce and Dennis have similar tendencies. Perhaps Judith's suspicion about Bruce's parents holds some truth. I exhale, fall into the sofa, and continue reading.

January 22, 1973

For the last two weeks, pressing matters at work consumed Bruce. I've been preparing for my trip to Italy in February, another production at La Fenice. And I can't wait to take part in Carnival again this year. Bruce and Mallory will attend again.

Mallory and I met for lunch today. Her new man consumes most of her time. She seems happier than I've seen her in a while. Maybe he's good for her.

I found the courage to ask Mallory about Bruce's parents. Her sentiment was similar to Bruce's when she revealed, "Mrs. Wheaton was frigid and religious. I suspect she was genophobic, and she didn't satisfy Mr. Wheaton. He was seen around town with other women. And there were rumors of divorce for one of his mistresses, but it never happened?"

Her next statement shocked me even more. She'd said, "On several occasions she overheard Mrs. Wheaton chastising Bruce for his sinful ways, and forbid him to leave the house until he repented for his sins. Bruce rebelled constantly and hated his mom for her prudish ways."

Her next revelation was unsettling.

"Can't you tell; he's still rebelling."

I asked what she meant, and she'd said, "Don't be coy with me Judith. He's sexually demanding. His appetite for sex is exhausting. Bruce's behavior may well be the result of his mother's punishments as a child."

I imagined Mallory and Bruce together. His demands must have overwhelmed her. Curiously, I'd found myself defending him. "He just needs a woman with the same passion. Maybe his behavior stems not from his mother but his father's sexual proclivities."

Her next comment bothered me in ways I hadn't expected. Jealousy rose with her admission."Well, Bruce knew how to keep me satisfied that's for sure; he's a wicked dish."

She saw upset on my face and instantly apologized. I was stunned, uneasy, and acutely curious why she'd broken up with Bruce. Shocked to learn Bruce ended their relationship, I feared what I've suspected for months. "Do you still have feelings for Bruce?"

"I will always love Bruce Judith, but I can't give him what he wants. Nonetheless, I want only the best for him. When he told me about you, I admit I was jealous, but I would never stop him from finding true love."

Her admission made me more ill at ease. Her friend dating the man she loves must be painful. I don't know if our friendship will ever be the same with this admission. How can it be?

Chapter 27

After two days, the storm has relented. Light streams through sky-lights and dormer windows, brightening the home lighter than when I first arrived. I stand and stretch my creaking limbs, and head to the patio for fresh air. On the beach, roaring waves have quietened to white-capped ripples, and strong winds are a gentle breeze, whirling salty mist from the sea. Detritus litter the yard with items blown from the beach and neighbor's homes. I place the patio chairs around the tethered-outdoor table, and survey the home, fearing damage, but sur-prisingly, not a single shingle was disturbed.

The ache pervading my legs for two days prompts me to rush up-stairs to my overnight bag and dress for a run. I ponder a circular route into town and back past Lighthouse Beach. At the front door, the downed power line causes me to worry about greater havoc on the island, but I can't bear another day without a run.

Stepping off the porch, I assess Starbuck Neck Road and begin a cautious jog. Turning on Fuller Street, a headwind lifts and flings my cap off my head. I double back, scuffle through puddles, zigzag, and tap furiously until my shoe pins the baseball bill. I tighten the cap's clo-sure and peer around to see if locals caught my comical chase. At the road's edge, a figure moves behind a hedge. I wait a moment with fear someone is watching me. I turn and glance at the hedgerow several times, then resume a vigilant jog.

At a slow pace, I continue past homeowners examining damage to their property. The nor'easter's aftermath obvious on every street—flooding, downed trees, power lines, ripped branches, torn home shingles, broken windows, untethered outdoor furniture, and garbage cans swept onto lawns and streets. I worry when a power line sparkles on a branch above. Carefully, I navigate the puddles and the roads, bypass severely flooded lanes, and shorten my run with a detour onto Captains Walk.

A headwind slams my body like a giant hand, pressing me back and fluttering my running jacket wildly like a mainsail. I catch my cap, holding it in place and lean into the force, pushing forward. I'd hoped to run farther than the 2.3 miles displayed on my sports watch, but fear conditions are too dangerous. Circling back, I turn right toward South Water Street with the sensation of eyes watching me. I glance back and then resume a quicker pace.

On South Water Street, a local surveying his property appears surprised to see me running and hurl a warning, "Be careful. Roads are dangerous."

I wave my hand, and say, "Good morning, I will," and continue on North Water Street's narrow lanes, past Captain Homes that once fascinated Judith. I study each detail, imagining fishermen decades ago, returning home after a long day at sea.

At twenty-two North Water Street, L 'Etoile Restaurant sits in a large, white, whaling captains home, a place often frequented by Judith, Aiden, and I in the past. Many summer evenings, under white tents and candlelight, we ate dinner, chatted and watched the harbor behind the restaurant. I wonder if Bruce had special moments with Judith at L 'Etoile. Suddenly, I remember Judith holding a man's hand as she pushed me in a stroller. *Was it Bruce?* How many childhood memories of Judith and Bruce have I lost?

In the harbor, boats rock quietly at their moorings. Toward the Harbor View Hotel, the lighthouse comes into view with astonished-looking hotel guests snapping photos of the skyline. As I turn onto Lighthouse Beach Walk, the source of their fascination appears in the sky. Large, billowing clouds spread open to azure, magenta, and orange heavens. In awe, I run across the well-worn dirt path, circle the lighthouse, and then double back toward the beach.

Dismayed by the gale's aftermath, I stare at dunes and seagrass swept out to sea by storm surge, eroding shorelines and leaving a flattened beach. Something sparkles atop the T-shaped sandbar adjoining the shore, twinkling from sunlight peeking through clouds. I wonder if its sea glass, but I'm not bold enough to traverse the sandbar, fearing a sudden drop-off into the cold water. As I resume my run, clay-like sand sucks at my shoes, and the headwind, now a tailwind pushes me toward Fuller Street Beach.

I veer in and out with the tide, remembering three summers ago with Hannah, Kayla, and Michelle. It seems yesterday, days after college graduation, the last summer before starting our careers, we ran along the beach, swerved playfully with the tide, and talked about our aspirations. Four idealistic women, untainted by life's cruelties, were ready to carve their niche.

"Vic, in two months we'll be working at a prominent hedge fund in New York City! I can't believe it!"

Kayla's high squeal resounds in my memory. Ecstatic about our offer from Wheaton, we planned our careers that summer. She would work and attend law school, and I would pursue my masters part-time while working as a full-time Analysts. Hannah's summer internship at the New York Times turned into a full-time position as a journalist. Michelle, still uncertain of her career path, decided to travel before choosing a career. I ache with the memory and yearn to turn back time. The memory of Kayla's excitement that summer and the brutal end to her short life seem discordant, heartbreakingly impossible, but it happened. My throat lumps, but I stifle tears and push forward toward the house.

In the distance, beautiful Cape Cod homes bordering the beach glisten in daylight. I imagine Judith's thrill the morning she slipped from Bruce's bed as she admired each home. As I grow closer to the house, a vague memory of a man walking along the beach with me atop his shoulders emerges. It wasn't Aiden. The hands securing my knees were lighter, and sun-kissed forearms bore golden hair. *Was it Bruce?* There's a growing need to remember my childhood. Something scratches my mind, irretrievable memories I may never recapture from earlier years.

In the near distance, between my house and the Greene's home, a man watches me, then quickly, disappears around the corner. Uneasily, I resume a slow walk and then a jog toward the house. On Starbuck Neck Road, a man walks around a parked white NSTAR bucket truck ready to restore electricity to the area. On the front porch, I take off my sand-encrusted running shoes and watch the whirring boom lift raise a lineman in the air. Surveying the Greene's front yard, I wonder if the man I saw from the beach was Mr. Greene. No, he wouldn't have walked away but would've waved hello.

Recalling the black Lincoln Town car in Central Park, fear gnaws at my stomach. I survey the area, wishing for Bruce's men's protective surveillance. *Was the man on the Greene's lawn Bruce's security?* I picture Kimura's men lurking inside, and cautiously, enter the home. By now, I'm positive Bruce's men told him of my escaped by ferry. After countless trips with Judith to the island, Bruce knows my precise refuge. I push aside my fear and head to the kitchen.

Chapter 28

After the run, my appetite has returned with a craving for Aiden's cheesy mushroom omelets, which I haven't had in over a year, not since Judith. Aiden always stocks the kitchen with breakfast basics. In the fridge, I grab two eggs, Provolone and Swiss cheese, a red bell pepper, shiitake mushrooms, and search the pantry for onions and garlic. I start preparing ingredients when my cell phone beeps intermittently on the coffee table. I sigh, retrieve the mobile, and notice five texts from Hannah and Michelle, and several voice messages from Aiden, Bruce, Chase, and Kevin. I sigh again, and deliberate calling Hannah, but mentally, I'm not ready to deal with her pain or talk about Kayla, so I place the phone on the counter.

The water pipes grumble and groan as power surges through the home. Lights flicker on and off several times before the rooms brighten. I begin chopping peppers, onions, and mushrooms, unaware the front door opened and closed. Startled by footsteps, I turn quickly, wielding the chef knife as protection.

"Oh, my God! Anne, you scared the crap out of me!"

Frozen and wide-eyed, Anne stares at the chef knife in my hand.

"Oh, I'm sorry." I place the knife on the counter and embrace her tightly.

"I shouldn't have barged in like this. When I saw the lights on, I came to check it out. I had no idea you were home. I hope you don't mind me using the keys Aiden gave me."

"No, Anne, of course not, you're like family. Aiden said you would keep an eye on the house."

"Dear, I'm so glad to see you. I wish I'd known you were coming."

"It was an impromptu trip."

She frowns. "Is everything okay?"

"Yea, it's just the storm … had me edgy for two days," I lie, concealing growing concern about the Kimura family. But it's not too far from the truth given I thought the storm would rip the house apart. "I wasn't prepared for a nor'easter when I arrived."

"You've come at the worse time," she says, strolling toward the kitchen island. "They've been forecasting this storm for days. And another one's headed our way tonight. Weather is so unpredictable with global warming."

"Well, I'm just happy it let up for a while. I was dying to run and finally got out this morning—"

"Vic, that's dangerous with all the downed power lines," she says with a scowl. "Sweetie, you could have gotten hurt."

"I was careful. You know me, I'll run through a thunderstorm if I have to, but I'm always cautious. Besides, I ran the last couple of miles on the beach. I couldn't believe the storm eroded the shoreline so badly, and that sandbar, I've never seen one so large."

"Shorelines are disappearing. That's a major concern around these islands, especially after Arthur and Sandy hurricanes. The Town Council started initiatives. Hopefully, it'll prevent further erosion."

I'm amazed Anne's aged so well. She must be the same age as Judith. But at sixty-five, she looks fifty. Her big, brown eyes are too large for her small, oval face, and remind me of summers she babysat me as a child. There's not a gray strand on her head, and I wonder if she uses hair dye. The New England accent, like many of the locals, is stronger than ever. Anne is one of Judith's closest friends and like a member of the family. I realize I haven't spoken to her since Judith's funeral and wonder how she's handling her friend's loss. "Anne, I'm so sorry I haven't called since mom's funeral—"

"Stop it, Vic, there's no need to apologize. I know this is difficult for you. Aiden said you were having a hard time getting back here, which is understandable. This place was Judith's love. Being around her possessions must be painful."

"Yes, but I'm glad to be back."

"And I'm glad you're back, but I wish you'd come at a better time. The island can be depressing this time of year."

I sigh. "I know, but I needed to get out of the city."

"Is something wrong?"

Dreading more words of pity and condolences, I wavered before mentioning Kayla's death. *Oh, no!* How could I forget? Anne doesn't know about Kayla. And then I remember Kayla's fondness for Anne. How could I forget? "Anne, have you heard—"

"I know, Vic," she says before I finished my words.

"You know about Kayla? How did you hear so soon?"

"Aiden. When he called to check on the house, he told me. I was stunned speechless such a vibrant girl was gone. Aiden seemed confused about her death. Do you know what happened?"

"No, we only know it was a gunshot," I say glancing sideways with the lie.

"But who would shoot her?"

I focus on the chopped red pepper afraid she'll see the lie on my face. "I don't know. She was just in the wrong place at the wrong time, I guess."

"I'm so sorry, Vic. Anne studies my face with her big eyes narrowed. You two were so close. Kayla was much too young and passionate about life. So much promise gone. It's just unbelievable,"she says, raising her arms with a confounded flop to her hip. Glancing around the kitchen, she asks, "Do you need anything—groceries or necessities?"

"No, but thanks for asking. Aiden stocked the kitchen well before he left."

"Well, if you need to talk, Vic, I'm here."

After two days of solitude, I sorely need company. "Would you like an omelet?" I ask, hoping she says yes.

"I'd love to, but I've already had breakfast with Gerald. But I could do with a cup of coffee."

"Good drip coffee, I've been drinking instant since the outage."

Placing the keys on the counter, she continues to the cabinet and pulls out the coffee beans as if she'd prepared coffee in the home a thousand times. She exclaims, "There's nothing like a good cup of drip; instants just not the same." Heading toward the pantry, she comes back with the coffee filters and chuckles at my curious expression. "Dear, I've had coffee with Aiden many times. I know where he keeps everything."

"Oh, I'm glad you visit Aiden. I'm always worried he's alone."

"Aiden..." she chuckles "... hardly" He's never alone. He's got poker and fishing buddies on the island. That man's never without company."

I knew Aiden had fishing buddies, but I never imagined him a poker player. Not a man who spends his time listening to classical and opera music. Poker is so uncharacteristic, but so is fishing. "I guess one never knows everything about their parents. Well, I'm happy he has buddies to keep him company."

Anne pours coffee beans into the grinder, and I continue slicing mushrooms for the omelet. After adding water and coffee grinds to the coffee maker, Anne strolls toward the family room, and stares at the cushions and diaries in front of the sofa. "Aren't these Judith's? I recognize the painting on the box. Judith told me it's a replica of..." Anne presses her hand to her lips. "My memory has gotten so bad. Oh, the Palazzo Pisano. Hmm, the full name slips my memory."

"Moretta. Palazzo Pisani Moretta. The artwork is by Tiepolo."

"Look at all those journals," she murmurs and shakes her head. "Your mom was so disciplined. I tried, but never had the patience."

"Hmmm, I just realized I'd never seen Judith write in her diaries ... Never. Isn't that strange?"

"You wouldn't have," she says, staring at me with puckered lips and tapping her index finger on her lips. "From what I remember, your mom recorded her day every night before she went to bed. You were probably sleeping when she was writing."

Some nights as a child, I'd catch light shining under the library door. Was it Judith's nightly ritual, poised over her diary, deliberating and writing events of another day, or did words spill onto paper with the speed of memory? Was her writing revealing? Did it help her make sense of her life, a form of therapy? Putting her misgivings on paper must have offered some insight. Much like my running, her writing was therapeutic. "Well, Aiden just recently surrendered the diaries. He said Judith wanted me to have them."

Anne glides her hand over the box. "There must be many stories of her trips to Europe. Oh, and the Venice Carnival," she says with an inquiring squint.

I smirk. "Yes, lots," I say, pursing my lips. "Did you ever go with her to Carnival?"

"No, but I always wanted to. I just never found the time," she says, admiring the diaries.

Anne's expression freezes with a faraway glare as I continue beating the eggs. "When did you meet Judith?"

"Wow, I met your mom the same year I got married in 1972. She—"

I raise my brows with Anne's abrupt halt. "Anne?"

"I met your mom long before Aiden."

I sense her hesitation. "Anne, it's okay. Aiden told me about Bruce and Judith. It's in her diaries as well."

She places her hand on her heart. A tinge of guilt, not relief mars her face. "Thank goodness. I wasn't sure you knew."

"Did you know Bruce?"

"I met Bruce before I met Judith, the day he purchased the home. He was standing in the backyard, surveying the property. At the time, Gerald and I were newlyweds, and we came over to introduce ourselves. I was in such awe," she says, feigning a swoon. "He's such a handsome man. Gerald was so jealous when he saw Bruce's effect on me. I laughed and planted a big kiss of assurance on Gerald's lips," she says with a wistful glare. "I was happy someone finally bought this property. When the Simons, the previous owners, passed away, the property sat empty for two years before Bruce purchased it. This house was always so alive with children. It was unfortunate when they moved away. They couldn't keep the home any longer."

"Was the house always so beautiful?" I ask, folding the chopped vegetables into the cheese and eggs.

"The Simons kept it well, but Bruce remodeled the interior to sheer perfection. A few months later, Judith arrived. They were such a beautiful couple. I could've sworn they were newlyweds. You can imagine my shock when I discovered they weren't. You could tell they were in love. Gerald and I made a bet they'd marry before long."

"Were you surprised when they didn't?"

"No. As time passed, Judith changed. Your mom and I talked extensively. I believed she needed another female to confide in. We would talk about everything when we sat on the beach—the opera, her childhood, and silly women issues. I would blush something awful when she talked about her love life with Bruce. I admit I was a little jealous," she says modestly. "Gerald and I love each other, but our passion was tame compared to your pa—Bruce and Judith's," she says, catching her slip. "She told me Bruce's passion consumed her, and sometimes she felt she'd lose herself. Although she said he was demanding, all I saw was Bruce's love and respect for your mom. But, I guess no one ever knows what happens between a man and a woman in private."

I wonder if she'd feel the same if she read Judith's diaries.

"Ooh, such a striking man. He'd make a woman weak-kneed when he walked in a room. Even me, I admit. Oh, and those stares Bruce gave your mom, I swear it was so passionate I had to leave the room," she says with a chuckle.

I bet, I thought, recalling Bruce and Judith's steamy sex. I imagine Bruce's burning eyes and envision Anne blushing with such a passionate display. I giggle inwardly. "Is that why you thought they were newlyweds?"

"Yes, so much passion burned in their eyes. I couldn't understand Judith's concern. It was obvious he loved her. In retrospect, I believe Bruce would have done anything for your mom."

I realize she slipped a moment ago. She knows Bruce is my father. "Judith must have revealed much to you over the years. Did she talk about my father or her pregnancy?"

Her eyes flit to and fro, unable to hold my gaze.

"Anne, I suspect Judith revealed Bruce is my father."

Again, relief crests her face. "Whew! I wasn't sure if Aiden told you. Such a complicated bond your mom and dad had."

"So I've been told." *What's with that word?* How about unconventional, deviant, unfaithful. I'm sure there are better words than complicated to describe Bruce and Judith.

"I hope you don't mind my frankness. I admire Aiden, and I respected your mom's choices, even though I believe she made some bad ones. I guess everyone makes bad choices once in a while. Often, I worried about Judith's decision to marry Aiden when her love for Bruce was obvious. One day I asked if she was sure of her decision. I sensed her doubt. She told me Aiden allowed her freedoms that Bruce didn't. She feared Bruce would hinder her career if she married him. She was right. An opera career is demanding. I believe Bruce wanted a typical wife at home, not traveling all the time. Aiden, on the other hand, was supportive. He admired her work and only wanted her to succeed. I don't believe Bruce was as supportive as Aiden."

"Did you know she saw Bruce after she married Aiden?"

"Know? I was here," she says candidly. "After your birth, they visited the island often. People on the island thought Bruce was her husband. After Judith married Aiden, I found it strange, baffling, and bothersome when she revealed Aiden knew she spent time with Bruce. For years, I thought about what Judith told me."

"What was that?"

"Judith used the fireplace as a metaphor for both Aiden and Bruce. She said Aiden is the foundation that holds the structure in place. And Bruce is the fire, the flame that needs tending. At the time, I didn't understand what she meant, until years later." She pauses with a sudden realization. "Oh dear, I'm rambling on again. I think it's old age," she chuckles, "I just can't keep my mouth shut."

"No, don't stop. There's so much I don't understand about Judith. You were one of her closest friends. I need to learn more from people who knew her best. You said you didn't understand the fireplace metaphor until later. What was your final interpretation?"

"I didn't understand fully until years later. Judith told me Aiden assuaged a wildness she was trying to tame and worshiped her talent. She never spoke of Aiden as a woman would a lover, but as a mentor, a friend. On the other hand, when she spoke of Bruce, it was with passion. Honestly, I believed Judith feared passion that drew her to Bruce. Years later, when she was ill, she spoke often about her teenage years. Mostly, she talked about her mother's heartbreak after her husband's infidelities. She said she'd never love a man as deeply as her mom loved her father. She said her mother was never the same after the marriage failed. The heartbreak and depression worsen her mother's cancer. Judith believed her mother lost her will to live." Anne sighs and scratches her brow. "I suppose Judith chose Aiden because she was searching for that father figure she never had. She feared loving Bruce, believing he would eventually abandon her like her father had her mother."

"I didn't know. Judith never talked about her father's infidelities. I'm just learning about Bruce through her diaries. But, I believe you're right. Do you think she loved Aiden?"

"Honestly, she loved Bruce, but it scared your mother. Her bond to Aiden struck me as a friendship, a partnership, but I could be wrong."

Anne's assertion doesn't surprise me after reading Judith's diary. Remembering Bruce words when he discovered Michael Katz's book on Judith's coffee table, I realize Bruce was right. It was Judith who needed to see an analyst. Perhaps she didn't marry him, fearing the same fate as her mother. A burnt egg odor pulls me from thought. Quickly, I turned the browned omelet over just in time.

"Vic, do you remember the time you spent with Bruce as a child?"

"I did?"

Anne's chest heaves with her loud inhale and exhale. "Yes, you did, and he loves you, Vicky. He was a proud father when he walked with you and Judith in town. That's one reason locals thought they were a married couple, but Judith and Bruce didn't care. You and your dad were a lovely sight when you clung to his hand. Poor Judith, it was difficult whenever Bruce returned to Greenwich. Your screams were so piercing; she'd rush about the house trying to find a toy to stop you from crying. Later on, Bruce learned how to sneak out without you noticing." She smiles at me like I was still a child. "You were so attached to Bruce, probably more so than Judith at that age."

"Wow ... How old was I?"

"Bruce was in your life the moment you were born."

She stares with an odd expression, and I wait for a mind-blowing revelation, but her expression fades.

"But, after you turned four, Bruce was rarely around. I asked Judith why, and she said you needed to bond with Aiden. Vic, Bruce loved you so much. It was obvious he was your father. Frankly, I feared for poor Aiden. With your birth, Judith and Bruce's love grew stronger. I often thought with their growing affection, she'd leave Aiden, but she never did."

"Anne, I have no memories of Bruce, but there's one memory of a man carrying me on his shoulders on the beach. But I can't determine whether it was Aiden or Bruce."

"Aw! That was Bruce. I used to watch him run on the sand with you on his shoulder all giggles and sunshine. Constantly, Bruce teased you to hear your sweet giggle."

Finally! Anne's affirmation assures me the fleeting memory of Bruce is real. I suspect there're many moments with Bruce I'll never recapture. "What about Aiden, did he spend time with me here ... on the beach?"

Anne takes a sip of coffee and shakes her head. "No, rarely, well not at that stage of your life. I'd often wondered why? Later, Judith revealed when Aiden discovered the home was a gift from Bruce, he was uneasy staying in the home. But Aiden knew Bruce visited you and Judith here."

"God, Anne, why would Aiden stay married to her?"

"Vicky, it's not for us to judge no matter how wrong it seems. Judith, Aiden, and Bruce's arrangement were explicit. There were no secrets or delusions. Whether they were happy, is something only they know."

Placing the omelet on a plate and pouring a cup of coffee, I sit next to Anne, yearning to hear more about Bruce. I've never been more grateful for her friendship with Judith than now, positive she'd retained memories I'd forgotten. "Anne, can you tell me more about Bruce."

After an hour, Anne painted lost childhood memories of a man I'm beginning to embrace.

Chapter 29

Harbor clouds bode another storm. Shivering from the drastic drop in temperature, I wrap my arms around my waist and watch dusk grow dark and cold over the island, then head back inside. I close the patio doors and switch on the back and front porch lights. Needing to unwind, I pour a glass of wine and stroll to the sofa, pondering Anne's elucidation of my infancy and my swelling empathy for Bruce. When Judith ripped him from my life, did he protest? Bruce and Aiden's pain at Judith's hand, I can't imagine. "What do you make of this mess, Kayla?" I whisper, imagining her replying, *"Unbelievable!"* Judith and Bruce's affair would have intrigued her to the point of unrelenting probing, and a diagnosis of Judith as phobic, fear of love or passion if there's even such a disorder.

Alcohol courses through my veins, freeing tears I'd suppressed with Judith's diaries. I wipe my eyes and stare at the box beside my feet, wondering what I'll discover tonight. Randomly searching through many pages, I skip years of Judith's stage life, erotic escapes with Bruce to Venice, and their weddings to Aiden and Mallory. After their nuptials, they maintained a sporadic affair with months between each rendezvous. My eyes stop on an entry dated September 3, 1986, which mentions Mr. and Mrs. Kimura. Bruce revealed the night of our meeting, Judith wasn't aware of Mr. Kimura's blackmail, except for a brief encounter at his dinner party. Curiously, I explore the entry, seeking hints of Judith's knowledge about Michelle's family.

September 3, 1986

Aiden's away on business in California, and I'm missing his company. With our busy careers, every minute together is scheduled. Our sex life, though consistent, lacks fervor, leaving me frustrated. I try not to compare Aiden to Bruce, but now and then, I wish he was more passionate. Aiden pictures me a virtuous woman, worshiping my talent, not my femininity. I laughed at his belief that overindulgence in sex and stimulants affects my talent. The asceticism he believes I must assent to is shocking. Some self-indulgence is necessary. I wonder if his view of me has changed since marriage. Although he lacks Bruce's passion, he's ardent in other areas of our marriage.

Today, Mallory invited me to another dinner party, and foolishly, I accepted. I haven't seen Bruce in a while and dreaded being near him now that we're both married. As soon as I'd entered the home, inquisitive brows altered Bruce's expression. Had Mallory failed to tell him I was coming?

Later, Mallory introduced me to an interesting Japanese couple she'd met at Carnival, Mr. and Mrs. Kimura. I was shocked by their age difference. She's almost a child at twenty. Mr. Kimura must be at least forty, a twenty-year difference. They recently adopted two boys and are considering adopting a baby girl. I'd asked them why three, and Mrs. Kimura said she's always wanted a large family. She'd also mentioned adopting allows them to help the less fortunate; such an altruistic deed. I couldn't imagine adopting and not having my own. And for the first time, I yearn for a child.

Mrs. Kimura invited us to lunch in the city. I look forward to making a new friend but worry about spending time with Mallory. Later in the evening, I noticed Mr. Kimura and Bruce engrossed in deep conversation. Bruce appeared displeased. Another expression I couldn't discern covered his face. Even now, I wonder what they spoke about. Mallory was missing most of the evening, which is unusual for her. Later, I found her showing Mrs. Kimura around the estate. Bruce must have seen me leave the great room. When I turned around, he was at my back. I'd avoided him most of the evening because of Mallory, but I couldn't resist when he led me toward the maze in the backyard.

Inside the maze, Bruce revealed he'd made a mistake marrying Mallory. He'd voiced anger toward my marriage to Aiden. I sensed his frustration and felt culpable. When Bruce placed his hands around my waist, I didn't protest.

"Does Aiden satisfy you, Judith?" He'd asked.

I refused to talk about Aiden, and didn't answer his question, but retorted, "Does Mallory satisfy you?"

Swiftly, he pulled me to his body, kissing me harder than ever. I should have pushed him away, but I didn't. My marriage to Aiden hasn't suppressed passion for Bruce.

"Do you love her?"

"Why do you care, you're with Aiden." His words aroused anger and lust. Swiftly, he turned me around and lifted my dress as he'd done years before our marriage. I welcomed his mouth,silencing my moans. When we finished, he'd said, "It's always been you Judith, not Mallory I love. I suspect your passion for Aiden isn't as strong. Why did you marry him?"

I couldn't answer his question. My response would never make sense to him. God knows I've asked that question many times the last two years.

Before I could answer, he'd said, "This is wrong. I could bear this when we weren't married to others. Aiden and Mallory deserve people who love them."

After painful words, he left me in the maze. An irrational fear crept over me. I'm married to Aiden, but I fear losing Bruce. Shouldn't I fear Aiden leaving me? My mother loved my father so deeply, when he left, it destroyed her. She became depressed, losing her will to live. I won't allow fear to cripple me as it had her.

As I'd turned to leave the maze; a man standing in the dark startled me. I believe it was Mr. Kimura. Embarrassed, I'd hurried from the maze, hoping he hadn't witnessed the entire scene with Bruce.

* * *

Mr. Kimura. Did he know about Bruce and Judith? Was this the black-mail he held over him? Maybe Bruce was protecting Judith from harm as well. Only questions Bruce can answer swirl in my mind.

Finally, I understand why Judith didn't marry Bruce—a fear of lov-ing too much and being abandon like her mother. Had she chosen Aiden because he loved her more than she loved him, believing he would never leave her? *Poor, Judith.*

At last, Bruce's conscience reared its pesky head. I recall what Bruce and Aiden told me that the affair continued for years. Bruce's love for Judith defeated his conscience. I open the diary to the next entry, noticing the scene in the maze fueled their next escape to Martha's Vineyard. Thumbing through several more pages, I find another entry about Mrs. Kimura.

October 15, 1986

Today, Mallory and I attended a lunch at Lea Kimura home in Green-wich Connecticut. The home is just as grand as the Wheaton estate. De-spite her wealth, Lea appeared sad, and I wondered if it was the absence of her husband. She'd explained, "My husband is never at home. He's al-ways traveling abroad to attend his businesses. My life consists of raising our adopted sons." When I'd asked Mr. Kimura's line of business, she'd stumbled. "Line-um ... well, he owns various manufacturing companies." She diverted the conversation as swiftly as it had begun, back to her two sons. Her husbands business must be lucrative, I'd concluded after ex-amining the home and servants. Later, I discovered Lea's marriage is an arrangement made by her parents. The idea of a loveless marriage made me cringe. Perhaps they've grown to love each other with time. A smile lit Lea's face when she mentioned they're adopting another child, "A girl this time," she'd said. When I asked why she didn't give birth to her own, she'd explained, "A medical condition prevents me from carrying full-term. We've tried several times, but I would always miscarry." Maybe that's the sadness in her eyes, or is it the absence of her husband?

I was troubled by the number of guards around the home. Why would they need so much security? As we were leaving, Mallory joked, "You'd think Mr. Kimura is the Prime Minister of Japan." And for some reason, I replied, "Or a drug lord." I don't know what possessed me to say that.

After leaving the Kimura's home, Mallory grew quiet on the ride back. And then, out of the blue, she asked, "Judith does my marriage to Bruce bother you?"

I was stunned. Before I could answer, she said, "You're probably wondering why I married a man who loves someone else."

I was shocked, and a second response failed me.

"I've always loved Bruce, and want the best for him. When you married Aiden, Bruce was devastated. I was angry you discarded his so easily, and still, you toy with Bruce's emotions."

I couldn't say anything because she was right. I'm surprised she knew Bruce, and I are still together. I anticipated angry words, a slap or kick from the moving car, but she kept talking.

"Judith, I know Bruce still loves you. Bruce and I have been best friends since school, and I'd hoped that would be enough to sustain our marriage. You might find it strange. Our marriage is not traditional. We're partners, friends, and allow each other freedoms as long as we're honest with each other."

My mouth flew open at her admission. They've given each other permission to see other people. Why would she enter a loveless marriage and then allow him to see other women? She's beautiful and could find someone with deeper affections than Bruce.

"Why would you marry Aiden when you're in love with Bruce?" She'd asked.

I grow weary of that question. I owe no one an explanation about my marriage to Aiden. But I couldn't lie to her. I feel securer with Aiden, but I also love him, just differently than Bruce. Why would you marry a man who's in love with someone else? You've shortchanged yourself. You deserve better, Mallory."

Quickly, she'd replied, "You chose a man for security, not love; you've shortchanged yourself more than I ever could." Her next response sounded well-rehearsed as if she'd tried to make sense of her marriage to Bruce a thousand times. "I'd rather be with a man I love than with someone I *don't. Besides, Bruce deserves to have a family of his own, and I'd like to give him that. With time, I imagine children will create a stronger bond."*

For the rest of the ride, I sat quietly. I'd never considered Bruce's need for children.

* * *

There, finally, they've said it! They're both rsponsible for the mess they'd created, and I'm certain they regretted their decisions years later. *But would they admit it?* Did Bruce want to have children with Mallory, or was it a ploy Mallory used to hold on to Bruce? Well, at least Judith's intuition about the Kimura's line of business was correct. If only she'd used that keen intuition and said yes to Bruce's marriage proposal, then everyone would've fared better. *Aiden forgive me!*

November 21, 1986

Today, Aiden and I threw an intimate dinner party for the Kimuras. They're such an odd couple. They never make direct eye contact or show signs of affection. Lea Kimura appeared shy and uncertain in her husband's presence. I attributed it to their age differences, or perhaps it's cultural.

Mr. Kimura bombarded Aiden with business questions all evening. Lea and I discussed several operas. She was fascinated and saddened by Violetta, and Alfredo's doomed love in La Traviata. She believes a man wouldn't marry a courtesan in real life. I know little about her culture, but I have heard that Geishas marry their patrons. I have no proof to substantiate that claim, so I'd smiled in acknowledgment and changed the topic, telling her about the Venice Carnival in January. She seemed interested in attending until she'd glanced at her husband and said, "It wouldn't be possible this year."

I wonder if she needs permission from her husband. I would never be in a controlling marriage, what a horrible way to live.

Later, Mr. Kimura followed me into the kitchen. I felt uneasy alone with him. He'd asked too many questions about the Wheatons and had expressed with unwavering eyes, "You appear close to Mr. Wheaton." His comment appeared an insinuation. Now, I'm certain it was him in the maze. Later that evening, he'd continued prying for information about Bruce's personal life, and my suspicions grew. I'd asked, "Why are you so interested in Bruce Wheaton?"

Warmth in his eyes froze to black ice. "Wouldn't you want to know about the person managing your investments?" He'd asked with a wink and wicked grin. A wink that revealed he's aware Bruce is my lover and a grin so thick with malice it made me shiver.

* * *

I imagine Mr. Kimura's eyes and lips, black ice and sharp daggers, sending shivers down my spine as it had Judith's. Although Judith had nothing to hide, Mr. Kimura couldn't have possibly known his threat was ineffective. Aiden and Mallory already knew about Judith and Bruce's affair. Some other threat forced Bruce into silent compliance. Some extortion so strong, it's held Bruce captive for years.

I wonder if Aiden continued to speak with Mr. Kimura after that night. Filled with questions, I retrieve my mobile and phone Aiden. In the background, raucous voices sail through the speaker.

"Hi, dad. What's all the noise?"

"Hey, kiddo, I'm watching football with friends. Vic, I've been calling for two days. Why haven't you returned my calls?"

"I'm sorry. After Kayla's funeral, I needed time alone. I'm in Martha's Vineyard."

"During a nor'easter? You've picked the worst time to visit the island, but I'm happy you made it back. Are you okay being alone?"

"I've been better. Judith's diaries kept my mind off Kayla and the storm."

"With the weather, I imagine you have plenty of time to read."

"Nothing but time ... Aiden, have you ever read Judith's diaries?"

"No. As I told you, there's no need. Judith and I discussed everything. I trusted her. Besides, I don't want to go dredging up the past."

My intuition jabs at me. I believe Aiden's in denial. I'm beginning to sense his refusal is out of fear—fear he'll discover truths Judith never divulged, something to change his view of his marriage. "I thought your curiosity got the best of you at some point."

"Kiddo, are the diaries helping you understand Judith any better?"

"More than I hoped," I say with a frown. The sexual content in Judith's diaries would horrify Aiden, and I'm not going to mention it ever.

"You sound a little strange. What's going on?"

"Do you remember Mr. and Mrs. Kimura?"

"The Kimuras? Michelle's parents?"

"Yes."

"Years ago, I met them once or twice. They were mostly friends of the Wheaton's. If I recall, Judith thought they were a strange couple."

"Why do you say that?"

"Well, at one time, Judith tried to build a friendship with Mrs. Kimura, but after a while, she said something wasn't right. She became suspicious and stopped inviting them to events. Why do you ask?"

"Do you remember cooking dinner for them?"

"Honestly, Vic, these days I can't remember where I leave my reading glasses. How am I going to remember twenty years ago?" He chuckles. "Oh, wait, there was that one time Judith invited them to dinner. It was so long ago I'd almost forgotten. Why the sudden interest in the Kimura family?"

"Judith mentioned them once or twice in her diary. I thought you might remember occasions spent with them."

"Not much. But I recall right around the time Judith gave birth to you, Mr. and Mrs. Kimura adopted Michelle."

"Were Judith and Mrs. Kimura good friends at the time?"

"No, but Mrs. Kimura kept in contact with Judith over the years. Judith kept a casual acquaintance, nothing more. Even with your mom's standoffish ways, Lea continued to call. She even sent a beautiful gift for the baby shower and called to congratulate Judith after your birth. I was baffled she tried so hard when Judith didn't reciprocate the friendship."

"Why didn't Judith reciprocate?"

"She thought they were hiding something. She said they gave her the creeps. So you can imagine how irked Judith was when Mrs. Kimura called to discuss the college you were attending. She was hoping to enroll Michelle at Wellesley as well. Hmm, even today, I find her persistence strange. Your first day on campus, Mrs. Kimura called to tell Judith Michelle was in the same dormitory."

"I had no idea. I thought our meeting was pure coincidence."

"Vic, believe me, Judith had nothing to do with your friendship with Michelle, but I'm sure Mrs. Kimura did."

Voices cheer in the background and Aiden joins in. "Dad, get back to your game. I'll call you later."

"Okay, sweetie. Call me if you need to talk, and I'm glad you finally made it back to the house. Vic, before you go, are you coming for Thanksgiving next week?"

"Wow, next week is Thanksgiving? Well, I was hoping to stay a little while longer, but I'll try."

"I know Kayla's death has been devastating, but I don't want you spending the holidays alone, especially now. I've invited a few friends if you decide to come. But if you don't, I'll understand. Take as much time as you need."

"I'll try, dad."

I feel horrible keeping the truth from Aiden about the Kimura's money laundering and their role in Kayla's death. But I don't want him worrying or involved. He's the only family I have left, well, except for Bruce.

Chapter 30

Vexed with queries, I place the phone on the coffee table, settle on the sofa, search Judith diaries for entries about my childhood, and find a diary labeled 1990—my birth year. I finger through pages and stop on February 13, 1990, the day Judith raised the topic of a child with Bruce at Carnival.

February 13, 1990

Tomorrow is the opera's last day, and I haven't told Bruce about my plan. I'm still worried about Aiden raising another man's child. He's assured me he'd treat the child as his own, but the idea must disturb him on a deeper level. Anyway, Bruce might object. I've thought about trying to get pregnant without Bruce's knowledge, but that's wrong, immoral. Is it wrong wanting both as fathers?

Tonight we attended the Il Balo del Doge at the Palazzo Pisani Moretta. I've grown to love the balls and anticipate them every February. Each year feels new and different as if we're meeting for the first time. I've come to expect Bruce's demands. His sexual appetite has become my own. With every Carnival, our passion remains strong. At the ball, a young woman stared flirtatiously at Bruce. He leaned over and kissed me. She understood and looked away.

Much as our first night at the Palazzo Pisani Moretta, I found his hands on my thigh. But I've come to expect and desire his advances. Sensing my excitement, Bruce stopped and said, "Not until later." We've become that couple I'd blushed at years ago, displaying affections for all to see. But tonight, all I thought about was Bruce's child. Surrounded by Carnival's decadence, it was the perfect time to reveal my plan. I'd whispered, "I want your baby." I'd feared his reaction. He didn't appear shocked but stared with deliberation.

"What about Aiden?" He'd asked.

When I explained Aiden's impotency, Bruce's eyes brightened, and a smugness crept into his countenance with new hope I'd divorce Aiden for him."

With a smile, Bruce said, "I'd imagined you pregnant with my child for a long time."

February 14, 1990

Tonight was my last performance as the ill-fated seamstress, Mimi. Puccini's La Boheme has ended. This evening I ended the doomed love affair with Rodolfo; I feigned my last death in his arms. In some way, it's a relief. For months, the role has kept me depressed. Physically, I began to assume phantom symptoms of Mimi's tuberculosis. After the second week of production, an all-consuming weakness, fatigue, weight loss, and even phantom coughs overcame me. Although I realized it's psychological, I feared genuine illness. My doctor laughed and prescribed vitamins and rest while assuring me I'm perfectly healthy. It was the oddest thing, but the moment the final scene ended, and I left the stage, my energy returned.

Finishing a role I've played for months, feels like death. I'll miss the performers I've shared the stage with and our nightly celebrations. Mostly, I'll miss the daily routine, but again, I'll adjust. Bruce was in the audience tonight. At the curtain call, I heard his voice screaming above others. Brava! Brava! My affections deepened, I believe because of our unborn child.

Later, Bruce asked, "If it's a girl, what will you name her?"

I hadn't thought about names yet. Playfully, I suggested opera characters—Mimi, Violetta, Lisette, Juliet, Isabella, Sophie, and the list went on until I tired and jest, "If we're victorious tonight, Victoria would be fitting."

Bruce loved the name, but I preferred Violetta, my favorite role.

"And if it's a boy?" I'd asked.

"That's easy. Victor."

Then Bruce said, "Victoria Angelica." Instinctively, I knew that would be my daughter's name. For the first time, Bruce relaxed his control. He was merrier than I'd ever recalled. Maybe Mallory is right; conceiving Bruce's child will forge a greater bond.

* * *

As I'd suspected, Judith named me Victoria to signify her victorious conception. I'm glad Angelica was Bruce's idea. *Did the hotel ceiling contain pictures of angels or cherubs?*

I thumb through diary pages to my birth date, December 1, 1990. Between the pages lays a faded Martha Vineyard Hospital letterhead containing a sloppy version of Judith's penmanship. I assume with her hospital stay, she hadn't brought her diary and needed something to write on, and managed to transcribe words from the stationery into the journal.

December 1, 1990

I'm writing from my hospital bed. Today is Victoria Anjelica Powell's birthday. She came into the world unexpectedly, during a raging storm, delivered by her father's hands at 11:22 A.M. I'm tired, sore, and drowsy. And soon the medication will put me to sleep. So, I'll make this brief.

I'd planned a hospital delivery with Aiden at my side, but my daughter's birth didn't go as planned. Bruce and I were trapped on the island by an unexpected storm. My water broke, and like the raging storm, contractions came fast and fierce. Roadblocks delayed the ambulance's response. With or without a doctor, the baby was ready to arrive in the world.

I've never seen Bruce so scared. He'd rushed about the house and tried to remain composed, but I'd heard his voice tremble when he'd called Anne Greene for help. Swiftly, and before Anne arrived, the baby was on her way. Bruce stood over me, ready to bring her into the world. I've never felt so much pain. I couldn't breathe and feared I'd lose the baby or die giving birth.

"Breathe baby, breathe," Bruce had said, trying to calm me.

I continued to breathe, and my eyes never left Bruce's face.

"I see her," he'd screamed with relief.

With his reaction, I'd breathe, laughed, and cried all at once. Wanting the baby out of me, I'd pushed forcefully, while he'd coaxed me through the pain.

Anne arrived just as the baby appeared. Her eyes flooded with tears.

Exhausted, I'd watched Bruce's face soften. For the first time, tears roll down his face in my presence. He was the first person Victoria saw when she entered this world. So small and fragile, I couldn't take my eyes off the tiny person placed in my arms. Her heart-shaped lips are mine, but her eyes are her dad's. Bruce had searched and found the birthmark on her neck—the small port-wine infinity sign—a trait from her father. I'd held her tightly until the ambulance arrived and couldn't let go when they took her from my arms. I can't wait to see her when I wake up. Aiden will be just as thrilled when he arrives in the morning. Victoria has two fathers who will be there for her always, unlike mine, who abandoned me for a new life.

* * *

Ink blurs with my tears in a bluish haze down the page. I dab the page with my fingertip, then wipe my eyes, imagining Bruce bringing me into this world. *The first face I saw.* Overwhelmed with emotions, I question why no one told me. Why didn't Anne tell me earlier Bruce delivered me in this house? I've always believed a doctor delivered me at Martha's Vineyard Hospital, not my father. *The birthmark.* Slowly, I trace the port-wine infinity sign, proof that Bruce is my father. I stare at smeared words on the page then continue to read, discovering Bruce left the island before Aiden arrived the next morning. Judith colored the truth for Aiden's sake, never telling him Bruce delivered me. Like mother, like daughter; Judith and I forever shielding Aiden from pain.

Chapter 31

Imbued with mixed emotions, I stare blankly around the room envisioning my parent's fear the stormy day I was born. Earlier, Anne had said *Bruce was in my life the moment I was born.* At the time, I didn't catch the insinuation. Now, I know what she'd meant.

The phone vibrates on the table, and on the screen, Kevin Collin's picture appears. I clear my throat and take a deep breath before answering. "Kevin?"

"Vic, where've you been? I've tried to reach you for two days. Are you at your apartment?"

"Kevin, I'm so sorry, I'm in Martha's Vineyard. I needed some time alone."

"You shouldn't be by yourself."

"Why? Is something wrong?"

"I have news about the Kimura family. I've been working with the FBI who has been working on this case for years. They're close to bringing them in. Vic, they've informed me the entire family's involved."

"What about Michelle?"

"I'm not sure about Michelle. But her family has a long history of corruption. Did you know Michelle was adopted?"

"Yes, she told me in college. Why?"

"You're going to find this strange, but Michelle's parents aren't married. They're siblings."

"What! Are you certain?"

"The Kimuras are adopted, not biological siblings. There's no record showing they were ever married. They also changed their surname from Ogawa to Kimura, to disassociate themselves from their father's crimes, the Ogawa cartel busted over thirty years ago. Vic, the Kimuras have been adopting children for years, inducting them into their business."

"Are you serious?" Suddenly Judith's observation makes sense. She'd noticed the lack of affection between the two, and perhaps that's why Mrs. Kimura never conceived children. "Kevin, that's just odd."

"I would say so."

"Vic, I don't want to alarm you, but we lost their trail two days ago. The FBI raided their Greenwich home. There's no trace of them. Have you heard from Michelle?"

"No-um-yes, she's texted me, but I haven't read her messages."

"Can you check while I'm on the phone?"

"Okay, hold on." I click on my text messages and frown at the number of texts from both Michelle and Hannah. "Kevin, there are six texts from Michelle."

"Read them to me. We might find some clue of her whereabouts."

Michelle

Vic, call me as soon as you get this, it's urgent.

Sunday 5:00 p.m.

Michelle

Vic, where r u? Are you still at the Collins?

Sunday 7:15 p.m.

Michelle

Vic, I'm freaking out! I believe my brothers had something to do with Kayla's death.

Monday 10:00 p.m.

Michelle

Vic, you're scaring me. Hannah says she hasn't heard from you since the funeral. Seriously, call me back!

Monday 12:00 p.m.

Michelle

I don't know if you're getting my messages. I hope you're okay. I understand Kayla's death has been hard on you. Maybe you needed to get away. I hope it's someplace safe. I think I know where u r. If u r, I'm happy you made it back.

LYLAS

Tuesday 10:32 a.m.

Michelle

I'm not in my apartment anymore. My brothers showed up, but I managed to evade them. I've been driving around for hours. I need to get out of the city, but I don't know where to go. I broke it off with Taylor. I don't want him involved with my messed-up family. Vic, please call. I'm really scared.

Tuesday 11:08 a.m.

"Kevin, I'm worried."

"So is Taylor. I spoke to him earlier, and he has no idea where she is. Michelle called off the wedding after Kayla's murder. The poor guy's in shock."

"Does he know about Michelle's family?"

"He does now."

"Michelle said she confronted her mother when she found Kayla's letter in my apartment. Do you believe they'd hurt her?"

"I hope not... Does anyone know you're in Martha's Vineyard?"

"No, just Aiden ... Oh, and Bruce."

"Do you have any protection—a gun?"

"A gun, are you serious? Now you're scaring me."

"Good! You should be."

"Do you think I'm in danger?"

"Vic, anyone who knows the truth about the Kimura family is in danger. I don't know what they're capable of."

I envision the steel box containing the gun in the master suite. Now I have no choice but to enter a room I've been avoiding since my return. "Aiden keeps a handgun in the closet."

"Get the gun and keep it close. I've got to go, but I'll call you as soon as I can. Oh, if Michelle calls, phone me right away."

"I will."

Growing fear sends me scurrying and checking all the windows and doors. I draw the shades and curtains, rush upstairs, and hesitantly, enter Judith's room. All her belongings are still in place, even her clothing inside the closet. Aiden hasn't discarded a single item. On the top-shelf, is the metal box where Aiden keeps the gun. Years ago, he told me my birthday is the code to open the lock. I reach for the box, disturbing Judith's clothing with my elbow. A citrus fragrance emanates around me, her favorite perfume. I run my hand across the green lace cover-up she often wore on the beach. As I stand immersed in her favorite scent and clothes, a pining jolts me deeply. I'll never have the chance to tell her I'm sorry for my horrendous teenage rebellion. I avert my eyes back to the metal box, enter the code, and remove the gun and ammunition. Before I exit the closet and the room, I glance around at a place I ran to for comfort as a child, a room that caused suspicions and anger, and a room that's more home than any place I've known. The room Judith and Bruce brought me into the world. I close the door and rush downstairs.

At the dining table, I load the gun as Aiden showed me years ago with Judith's fearful protest resounding from the past. She hated the gun in the home. But Aiden assuaged her concern with fear-based tactics, painting a deadly home invasion. She conceded.

I carry the gun to the foyer console, place it in the drawer, wander toward the front door, and check the security system. The green light shows it's armed, but Kevin's words hold me fearful. I reprove my stupidity for coming here alone. Stepping toward the family room, I peer through the curtains into the night. Waves roar and winds pick up momentum. Earlier, Anne said another storm is coming, but I hope not as severe as the previous one. On the other hand, it would prevent Kimura's men from getting on the island.

Michelle, where are you? I hope she is somewhere safe. Immediately, I dial her number, and the call goes straight to voicemail. "Michelle, I got your texts. I'm in Martha's Vineyard. Call me when you get this message." I hang up and begin to read Hannah's texts.

Hannah

Vic, where did you disappear to after the repast? If I know you, you're someplace alone with your grief. I'm here if you need to talk. LYLAS

Sunday 7:15 p.m.

Hannah

Vic, Michelle just called. She's frantic. Call her back. She sounds so scared. I'm calling Kevin, maybe he can help.

Monday 12:15 p.m.

Hannah

OMG, Vic, why didn't you tell me BW is your father? I just spoke with Kevin. He thought you'd told me. I'm stunned! OMG! Please call me soon.

Monday 1:30 p.m.

Hannah

Vic, Kevin filled me in on everything. I made some calls to Frank, the reporter I told you about. Mr. and Mrs. Kimura were a part of the Ogawa Cartel brought down by the FBI over thirty years ago. Kevin is working with the FBI. I'm worried about you and Michelle.

Monday 6:30 p.m.

Hannah

Vic, where r u? Did you turn your phone off? I hope you get this soon. I'm worried. I believe I know where you are. Every time you have a problem you run to Martha's Vineyard. Have you finally gone back? Please call!!! LYLAS

Tuesday 11:00 p.m.

Hannah

Michelle texted me a few minutes ago; I was afraid to tell her where you might be. Her family may be trailing her.

Tuesday 11:15 p.m.

Hannah

Vic, I've been in the car an hour, I'm headed to the vineyard. I hope you're there.

Wednesday 1:00 p.m.

I glance at the time and realize Hannah will be here soon. I dial her number, and the call goes straight to voicemail. "Hannah, I got your text. I'm waiting at the house."

"Her family may be trailing her." Hannah's words seep into my mind, but minutes too late. I've already told Michelle I'm here. Anxiously, I turn toward the console, wondering if I should put the gun someplace else. I leave it alone, and pace in front of the fireplace, wondering where the Kimura family disappeared. Perhaps back to Japan, I hope.

I check my voicemail and play Chase's message first. His voice sounds through the phone. "Victoria, I've been calling your home phone, but you're not returning my calls. I hope you're not having second thoughts about us. Call me soon."

"I wish I could, not yet." *Maybe I should text him; let him know I'm not having second thoughts.*

The next message plays, and it's Bruce's somber voice. "Vicky, my men told me you took the ferry at Woods Hole. That's not the safest place to be." A deep sigh escapes through the speaker. "I wanted to tell you before, but since Judith's death, I didn't see the point. Mr. Kumura has known about me and Judith and Martha's Vineyard for years. But don't worry; my men are still watching over you."

Bruce's message confirmed my suspicions. Had Mr. Kimura threatened Judith's life? Was Bruce talking about Judith when he said he'd do anything to protect his loved ones? Is Bruce aware the Kimuras are missing? Where could they've disappeared to? Remembering the proximity of the Kimura home's to the Wheaton estate, I begin to worry for his safety. I call Bruce, and the servant picks up. Before I can say hello, he states, "Mallory and Bruce are out for the evening."

No, she can't be. Mallory is visiting friends in Italy until February. And why did the servant pick up? Calls usually go straight to voicemail when Mallory and Bruce aren't home. *Something's wrong.* I dial Bruce's cell phone. It goes to voicemail. "Bruce, I received your message today. Sorry, I didn't call back sooner. Please call me as soon as you get this message." I dial the Wheaton estate again. The servant answers, but I interject before he speaks. "Hi, is everything okay there?"

Ignoring my question he states, "Mallory and Bruce are out for the evening."

His voice sounded forced. *Something's not right.* Quickly, I call Kevin, growing impatient on the fourth ring. "Come on, Kevin, please, pick up, pick up."

"Kevin Collins."

"I'm so glad you answered. Something's wrong at the Wheaton estate. The servant's voice sounded strange. I believe he was trying to tell me something. He kept repeating Mallory and Bruce are out for the night, but Kevin, Mallory is in Italy. Do you think the Kimuras would hide there?"

"I don't know, but it's worth a shot. I'll get the Greenwich police there as soon as possible."

"Thanks, Kevin. Keep me posted."

Suddenly, I'm afraid of losing Bruce. A man I haven't spent enough time with and would like to know better.

Chapter 32

Gravel crunches under a car rolling into the front yard. The car stops, and the car door opens and closes swiftly. Footsteps stomp up the stairs and across the porch. Panicked, I rush for the gun. The doorbell chimes several times, followed by Hannah's loud voice.

"Vic, it's me, Hannah!"

I exhale, gather my composure, and return the gun to the console. Hannah storms into the foyer appearing as if she'd ran from Manhattan. Her one-sided braid unravels with wisps falling messily about her face. Familiar vanilla and raspberry fragrance permeate the foyer; evoking happy memories.

She drops her bag and shudders with her ears to her shoulders. "It's freezing out there, and it's starting to snow." She grabs and squeezes me tightly. "You scared me to death!" She exclaims.

Hannah's perfumed scarf brushes my nose with a scent redolent of Bella Sorelle's carefree days. A trail of shedding mohair lines my lips and nose when she releases her embrace. "Hannah, I'm sorry. Did you get my voicemail?" I ask, wiping mohair from my lips.

"I did, just as I entered Edgartown. I was relieved I didn't have to check into a hotel."

"Who's watching the twins?"

"Paul is. I didn't tell him I was coming here. I just left," she says with an annoyed eye roll and head shake. She stares sadly. "I still can't believe Kayla's gone. As I approached the house, all I heard were her ecstatic screams. Remember how she'd yell, 'We're here! Beach here I come!' And we'd get annoyed at her loud screech. Well, as I was nearing Starbuck Neck Road, all I wanted was to hear her voice one last time. I miss her so much, Vic."

The memory squeezes my heart. I picture Kayla's face lit with excitement the last time she came to the Vineyard. She wore a floppy straw hat, bikini beneath a sundress, and beside her, sat a beach bag filled with summer essentials. The moment the car stopped, she leaped from the seat and ran straight to the beach. Her white dress streamed behind as she yelled, *"Yahoo!"* I'll never forget that image of Kayla.

"You okay?" Hannah asks.

"Yep ... I just realize how much I miss the four of us together."

"Me too ... Well, it's only three of us now, four Bella Sorelles no more."

"No, we will always be four."

"Okay ... Well, I guess we can call ourselves the Four Bella Sorelle, even if Michelle doesn't appear," she says, twisting her lips.

"Hannah!"

"I'm sorry. This is so unfair. Kayla was just finishing law school, just starting her life. It's not right!"

Her expressiveness stuns me. Hannah is always stoic in any crisis. Motherhood has softened her edges. Unlike the impassive girl from college—always cracking jokes to hide her true feelings—a new emotional Hannah has evolved. Now, I'm the comical one, trying to make her laugh. "Should I get out of the way? Do you want something to throw?" I ask, feigning a Hannah, as we called her comical asides in college.

Hannah laughs. "If I need to throw something I'll give you heads up." She stands akimbo, wielding an astute glare. Hannah's uncanny intuitiveness zooms in, sensing my edginess. "What's wrong?"

"Something's going on at the Wheaton estate. I just called Kevin, and I can't reach Bruce."

"When will this mess end?" She asks, slinking down the hall toward a closed door. Removing her boots, unwrapping her scarf and coat, she places them in the closet. The yoga pants and frayed oversized sweater tells me she left her apartment in a rush with no forethought to her outfit. "Vic, don't worry... Kevin knows what he's doing."

"I hope so for Bruce's sake."

"There's nothing you can do but wait," she says, pulling me toward the family room.

"I guess," I mumble. "It's been two days since Michelle's last text. Have you heard from her?"

"No. Not since Tuesday."

"This is crazy! I've been on autopilot for days, dodging one brutal blow after another—the money laundering, Alex and Kayla's death, discovering Bruce is my father, Michelle's family is part of a drug cartel. And now Bruce is missing, and the Kimura family is on the run. Geez, and they know about Bruce's affair with my mom and this house. Hannah you shouldn't be here it's not safe."

"Whoa—whoa—whoa—Vic, stop. Take a deep breath," she says, raising and lowering her hands slowly.

"I'm fine," I lied, catching a lung-full of air and releasing it slowly and breathing deeper again. "Okay, we'll wait until Kevin calls."

Peering around the room with furrow brows, Hannah asks, "What have you been doing here alone?"

I ponder her reaction to Judith's diaries, my foray into my mother's sex life. Will she think my behavior iniquitous? No, she won't. She'll probably laugh at my embarrassment. Hannah's brutally honest with her opinions and always conveys them with a tease rather than a blow. "Well, you might find it odd..."

"Find what odd?"

"With the nor'easter I was inside two days with nothing to do. So it gave me time to read Judith's diaries."

"Diaries?"

"Yep," I say with a sheepish grin. "Hannah, it's embarrassing, and there's so much sex!"

"Hmmm..."

"I felt like I was sinning just reading them, but I couldn't stop."

Hannah's brows arch. "How Freudian," she says with a giggle. "Vic, there's nothing wrong with reading about sex," she assured, but her expression and words are incongruous. The sudden twitch in her lips tells me she's trying to suppress a laugh. Her face alters comical, and I snicker then release a much-needed laugh. Our amusement bounces off high beams spilling across the room.

"Vic, it's' okay," she says, tapering her laugh. "Anyone would be freaked out reading about their mother's sex life. I know I would. Wow, that's gotta be strange."

"Strange ... how about wicked, or depraved." I frown, pondering the nebulous line between depravity and curiosity. *Does curiosity breed depravity*? "Once I got over the shock, her writing explained a lot. God, I wouldn't have read the diaries if Aiden and Judith had been honest about Bruce. I just wanted to know more about their affair. I felt I was reading about a different person, not Judith."

Hannah slides into the sofa, tightening her braid and examining my face. "How did you get the diaries?"

"Aiden. After he told me Bruce is my father, he produced this box filled with Judith's diaries. Judith wanted me to have the journals if I ever discovered the truth about Bruce."

"Wow, that must have been a shock. How are you handling it?"

"Of course, I was angry and stunned, but after talking to Bruce, and reading the diaries, I've grown less critical and more empathetic. I learned a lot from Anne Greene today."

"Anne ... your next-door neighbor?"

"Uh huh ... She's been Judith and Bruce's friend for years. You won't believe it, Hannah. This house was a gift to Judith from Bruce when he proposed to her. All these years, I thought Judith purchased it."

"Wow! What a gift ... What happened? Why didn't they marry?"

"That's a question only Judith and a therapist can answer, but I believe the root of her rejection was psychological. Judith had a fear of marrying a man like her father and becoming like her mother. Well, that's what her writing reveals. I'm just starting to grasp her fear. Can you believe she rejected the proposal of the man she was madly in love with?"

"Her fear must have been overwhelming. So how did you come into the picture?"

"That's what I asked when Aiden explained he's impotent."

"Oh, wow ... I need alcohol to chase this down," she says, quickly scrambling toward the wine cooler.

"There's a bottle in the fridge I opened earlier."

Hannah grabs Judith's favorite wine from the fridge, two goblets, and brings them back to the sofa. Filling both wine glasses to the brim, she takes a thirsty sip and slides into her spot, as if resuming a juicy novel. "So, Aiden can't have children?"

"Unfortunately, no."

Twirling the braid around her finger, she takes another sip of wine. With her bottom lip pressed to the glass, a hollow question escapes. "So, Judith was still sleeping with Bruce?"

Given what I've learned the last couple of days, oddly, I'm feeling the need to defend both Aiden and Judith. Only a few days ago, I would have condemned her deceit and protected my cuckolded father. However, given what I know, neither Aiden nor Judith was deceitful nor deceived, but informed. "Well, it's a little more complex than that. Aiden was fully aware. It appears Judith never stopped seeing Bruce while they were married. Well, to make a long story short, they had an agreement with Bruce, and here I am."

Two frown lines crease between HAnnah's brows. "Hmpf, so, Aiden just allowed his wife to bear her lover's child? That's unbelievable, especially Aiden's willingness to share his wife. Who does that?Aiden must be confident or spineless to allow Judith's indiscretions."

I'm not sure if it's Aiden or Judith's behavior she disapproves of, but I believe they were both at fault. "Believe me, Hanna, I was just as horrified. I'm trying to understand, but Aiden and Judith did have a strong marriage, regardless of her love for Bruce," I say, realizing how absurd it sounds.

"Judith's life seems more tragic than the operas she performed," Hannah says in jest. "The Trials and Tribulations of Judith ... le prove e le tribolazioni di, Judith."

I chuckle because it's true. Judith's life was as tragic as her opera roles. A sudden ache rises in my core, but I hide pain and mimic Hannah in a sweeping tone, "Due amanti di Judith (Judith's two lovers) ... Gli amori di Giuditta di (The Loves of Judith)." Our laughs spill across the room and squash my pain. Laughter is just what I needed. Taking a sip of wine, I relax into the chair.

"I have to thank Judith for pressing me to study Italian. Your mom made a great impression on me. She was so strong-willed and independent. She helped me understand that I can achieve anything if I want it bad enough. I've used her mantra in every aspect of life and achieved everything I wanted—a career, a husband, and now, two screaming babies."

Remembering the last tearful meeting with Hannah, I laugh inwardly, picturing her crying over the twins. Did she get what she wanted, or thought she wanted, and now, regrets? "Yes, Judith was persistent about knowing more than one language," I say, remembering how she hounded me to the point of rebellion in vocal and music training.

"Well, thank you, Judith Powell," Hannah says, toasting the air. "Although sometimes she was a little over-the-top."

"Hannah, all kidding aside, my parents had their problems."

"Honestly, Vic no one's perfect; everyone has a personal battle."

"You sound like Anne."

"Well, she's an intelligent woman, thanks for the compliment," she says, leaning over and sweeping her hand across the diaries. "There are so many. How much have you read?"

"Enough. It was selective reading. I had pressing questions, so I skipped a bit until I found what I needed."

"Well, after two days, maybe it's time to take a break from the past," Hannah says, glancing at the patio doors. "Wow, do you hear that?" She asks, rising from the sofa and peering toward the dark beach and roaring waves. "I made it just in time. It's snowing harder. Have you seen the weather report?"

"No, electricity was out for a while, and I haven't turned on the television since I arrived. But Anne did say another storm is coming."

Hannah clicks on the television, and flips through channels, searching for local weather reports, and pauses on NBC's live broadcast from Greenwich Connecticut.

"Hold it!"

"What..." Hannah screeches.

"Isn't that the Wheaton estate?"

"Oh my God..."

"Turn it up."

At the bottom of the TV, headlines roll across the screen.

> *Bruce Wheaton, prominent Hedge Fund owner's estate in Greenwich Connecticut, has been swarmed by FBI agents and local police.*

The news reporter states, "After FBI seized the home, hostages were released. Earlier today, not too far from the Wheaton estate, FBI, stormed the home of a prominent businessman with known ties to a drug cartel. NYPD traced them to the Wheaton Estate. Inside, two shots went off, and two are injured. There's no further information on their identities."

FBI agents lead Mr. and Mrs. Kimura in handcuffs from the home, trailed by four other handcuffed men.

The news reporter reveals, "Police confirmed the two victims were Wheaton servants."

Relieved Bruce wasn't one of the victims; I exhale a long-held breath and launch from the chair when my mobile rings with Kevin's picture, tripping over my feet and catching my fall on the coffee table's edge.

"Kevin, I saw the news."

"Thanks to your call we got them."

"Did you find Michelle?"

"No, she and her brothers are still missing. So you haven't heard from her?"

"No, nothing since we last spoke…"

"Hmm, well, I'll keep you up-to-date on my end. Call me as soon as you hear from her."

"Okay, I will. Kevin, where's Bruce?"

"We don't know. He wasn't in the home. I'd say he was damn lucky. Vic, I know you want to believe Michelle is innocent in all of this, but be careful. If she shows up, just play dumb again, okay."

"Okay, Kevin." I continue watching the news for more updates.

Hannah stares wide-eyed in my direction. "What did Kevin say we should do?"

"Nothing, just wait…"

Chapter 33

Television stations reiterate the Kimura capture nonstop. I sit engrossed in the news while Hannah showers. For twenty minutes, I channel surface for updates and worry about Bruce and Michelle. Finally, Hannah saunters downstairs dressed in black, drawstring pants and a long, gray cardigan that covers weight she'd gained during pregnancy.

"Is there any more news?"

"No, just the same story ... Nothing new."

My cell phone rings and Hannah reads the display. "Who's Chase Dillon?"

"So much is going on; I haven't had time to talk about Chase."

"Aren't you going to answer?"

"No, I can't talk to him right now."

"So, who's Chase?"

"He's a doctor I just started seeing."

"Okay, now I want to hear everything," she says, scooting back on the sofa and crossing her legs in an Indian pose. "Come on, spill it."

"Hannah," I whine. "There's nothing to tell."

"Vic, when you give your cell number to a man, I know there's more going on. So, come on, spill it."

I scowl at Hannah, recognizing her insatiable need for romantic stories. Often, I've teased her about the number of romance novels she devours. Maybe her marriage lacks the passion she craves. Then I remember the look in Paul's eyes the night I left her condo. Has romance dwindled in their marriage?

"Is he cute? Have you had sex yet? Tell me?" She pleads.

How can I discuss Chase when Michelle is missing? It seems wrong to talk about men and sex when she could be in trouble. Nevertheless, Hannah's inquisitive eyes goad me on. I sigh and give her what she wants in a singsong voice. "We met while running in the park. And yes, we had incredible sex before and after Kayla's last phone call," I say with a forced grin.

Hannah's mouth drops. "Vic, I'm so sorry."

I recall the scene with Chase in my foyer for the first time since I left the city. "I'll never forget my first sexual encounter with Chase. It was a devastating day. I'd just attended Alex's funeral and then later learned from my father that my boss is my real father. Several hours later, I lost all sexual control and bedded Chase, and then the day climaxed with Kayla's frantic phone call. It was mindboggling."

"This happened in one day?"

"Yep, just as the Tarot cards predicted."

"Wow, that's a load for anyone."

"Hannah, I was wrong about Judith. I was angry with her, believing she'd had many affairs. I was determined to be different from her. But my resolve flew out the window with Chase. Hannah that night was so erotic. When he walked into my apartment, I felt like someone took control of my body. We attacked each other before my front door closed."

"Whew! All that pent-up lust will make you do crazy stuff," she says with a chuckle. "Vic, I've always wondered about your reluctance when we introduced you to all those gorgeous hunks. At first, I thought you were just career-driven and didn't want any distractions. But after a while, after too many rejections, I started to believe it was something else."

"You weren't too far off. I wanted to focus on my career, not men. Wow …"

"What?"

"I just realized I'm a perfect case for Dorothy Dinnerstein. Judith's affair with Bruce influenced all my relationships."

"Well, now that you know the truth, it's time for some much-needed-steamy fun!" She states loudly.

"You're right. Hannah, I wish I could rewind time to Kayla's phone call. There was fear in her voice. I knew something was wrong. If I'd told her to come to the apartment, she might still be alive." I imagine Kayla rushing to my door and the Lincoln Town car following her. If I'd called the police, would she still be alive? "I feel horrible I didn't take her call seriously. I should have after the Tarot reading. It predicted a new lover and the death of a friend simultaneously. I've been avoiding Chase since I left the city."

"Vic, Kayla's death is not your fault. There was nothing you could do. Kayla brought this on herself. She wouldn't want you sacrificing your relationship with Chase. She's probably screaming from the heavens, 'Girl, are you stupid!' Don't let Kayla's death interfere with your love life. You should call him. You don't have to tell him what's going on; just let him know you're not avoiding him. And stop with the self-recrimination."

My eyes flood, imagining Kayla screaming from the heavens. "I'll call him; just not this minute, not until I hear back from Kevin."

"Oh, I almost forgot; I made your favorite dessert, tiramisu." Jumping off the couch, she shuffles to the foyer and slips on her boots and coat. "Be right back..."

"Where're you going?"

"I left it in the car."

Remembering Hannah's penchant for baking when she's sad or stressed, I imagine her poised over the expensive stainless steel mixer, whirring with ingredients, mourning Kayla's death and worrying about the safety of her two friends, unaware of assorted baked goods overflowing the kitchen. Years ago, she explained baking is cathartic; her therapy when she's sad.

On the television, Bruce and Mr. Kimura's photos appear. Quickly, I turn up the volume just as a CNN reporter announces "... no known link between Bruce Wheaton and the Kimuras." My heart sinks when pictures of the two victims appear. "During the siege, Roman Vargas, twenty-five years old, and William Wisnewski, forty-five, were in the home and are the only fatalities." I recognize the young servant who escorted me to my room during the company weekend. For several minutes, I flip through several channels, hoping for more reports. With no success, I return to CNN for updates.

A long shadow moves swiftly across the patio windows. I stare unblinking, waiting for it to reappear. Every muscle tightens with alarm as I tiptoe toward the curtain, peek through folds, and scan the area. Huge chunks of snow fall diagonally, blanketing the dark backyard. I scan the area then slowly close the curtains. *What's taking Hannah so long?* Worried, I head toward the front, but the phone stops me. Bruce's number displays. Swiftly I answer, "Bruce, where are you?"

Bruce's voice leaps terrifyingly through the phone. "Vicky, get out of the house. Don't go to the front. Get to the Greene's now!"

A scuffle sounds from the front door. I race toward the console, but before I can reach the gun, a fierce blow shakes the door. I rush toward the patio into twenty-degree weather. Cold wind bites through my T-shirt and leggings. My bare feet sink through snow-covered grounds. Noticing a dark figure in the Greene's backyard, I stop and look toward the front yard. My mind screams, *run*! Lights inside the Greene's home darken. *Something's wrong.* Peering left to right men emerge on both sides. I run in the only direction possible, toward the pitch-black, roaring surf.

* * *

Raging winds push at my back, snow pummels my face, and my heart roars like waves pounding the shore. Menacing silhouettes wielding guns, surround me in every direction. There's nowhere to escape except the dark, frigid sea where I'll succumb to hypothermia. And if I run along the shore, Mr. Kimura's men will outrun me or shoot me in the back. When one of the men lifts his gun, I race into the water and dive into a rolling surge which sweeps me out and under the water.

Icy daggers puncture my skin with lightning shock. My lungs constrict. My heart flutters. A rolling breath swells and freezes in my chest. I gasp and sputter frigid air tightening my lungs. Jerky gags follow then panic sets in, but I can't let it. *Breathe! Breathe!*

For several minutes, waves carry me as I regulate my breath. Body heat escapes in a cloud around my head. Snow obscures my vision, shrouding the dark beach, and several men waiting for me to emerge or perhaps drown. A bullet skips the water close by and then another. Can they see me in the dark? I swim further out, away from their view. In the distance, two men race from the Greene's backyard, following at a distance behind the men surrounding the beach. I tread water for several minutes, aware of hypothermia the longer I remain in the water. *I don't want to die like this.*

I swim horizontally to the shore toward the flashing lighthouse. Snow begins to fall hard, clumping and icing my eyelashes, then a wave bigger than the last pulls me under again. I hold my breath and close my mouth and remerge above water with chilly daggers lancing clear to my marrow. My teeth begin to chatter uncontrollably. *Swim, keep swimming!*

With leaden extremities growing cumbersome by the minute, I keep moving until a third wave grabs my weakening limbs. I thrash with clumsy efforts. *Don't panic!* Pins and needles prick my skull and light-headedness creep into my senses. Soon hypothermic confusion will take over. With diminishing strength, I kick like the devil toward the lighthouse.

Lighthouse beams rove ahead, glistening something in the distance. *The sandbar!* It's the object I saw on my morning run. A whir sounds above, and I stare up, blinking snow from my eyes. The sound grows closer then fade in the storm. For a moment, I float on my back and picture the next wave pulling me farther out, my mind losing consciousness, and slipping into a *permanent deep sleep.* The next morning, my lifeless and discolored body would wash onshore. The thought is horrifying. *I'm not ready to die.* I kick harder toward the sandbar with numb limbs growing heavier with each stroke.

Finally, ahead, lays the sandbar. Like a seal, I slide out of the water in a shivering frenzy. My feet and hands throb with incipient frostbite. I roll into a ball and pull my knees into my chest for warmth. Lighthouse beams spindle over the sandbar, sparkling something in front of me. I dig the object from its gritty hold, a large diamond ring. Waves crash and rise over the sandbar, splashing my body again.

In the distance, several men arrive on the beach and confusion ensues. Three shots ring out, and two men fall as a whirring grows closer and louder. Above, a helicopter casts light on the chaos. More men enter the beach and three men race in my direction. When another shot rings out, a man dives in the water. In the distance, a familiar voice calls my name, but cold has claimed my strength, and unconsciousness threatens to consume me. Unable to stand, I lay wrapped in my arms, knees pushed to my chest, trying to create warmth. Somewhere nearby, "Vicky," floats in the air. I open my eyes and stare into the dark heavens. Snow falls around me, blanketing my body. When the shivering stops, hypothermia's icy hands render me unconscious.

"Vicky!"

Chapter 34

Vague voices overlap somewhere near. I open my heavy eyes to three blurry figures swimming into view. Anne glances up and jumps from the chair, followed by Hannah and Bruce.

"Hon, how're you feeling?" Anne asks.

"Vic, I was so worried," Hannah reveals and grips my hand.

"Welcome back, Vicky," Bruce says.

"Where am I?" I wince at the pain croaking like a frog from my throat.

"You're in the hospital," Anne reveals.

I assess the room, I.V., and bandage on my right shoulder.

"How are you feeling?" Bruce asks.

I swallow hard wetting my dry prickly throat before answering. "Like a thawed-out fish," I say and wince at the pain. Laughter escapes around the room, and I laugh despite my raw throat. "Did they get them?"

Bruce nods. "Yes."

Then I remember his phone call before I bolted from the house. I hold my throat to suppress pain. "How did you know they were at the door? Where were you calling from?"

"I was close," he says, turning as Anne approaches with water. Taking the glass from her hand, he places it to my lips. "When my men informred me of your getaway by ferry, immediately, I got a flight to the island and arrived the same night as you. Vicky, I've only been a few yards away thanks to Anne and Gerald taking me in ," he says with a smile at Anne.

"Anne, you knew the entire time?"

Remorse creases her oval face. "I'm sorry, Vic. I promised Bruce to keep quiet."

"So, you knew earlier it wasn't a prowler in the house?"

She nods her head and frowns. "Well, I had to pretend. But I knew you would need company after the storm. Well, you know the rest. You gave us such a scare when you ran into the water. Why didn't you come inside the house?"

"I couldn't. A man was on the patio, and when the house darkened, I was afraid they'd captured you."

Bruce shakes his head. "That was my man. You took off before he could stop you. We wouldn't have let them harm you, Vicky. We were ready to move if they tried."

"But there were so many."

"When you ran, my men and I followed. My eyes stayed on you the entire time until that wave swept you under. I thought I'd lost you until the beam from the lighthouse caught something shining on the sandbar, and then there you were, climbing out of the water," he says, placing the glass of water at my lips.

I recall two men racing from the Greene's backyard, staying behind Kimura's men. "So, you dove into the water?"

"No, that was Mr. Kimura's man. He dove in when the FBI swarmed the area. I raced toward the sandbar and found you unconscious. This was in your palm."

I stare at the sparkling diamond ring that guided me to safety. "It was on the sandbar."

"A lucky charm ... You should keep this. Maybe it will bring you more luck," he says, placing the ring in my palm.

I study it closer. "It looks expensive. Someone's missing this."

"Well, their loss is your fortune," he says with that look that worried me in the past, but now I understand is fatherly love. "How are you feeling?"

"Tired, achy..." I say touching the bandage on my shoulder. "Why is my shoulder bandaged?"

His eyes arch and he stares at me unblinking for a second. "You don't know?"

"Know what?"

"You were shot."

"Shot? I couldn't have been." The moment I plunged into the water, I was sure the bullet missed me.

"The proof is under the bandage," Bruce says.

"I thought the stinging pain was from the frigid water. How's that possible?"

"Adrenaline can block the most acute pain, especially when you're fighting for your life."

"I felt the cold water stab my chest. When I couldn't breathe, I thought I'd die from shock. I knew if I didn't get out of the water fast, I'd die. And I didn't want to die like that, so, I fought through the pain."

"There you go! Your pain was second to your survival."

"Was it bad?" I ask, touching the bandage."

"It went straight through your shoulder. You're lucky it didn't hit a major artery ... Well, you're alive, and that's all that matters" he says, squeezing my hand. "Hypothermia would have claimed you if I hadn't found you in time."

Tiny threads tickle my throat, causing me to choke and cough. Bruce lifts the glass to my mouth, and I swallow swiftly. "Was I in the water long?"

"I would say twenty minutes. That's long enough for hypothermia to set in, especially given your skimpy outfit and loss of blood. But you survived, and that's all that matters."

I can still feel the icy grip claiming my senses—intense shivers, fluttering heart, numbness, and the overwhelming drowsiness lulling me unconscious. If Bruce hadn't seen the glimmering ring, I wouldn't be alive. I could have died on that sandbar undiscovered till morning. "Thank you," I murmur.

He squeezes my arm fondly. No words are necessary, and I know he would have protected me regardless of danger.

Hannah brushes my arm. "Hannah? What happened? How did you get away?"

"I was never in danger. I could have died of a heart attack when the FBI grabbed me. I threw tiramisu in their faces and tried to escape."

I sputter a laugh. There's comical Hannah, making everyone chuckle.

She snickers. "What a mess! Tiramisu flew everywhere, and I blinded one agent. Vic, I tried to warn you, but they cupped my mouth before I could scream. They told me they were FBI and I realized what was happening. When they got into the house, you'd already taken off."

Bruce chuckles. "Hannah put up a good fight. She almost made it back inside the house," he reveals. "She was desperate to get to you regardless of her safety."

I laugh, picturing Hannah's indomitable struggle with tiramisu as a weapon.

"When I realized they were struggling with Hannah, I knew they wouldn't get to you in time. So, that's when I called you. You were fast," he chuckled, "too fast to stop running to the beach."

"How long has the FBI been on the island?"

"The night you arrived, two agents took the flight with me. You dodged the others at the ferry."

"Those weren't your men?"

"No. Agents have been trailing you since our visit. They knew the Kimura men would follow you."

I realize it took great courage for Bruce to involve the FBI and to protect me. "When did you call the FBI?"

"When my man returned with the file you gave him, I paced all morning deliberating my next move. I read the note you wrote on Mark Ames business card and called him without hesitation. Vicky, when it comes to your life, there was only one choice. The note was the kick in the ass I needed," he said with a guffaw. "You're right; turning a blind eye is a slow death. It's been eating at my conscience for years. Your words and Kayla's death gave me the courage to end Kimura's threats." He sighs deeply. "But I'll always regret not saving Kayla's life."

"Why didn't you tell me?"

"Mark Ames said it would only make you nervous. He assured your safety and had agents shadow every move you made."

"Did the FBI follow me this morning on my run ... Were they also watching me on the beach?"

"Yes, but it was me you saw from the beach. I was hoping you didn't recognize me. You reminded me so much of Judith. She would always take strolls on the beach in the morning."

I run my fingers over the diamond ring, pondering my next question. "Did Mr. Kimura also threaten Judith's life?"

Bruce peers at Anne, and then Hannah. "Can I have a word alone with my daughter?"

My daughter warmly jolts me.

Hannah and Anne throw me a smile and exit the room. Bruce waits for the door to close.

"This has always been about saving you and Judith," he says sitting on the bed. "The threats Mr. Kimura made years ago were direct threats against you and Judith. I had to protect you. If I'd gone to the FBI, they would have killed you both. For years, I've been silent fearing for your lives. If Kayla hadn't been so brave, and you hadn't written that note, I probably wouldn't have gone to the FBI."

"How did Mr. Kimura find out about me?"

"Mr. Kimura was a sly one. He had suspicions about Judith and I. One night he stumbled on the truth at one of my dinner parties."

"In the maze," I say without forethought.

"How did you know?"

I can't tell him I've read details of his love life, but I can't lie either. After all the secrets at my expense, I can't bear hiding another one. "Judith's diaries..."

He shifts uneasily and clears his throat. "How could I forget," he mumbles. "Did she keep them in a box with—"

"Tiepolo's Venus and Mars painting," I interject.

His face flushes, and then he clears his throat. "Yes. I gave Judith the box as a memento of our first meeting in Venice. I've always wondered what happen to her diaries. She was adamant about writing every night. "So," he says with narrowed eyes, "she mentioned the maze?"

I hold his gaze and feign nonchalance. "Yes, the diaries were revealing."

"I can imagine." His composure belies his tone. He clears his throat and smiles. "Hmm, well, I hope not too enlightening," he says, rubbing his stubbly jaw, and narrowing his eyes. "That same night Mr. Kimura saw us in the maze, he threatened Judith's life. From that point on, the Kimura men kept constant vigil over your mom and I. But I was sure he would never discover you're my daughter. Unfortunately, he did."

"How?"

Bruce turns around and pushes his hair up, revealing the port-wine infinity sign, just like mine. "Mallory realized you were my daughter when she saw your birthmark. Every Wheaton family member bears it somewhere on their body. Yours and mine are in the same spot."

"I'm still confused. How did Mr. Kimura find out?"

"By accident … Foolishly, Mallory brought Mrs. Kimura without an invitation from Judith to your fourth birthday party. Mallory discovered your birthmark that day and was livid. Mrs. Kimura must have sensed her concern, and followed her when she made a phone call to me. She overheard Mallory's conversation, and later that evening, Mr. Kimura called making more of his threats."

"Did Mallory know about the Kimura family?"

"No, it was better keeping Mallory oblivious. She and Mrs. Kimura socialized together a great deal. I believed keeping her close to Mrs. Kimura would serve an advantage. Besides, Mallory wouldn't have handled the news well. She would have gotten us all killed."

"What about Judith?"

"No, I didn't want her fearing for her life. I kept it secret, but she did question the constant security I traveled with." He pauses in thought. "I figure, after reading Judith's diaries, you know our history."

Steamy images of Bruce and Judith edge my mind. I hope the truth isn't written on my face. "Enough, but I haven't read every journal."

He holds my stare then sighs. "Well, I hope you have a better understanding of Judith, and she hasn't cast me in an unfavorable light," he says with another sharp squint. "Vic, I would have done anything for you and Judith."

"I know." After years of protecting us, I believe he would have given his life to keep us safe. *Does he know how much Judith loved him?* "Judith loved you immensely, Bruce. I believe, so much so, it frightened her."

"Yes, I know. Judith and I spoke at great lengths before she passed away," he says peering around the room, "in a space similar to this one. Days before her death, she revealed if she could do it all again, she would have said yes to my marriage proposal."

Finally, she admitted her mistake. How ironic. Judith confessed her love much too late just as Violetta had on her deathbed to Alfredo in La Traviata. I wish she had been brave enough to admit her wrongs long before her illness. Judith's revelation and the capture of the Kimura's bring a sense of completion. A victory Judith will never know or write in her diaries. The victory belongs to Bruce and me. There's some satisfaction knowing he's aware of Judith's love. I hope it's given him some comfort. Grasping the measures Bruce assumed to keep us safe, my love and respect are growing. "I wish I'd known when I was a child, that you are my father."

"I've always regretted that decision, but I made a promise to Judith and Aiden I couldn't break. I've always been in your life. You couldn't have known. Judith and I talked extensively about you over the years." His face brightens. "I saw your first performance on stage at school. I was sure you'd follow in your mom's steps. Your voice is beautiful, Vicky. Why did you stop singing?"

"I've often wondered about that. I was always comparing myself to Judith. I believed I could never be as good as she was. Honestly, I was rebelling. I was angry with Judith, and her constant badgering frustrated me. It was too much pressure. I lost my passion."

"You're only twenty-five. It's never too late to try again."

"No, that boat sailed a while ago," I sigh with certainty. "I just don't have the same fire Judith had." I pause, twisting the lucky charm in my hand. Lifting my eyes to his gaze, I reveal with difficulty my baseless anguish. "I must admit part of my rebellion was out of anger at Judith's infidelities. I was wrong. I remember your visits to the Vineyard, but I was too young to understand what was happening. For years, I hated Judith for cheating on Aiden."

"I'm sorry you suffered from our actions. We thought we were doing what was best for you," he explains. "If we'd given all the consequences more thought, we would have handled the situation differently. I regret you couldn't talk to Judith. She wouldn't want you harboring anger toward her. If she'd known, she would have told you everything."

"I wish I could have." I imagine my pain—ammunition backfiring in my life. Noticing Bruce's remorse, I reassure him, "I'm okay now. I've learned much from people who matter, and Judith's diaries revealed more than I'd expected." I glance at the ring, and then up at Bruce. "Eventually, would you have told me you're my father?"

"Eventually, yes, I would have. A few years before your mom became ill; we agreed to tell you. We just never found the right time. With her illness, she wasn't sure you could handle two devastating blows."

"Well, I guess fate stepped in."

"It did," he says, rubbing his chin again.

I notice his hands, the hands that brought me into this world, carried me as an infant and saved me from death. Loosening the blanket, I sit up and hold his hand tightly. I imagine much as I had as a child.

Chapter 35

Roughly, the day before the Kimura capture, Michelle was seized and beaten unconscious on her way to Martha's Vineyard. For hours, she lay bound in her car trunk near Woods Hole, Massachusetts. The brutal beating caused severe head injuries and has left her hospitalized for weeks. Now in critical care at Mount Sinai Hospital, her friends keep constant vigil, waiting for her to wake from the medically-induced coma. The FBI, anxious to interrogate her about the cartel, waits nearby for her recovery. With the capture of her parents, we've assumed the role of family, switching shifts, wanting to reassure her when she wakes she's not alone.

While waiting for Michelle's recovery, I've made peace with Kayla's death. For the first time since her murder, I travel the fated path I took that foggy November morning toward the wooded ravine. With dread, I descend the steep hill, and heart-wrenching memories reappear at the base of the ravine. The black Lincoln Town car is an enduring memory that will haunt eternally.

A part of me died with Kayla that morning, leaving a gaping wound. Days ago, a candle and flower monument replaced police tape at the spot her life ended. Hannah, Paul, Taylor and I, orchestrated a candlelight vigil at the exact moment of her death. We said our farewells, and I'd hoped to find closure the funeral hadn't provided, but it didn't. This morning, as I resume my daily run, I'm compelled to revisit the spot that haunts in my sleep.

Stanchly, I drift down the slippery ravine, retracing Kayla's treacherous steps—the last steps of her life, to the spot of her last terrifying breath. The brightly glowing monument is now a mound of rotting mulch. I sweep the area clean and replace dying flowers with fresh roses. Momentarily, the stream's peaceful babble is soothing. I imagine Kayla's essence still remains.

I run my fingers through the stream, refusing to believe her soul is gone forever but exists in a higher sphere. Today, I imagine her beside me, listening, empathizing, and acknowledging my remorse. There's so much I wish I could tell her. It's strange not being able to pick up the phone or hop in a taxi as I had in the past. "I miss having you as a friend. I'm so sorry I couldn't save you." I stifle a sob, imagining the execution-style murder. Angry words that have been trapped inside since the gun fired, rush from my mouth into the air.

"They had no right to take your life! Not Like That!" The ball trapped in my core since that morning dispels with every angry word. The painful weight, I've carried since her murder, lightens. "I hope it wasn't painful. I hope you felt nothing," I whisper into cold waters.

Across the ravine, raccoons wobble into view. The mother pauses with her kits, peering with frightened, yellow eyes. Alarmed, she freezes, examines the threat, and assumes a protective stance as her babies move away from danger. The raccoons continue along the stream, scouting for a safer haven with no guarantee of another day.

Kayla's words, the last time I saw her alive, the last time I exited her car pierce my mind. *Stop worrying, I'll see you tomorrow ... You're overly dramatic Vic. You're not going to lose me; so stop squeezing me like you'll never see me again.* But tomorrow never came, Kayla. I knew before I exited the car, you'd forge on single-handedly.

Closing my eyes, I whisper, "I'm angry but so proud of you. I'm so sorry you didn't get the life you planned—the life you deserved. I'm sorry we didn't get a chance to say good-bye." I stare at water coursing through my fingers. The words the Four Bella Sorelle often express flows from my mouth. "Love you like a sister and I always will."

As I rise from my crouch, a reddish glow wavers on the stream. Startled, I stare at vacillating crimson ribbons then look up at a scarlet bird perched above. *A red bird* stares straight at me. For a chilling moment, its coal-black eyes appear emerald green. Finally, it tweets and flits away. My mind refutes what my heart can't deny. It's unbelievable, but I know the red bird was a sign from Kayla. After Judith and Kayla's tarot card readings, my mind's open to all possibilities. *Kayla was here. She heard me.*

My heart is lighter with a sense of closure finally. Before I leave, I glance back and whisper, "Goodbye, Kayla. Thanks for being my friend."

Emerging from a place that's trapped me since Kayla's murder, I continue with a run never completed that foggy morning straight toward Mount Sinai Hospital.

* * *

Outside Michelle's room, Chase waits with coffee, a hug, and a kiss. Considering my demeanor with care, he asks, "Did it help?"

"It did," I say, laying my head on his chest. "I'm ready to move on." I want to tell him about the red bird, but not now, it's too soon.

"It takes time," he says, kissing my forehead.

I take the coffee and stare at Michelle's motionless body. The only sign she's alive is the machine monitoring her vitals. "Poor Michelle … Any change."

"No, not since your last visit. But her vitals are stable. Now that her family is gone, she'll need friends like you."

I frown at the thought of Michelle alone, no family. But they were never really there for her. Hannah and I will always be her family.

"I hate leaving you, but I have surgery for two hours," Chase grumbles. I lift my chin, and his lips meet mind with a lingering kiss. With difficulty, he pulls away with fingers interlaced. "Don't forget lunch in the cafeteria," he says with a wink as our outstretched arms and fingers release. He turns and disappears around the corner.

Although I've stopped counting morning rituals, my morning visit to the hospital has become a necessary one. My rituals were an obsessive-compulsive behavior used to control my life. Another constraint I'm relinquishing. Chase is teaching me to let go, be open, honest, and fearless. Although abandoning old habits is difficult, it's incredibly liberating. There's a reason Chase is in my life, to help me discover my true self, much as Bruce tried with Judith.

The crystal ball has cracked, allowing me to venture the right path. However, traveling a new path isn't easy. Before I become the new me, old issues need adjusting. I harbor no more anger toward Judith, just love, and empathy. Her parent's tragic marriage dictated her life. Her choices influenced mine, but I have time to learn and embrace change. Thanks to Kayla's bravery, and Judith and Bruce's affair, I've found the courage to loosen my constraints. And as prescribed by Hannah, I've allowed much-needed crazy, hot, steamy fun in my life. One day at a time, I'm creating better memories.

Epilogue

Three Months Later

Yesterday vanished, and today, I'm sweaty, breathless, and eager to catch a new sunrise over the floating city. I race up the Rialto Bridge just in time to witness night surrender dominance. A glorious orange magenta halo streaks Venetian skies, as the sun climbs the horizon. For several minutes, I watch multicolored ribbons disperse to navy-blue skies.

Brava! Brava!

Racing off the Bridge, I hurry to my next destination.

Minutes later, I'm in Saint Mark's Square, a place Judith photographed often. The Basilica's gilded domes and the Campanile loom high and majestic above the square. Turning in a circle, I search various shops and restaurants underneath the promenade, finding Caffe Florian in the distance. I stroll across the square, picturing moonlight shrouding two amorous costumed figures. Stopping at a column, I presume Bruce and Judith experienced their first kiss; I close my eyes and breathe in Venice. My moment interrupted by four merry costumed figures, laughing across the Piazza—perhaps starting their day, or ending a long night of Carnival festivities. I glance at my sports watch, hoping Chase hasn't wakened. Pulling my cell phone from my armband, I snap a picture of dawn illuminating St. Mark's Square then hurry back to Hotel Danieli.

* * *

Back in the room, water splatters in the bathroom, and for a moment, I consider joining Chase in the shower. But I'm captivated by light shimmering off the canal onto the ceiling. I fall onto the bed, and revel in the room's glow, more alive than I've been in a while. I bury my face in Chase's pillow, inhale his scent, and recall the passionate evening retracing Judith and Bruce's night years ago. The Palazzo Pisani Moretta's Saint Valentine Ball and a gondola ride to St. Mark's Square at midnight. The passionate kiss in front of Caffe Florian and erotic pleasures endured all night.

Just as I close my eyes, my mobile rings, and I roll over, catching the anonymous caller on the screen. "Hello."

Rustling sounds through the phone with scraping and scratching noise.

"Hello…" Just as I'm about to hang up, a voice answers.

"Vic? It's me, Hannah. Am I interrupting you and Chase?"

"No," I reply, reminded of Kayla's last phone call. I sit straight with a loud yawn.

"Did I wake you? I can call back later—"

"No, I'm fine. I haven't gone to bed yet. We were out all night, and I just got back from a run to catch a Venetian sunrise."

"I hope it was beautiful."

"Magnificent!"

"Did you receive my email?"

"I did and rushed out to buy the paper." The dog-eared New York Times peeks from my bag. "I must have read it ten times before putting it down. I'm so proud of you, Hannah! The article is flawless, accurate, and your portrayal of Kayla is perfect. She would be proud of you."

"This is the first article I've written close to my heart. I had to get it right for Kayla."

"And you did. So, Mrs. Wentworth, how does it feel being back at work?"

"I'm thrilled to be back at the paper. I wish it had been another reason and not Kayla's death that brought me back. Anyway, reporting the money laundering at Wheaton has been healing. I know it's what Kayla would have wanted. Somehow, I believe I've vindicated her death with the article," she says in a trailing voice.

"You couldn't have written it any better. Kayla would have wanted you as the journalist to expose the Kimura Cartel. Hannah, do you believe in fate or karmic justice?"

"Of course."

"I've thought about fate a great deal since Kayla's death. You ever wonder about our friendship and how all four of us came together on campus? It seemed our friendship was meant to happen. You and Kayla had much in common. She was the advocate for justice, you the relentless reporter bent on exposing the truth. Michelle and I were more connected than we knew. Her family's crimes impacted my world—two families tragically connected. If I hadn't met Kayla on campus, Bruce wouldn't have hired her. I have to believe we somehow saved Michelle from her corrupt family. Although nothing justifies Kayla's death, it's satisfying knowing her snooping eradicated a twenty-year injustice. Without her, Bruce would still be under the cartel's control. I wouldn't have discovered he's my biological father or learned the truth about Judith's affair. Michelle wouldn't have escaped her family's clutches, and you wouldn't have written the best article of your life. Hannah, Kayla's death has given me a new appreciation for life."

"After Kayla's death, I realize life is short. We have to enjoy the time we have left. You're right the Bella Sorelle's had a purpose. I hope you, Michelle, and I find a happier ending. I'm going to enjoy every minute with my new family. No more bitching and moaning about my lost freedom."

My first meeting with Kayla, on a clear Indian-summer day, comes to mind. She walked across the campus quad with red tresses shimmering in the autumn sun. She approached, and sat beside me on the quad steps. Before she could adjust her body on the cement slab, she'd asked remarkably, *"So, what do you have planned for the rest of your life?"* The ease with which she spoke drew me in. We spoke as if we'd been friends forever. I'd answered as naturally as our encounter. *"A career I'm damn good at, a man I love, perhaps a child or two, and good friends to share life."* In return, I'd asked, *"What does your ideal future look like?"* And she'd answered, *"Nothing grand; just to make a difference in other peoples' lives."* Her comment was as remarkable as our effortless friendship.

"Hannah, do you remember your first meeting with Kayla?"

"I'll never forget it. She gave me a piece of advice I've used for years. After months together on the campus newspaper, we rarely spoke to each other. One day she approached after reading one of my articles. She'd asked where that dynamic personality disappears to when I'm writing. I didn't take offense; I was just stunned. She said, *'Good article, good facts, but it lacks your witty personality and shrewdness.'* Kayla told me I should project my personality into my work; I would be more successful as a writer. And she was right."

"Kayla was blunt. I loved that about her. She never held back her opinions. I miss her so much, Hannah."

"We both do. Well, let's hope she's in a better place and smiling from the heavens. On a more joyous note, how's your romantic getaway with Chase?"

"I finally understand Judith's fascination with Venice. Carnival is unbelievable. We're having a ball, literally," I laugh. "I've never had so much fun in my life."

"Well, you deserve some fun. I hope it's as erotic as Judith's?"

"Hmm, maybe..." I say, glancing around the room. Two Columbina masks on the nightstand evoke passionate teasing and kissing in Saint Marks Square. Costumes strewn about the room and lingerie tangled on the floor arouse sensations of lace ripping across my chest and hips as Chase peeled them from my body. "Well, we're trying," I respond with a giggle.

In the background, Paul coos soothingly to the crying twins. "So everything's going well with you and Paul?"

"Better than ever ... Since I started working again, our sex life has improved, and Paul's spending more time with the twins. The babies wrecked our romance, but things are improving. We're even seeing the therapist you recommended."

"Hannah, I'm so happy for you."

"Vic, you know I love you like a sister and always will."

"Me, too Hannah."

"Well, I've got to go. Kiss Chase for me."

"Give the babies and Paul my love," I say disconnecting the call.

Love you like a sister, the term Kayla coined, remains on my mind after I end the call with Hannah. Thoughts soon turned to Michelle's precarious condition. She finally woke from the coma with no memory of anything or anyone. A stranger with a different identity woke in Michelle's place, a stranger named Aurora. Helplessly, we watched as she grappled with her new surroundings. Her doctor suggested we give her space and time to heal.

Outraged by Michelle's brutal beating and puzzled by the mysterious personality which emerged from the coma, Taylor remains by her side, but to Michelle, he's a stranger. Nevertheless, he keeps daily vigilance, hoping the amnesia is temporary, and the old Michelle will appear. It's a blessing Michelle has no recollection of the brutal beating or her family. The entire family will spend the rest of their lives behind bars.

The U.S. District Court charged Wheaton with failing to report millions of wire transfers and enabling drug laundering. Civil penalties amounted to the forfeiture of illegal funds and profits derived from trading. After a brief business suspension, and seizure of company records, FINRA, and the FBI gathered more evidence against the cartel. A few months later, Wheaton Asset Management resumed business for the first time in years without Kimura's threats. Because of extortionist demands, the murder of two employees turning evidence, and Bruce's willing collaboration, Wheaton was charged with only a minor civil penalty.

The Collins family, thankful Kayla's killers are behind bars, will always mourn their daughter's loss. Kevin Collins awarded for helping the FBI capture the Kimuras is now considering a career as a special agent.

The last several months, my bond with Bruce has grown stronger. After a frigid escape from the Kimura men, I spent the rest of the month on Martha's Vineyard. Finishing the diaries, I discovered more about my time as a child with Judith and Bruce. The journals served their purpose, revealing a woman I wish I'd known better. So, I've finally given the diaries to Bruce, the rightful owner. Judith did something right. She gave me two fathers who will always be a part of my life. Two men, I grow to love deeper every day.

I never resigned from Wheaton, realizing it wasn't a career change I needed, just more fun in my life as Chase predicted the first day in his apartment. So, I'm moving forward courageously. Judith and Bruce's affair inspired a desire to live passionately. My new mantra, once spoken by a wise man—Albert Einstein—is to learn from yesterday, live for today, and hope for tomorrow.

With an all-expense-paid vacation by Bruce to Italy, I'm discovering a part of me I feared too long. As the Tarot cards predicted, I've found love with Chase. Unlike Judith, I run toward life and love gobbling up every voluptuous moment. I said I'd never walk down the aisle in a ceremonial gown, and I won't. Chase and I plan to wed on a gondola ride through Venetian canals.

Lost in Venice outside the window, I fail to notice the quiet shower, but I sense Chase's heat and scent grow closer, inflaming arousal. He glides my sports bra off my shoulders. I close my eyes as he peels my leggings down my thighs. His breath, electrical pulses, rise from my ankle to my spine. I recall Bruce's whispered words to Judith. *"Watch the water and the gondolas and remember the view and sensations."* I surrender control and embrace erotic desires much as my father had years ago.

Dear reader,

We hope you enjoyed reading *Chasing Victoria*. Please take a moment to leave a review, even if it's a short one. Your opinion is important to us.

Discover more books by Denise E. Billups at
https://www.nextchapter.pub/authors/e-denise-billups

Want to know when one of our books is free or discounted? Join the newsletter at http://eepurl.com/bqqB3H

Best regards,
Denise E. Billups and the Next Chapter Team

About The Author

An author with a rare mixture of Southern and Northern charm, E. Denise Billups was born in Monroeville Alabama and raised in New York City where she currently resides and works in finance and as a freelance columnist. A burgeoning author of fiction, she's published three suspense novels—Kalorama Road, Chasing Victoria, By Chance, and three supernatural short stories, Ravine, Lereux, The Playground, and Rebound. An avid reader of magical realism, mystery, and suspense novels, she was greatly influenced by authors of these genres. She's a fitness fanatic, trained in ballet, modern, and jazz dance, and uses the same discipline to facilitate creative writing.

E. Denise Billups
www.edenisebillups.com

Books by E. Denise Billups

Novels
   By Chance
   Chasing Victoria
   Kalorama Road
Short Stories
   Ravine Lereux
   The Playground
   Rebound

Chasing Victoria
ISBN: 978-4-86752-687-3

Published by
Next Chapter
1-60-20 Minami-Otsuka
170-0005 Toshima-Ku, Tokyo
+818035793528
9th August 2021